Also by David Sheppard:

Oedipus on a Pale Horse
Journey through Greece in Search of a Personal Mythology

Novelsmithing
The Structural Foundation of Plot, Character, and Narration

THE MYSTERIES
A NOVEL OF ANCIENT ELEUSIS

Volume 1:
DAUGHTER OF DARKNESS

Volume 2:
THE DADOUCHOS

Volume 3:
THE TWICE-BORN
(at a later date)

by

David Sheppard

THE DADOUCHOS

Being the second volume of

THE MYSTERIES,
A NOVEL OF ANCIENT ELEUSIS

by

David Sheppard

Publisher Web site:
www.tragedysworkshop.com

Book Web site:
www.themysteriesofeleusis.com

FOR

All the brave women throughout history
whose stories have never been told.

Acknowledgements

The concept of this book is the outgrowth of a conversation I had with a friend of mine several years ago at a Starbucks in Boulder, Colorado. After listening to me talk obsessively about Herodotus, she suggested I write a novel set in ancient Greece. The essence of the story came to me immediately. She also midwifed it through the first draft. My sister-in-law, Nancy Sheppard, read it in episodes as it was written and offered encouragement. The expertise of my editor, Marilyn Mueller, has once again been indispensable. A special thanks to Richard Sheppard for the map and the cover design and illustration.

Author's Note

I am the author of *Novelsmithing, The Structural Foundation of Plot, Character, and Narration*. I used the methods of *Novelsmithing* to write *The Mysteries*. Since some instructors are using *Novelsmithing* in their creative writing classes, I thought it might be of benefit to expose a little of my plotting and research methodology. Therefore, I have provided some hints at story structure and the primary sources for *The Mysteries* at the end of the novel. I plotted Volumes One and Two of *The Mysteries* as one complete story and Volume Three separately. Practically all sources are a part of my home library. Anyone interested in the size and content of my library can find it listed at:

www.librarything.com/catalog/dshep/yourlibrary

For field research, I visited Greece twice, once for ten weeks in October 1993 and then for sixteen days in October 2009. I took a considerable number of photos and video clips, some of which I've provided for viewing at www.themysteriesofeleusis.com.

My readers can follow me on twitter at user name "novelsmithing" and on my blog www.novelsmithingblog.com. When I travel, I post at www.palehorseblog.com.

Ancient Greece in the 5th Century BC was a collection of separate city-states, loosely bound by a common language and religion. The ancient Greeks called the encompassing geographical area Ἑλλας, Hellas, and its people the Hellenes. No one called it Greece. I have used both: Greece/Greeks for narration and Hellas/Hellenes for dialogue.

MOUNT OLYMPUS ▲

DODONA •

THESSALY

MT.
PARNASSOS
DELPHI • ▲   BOEOTIA
                    THEBES •
ITHACA   PLATAEA •   KHALKIS •
          PATRAS • GULF OF CORINTH   AULIS •
                                 ▲ MT. KITHAERON
                            ELEUSIS •
                    ISTHMUS   ATHENS •
          PELOPONNESE CORINTH • SALAMIS • BRAURON
                                 PHALERON •
OLYMPIA •   MYCENAE • EPIDAURUS •
          ARGOS • NAUPHLIA •   SOUNION •

          TAYGETUS   SPARTA •
          MOUNTAINS

IONIAN SEA

EUBOEA

ANCIENT
GREECE
(HELLAS)

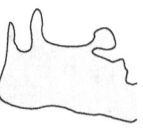

PROPONTIS

ABYDOS
HELLESPONT
TROY

LEMNOS

AEGEAN
SEA

ASIA

LESBOS
MYTILENE

SKYROS

SARDIS

CHIOS

SMYRNA

EPHESUS

SAMOS

MT. MYKALE

CYCLADES

TINOS

MYKONOS

DELOS

DODECANESE

KOS

THERA

RHODES

AEGEAN
SEA

KARPATHOS

CRETE

KNOSSOS

PHAESTOS

Table of Contents

The Dadouchos

CHAPTER 1: THE BURNING OF ELEUSIS

Myrrhine had left her housemaids and gone to watch Melaina and her girls cross the road. She saw them settle down on the hillside beneath the plane tree, along the bank of the cold, swift-running water of the Kephisos. Myrrhine had turned away, deciding they were safe. This was another of Melaina's favorite places, but one Myrrhine despised because Demeter's daughter had been kidnapped there. Myrrhine had been more vigilant lately, not letting Melaina out of her sight. Her daughter's abdomen was so large that a seizure now could injure her or the baby, and Myrrhine had little faith in the supposed healing at Epidaurus. But the invasion no longer seemed such a threat; last word had the Persians retreating from Attica, and the Spartans had been seen at the Isthmus with a small contingent on their way to Eleusis to bolster their own troops. She hadn't felt such relief in over a year.

The scorching heat was beginning to subside as sundown approached. Myrrhine's first indication that something was wrong came from dogs barking in the distance. She wondered if someone's sheep or goats had gotten loose. Sundown spooked animals. Myrrhine thought how proud she was of Melaina teaching her little circle of friends. Several mothers had changed their minds about Melaina because of their daughters' enthusiasm for learning, and they had made favorable comments to Myrrhine. Now, Myrrhine heard the sound of horses' hooves, and thought they were probably from Aeschylus' strong steed. He frequently charged through the city gates with news for the Hierophant and other city officials.

Just as she reached the city gate, Myrrhine heard the first scream. Horses they were, but not those of Greece. Persians sprang as if from the earth, shield-laden, rapiers rattling. The Persian cavalry came by storm, fearful to behold, and with the infantry in hot pursuit. Myrrhine panicked, fell into confusion and turned toward safety. Then, remembering her pregnant daughter in the path of the deadly charge, she turned back to save Melaina, realized the futility, and turned homeward again. She'd only taken a step when she heard Melaina's scream, her frantic plea to her long-dead father. Back Myrrhine ran toward the Persian onslaught, vowing to die with her daughter in her arms. Melaina was now obscured from view by the raging torrent of grim death descending on them.

Myrrhine felt an arm take hold of her. Aeschylus pulled her from the road, back through the city gates, and inside the stone walls.

"Melaina!" she screamed, hearing the gates thud to and clank behind her as the bolts shot home.

"To the docks!" cried Aeschylus. "Leave Melaina to us."

Myrrhine fled back into the city, past the Kallichoron Well where local women gathered to draw water and gossip. "Persians!" she shouted. "To your homes and children!" But Myrrhine couldn't force herself to the docks. From the propylaea, she ran to the Telesterion, the stone walls deep in shadow from the encroaching darkness. Searching frantically for the Hierophant, she found him running toward her, shield and sword in hand, and several more officials with him.

"To the boats!" she shouted. "Save yourselves!"

"Never!" he cried, flinging off his robe. "I go the way of Eleusis."

A stout arm grabbed Myrrhine from behind. She screamed, thinking it a Persian, but saw that it was young Sophocles.

"Follow me!" he shouted.

"No! Melaina!"

Persian shouts and the thunder of many feet swept her words away. Her father and the other sacred officials stepped forward to join soldiers manning the walls. Densely massed, they blocked the closed entryway. But brandishing two-edged axes, the Persians smote the wood doors through and off their hinges, hewed a hole in the stubborn oak beam, and breached the stone wall.

Sophocles jerked Myrrhine back from the action. They fled the temple, up the incline, and past the Cave of Hades to the hilltop overlooking the city. Myrrhine stopped to catch her breath and looked north to where she'd last seen Melaina. The air was filled with savage cries, women's plaints, and wailing. This way and that the people of Eleusis flew, some to the ships, some clambering west through the streets, all hoping to outrun the onslaught. From within the stone walls, the bewildered cries of children came, along with the shouts of husbands and fathers going rapidly to their deaths.

Myrrhine heard a loud pounding, the quick blows of a battering ram. Smoke from every quarter rose, black belching clouds laced with crimson quivering tongues. Persians spread like ravening wolves in a black mist. The myrtle grove rose in flame. The enemy drove from their pins sheep and goats, squealing pigs, cows, bawling calves.

Sophocles held fast to Myrrhine's arm, dragged her down the hill and along the street to the docks where the hordes were crowding aboard ships. She was crying now, burning grief gripping her throat.

The last boat pushed off as the first Persians descended upon them. Several soldiers rushed to their aid, but she realized Sophocles was no longer beside her. She ran to the water's edge, wondering if he'd boarded without her, but spotted him dragging a fishing boat from its storage hut. Myrrhine helped him pull it to the water's edge and climbed inside. Too late. Two Persians were upon them. Sophocles drew his sword and turned his rage on one. An arrow from some unseen bow took the other.

Now they huddled in the boat, young Sophocles madly rowing out of range of the whistling missiles. The boat pitched and swayed in the light surf, but Myrrhine's eyes remained glued on shore, hope of her father and Aeschylus escaping certain death dissipating in the gathering darkness. Once beyond any arrow's arc, she bid Sophocles stop rowing. "Wait for survivors. Perhaps someone will swim out to us."

No one came, though they waited as the sunlight failed, the landscape lit anew by towering flames. She studied the shore, memorizing every feature. She saw only Persians scouring the beach.

The other boats rowed on to Salamis, leaving Myrrhine and Sophocles alone, bobbing amongst the waves. Many times Myrrhine had witnessed her daughter's regard for Sophocles. She was surprised at how well, in spite of his youth, he'd acquitted himself against the Persian warrior. Then again, he was a veteran of the battle of Salamis.

A trireme came alongside, and the crew pulled them and their small boat aboard. Myrrhine recognized the captain as the Athenian general at the Isthmus, Kimon, who'd felt such affection for Melaina.

Myrrhine went to him. "Save my daughter," she begged, "set ashore your warriors. Save the daughter of Kynegeiros. The Persians have her."

"Eyie!" he said, raising his arm and sweeping the horizon to the east.

Myrrhine hadn't noticed anything but Eleusis burning. With the gesture, Kimon revealed the burning grain fields of the Thriasian Plain, Apollo's temple at Daphni in flames, and to the southeast, a new sun rising, the great conflagration consuming Athens.

Myrrhine paced the deck, speaking rapidly and to no one. She castigated herself for letting Melaina out of her sight. How could she possibly have let her beyond the city gates? If Melaina had been with her, Sophocles would have saved them both.

The trireme sailed unmolested southwest along the coast. Myrrhine stood alongside Kimon and Sophocles, judging Persian progress by the traveling wave of fire. They picked up survivors, some in small boats, and others who'd swum out to sea to drown rather than face the barbarian onslaught. The deck swelled with frightened refugees.

As the night labored away the hours, the trireme negotiated the zigzag strait of Megara, then turned west along the coastal town that centuries before had been the home of Kalchas, seer with the Greek forces at Troy. Soon Megara also cast the bright glow of flames out over the dark waters. Megara was the last city to burn. The wave of flame stopped there, and as suddenly as they'd come, the Persians turned about, retreated. The roar of the army faded as it swept back east.

"A foolhardy idea anyway," said Kimon. "Persia would have paid a more terrible price at the narrows of the Scironian Way than at Thermopylae. It would have cost them the war."

The trireme also turned about, renegotiated the strait, and came opposite Eleusis again as the sky lightened in the east. The flames had died to a glow, smoke no longer billowing, but now a rising mist of darkened hopes. As the pink glow of dawn revealed a smoke-burdened sky and the last of the Persian menace in the Thriasian Plain, Kimon ordered the ship in close to dock and put ashore an armed contingent to gauge their security should they decide to return.

A shout went up from those onboard when the troops reappeared with two survivors. Myrrhine's heart leapt seeing one was a girl, but it fell when she realized it was not Melaina's pregnant shape. It was Agido. But the dejected, battle-beaten man beside her was Aeschylus.

Myrrhine was the first off the trireme. Agido ran to her arms, and Myrrhine hugged her as if she were her own daughter. She knew how Melaina loved the little girl. But Agido couldn't tell what had happened to Melaina.

"She's lost her voice," said Aeschylus. "We survived hiding in the blacksmith's shop." Shame cut him short. "I didn't want to die. If I were a Spartan, they'd stone me." Then he spoke to Myrrhine's great fear. "We've seen nothing of Melaina, and Zakorus didn't make it." Aeschylus had already reverted to the Hierophant's given name, as was the custom once he no longer occupied the sacred office. "He fell during fierce fighting in the temple."

From the hilltop, Myrrhine surveyed the smoldering ruins of Eleusis. Heap upon heap of ashes, the strewn dead, the many shapes of sorrow. The blacksmith's shop was the only building still standing, Palaemon himself alive and well, said Aeschylus. They walked in the heat of glowing coals to his shop, but he refused to talk, instead working the bellows so that flames hissed and metal glowed white hot. He'd managed to save his wagon and two mules by tying them inside the smithy. Akmon and Damnameneus had also survived.

Aeschylus told a strange story of how the smith, when he saw the Persians coming, fueled the flames of his furnaces with wretched turkey wood, so the coals danced about sending sparks high into the air. He lit fires in all the smelters and pranced around them, agile as a deer upon his withered legs, waving his arms as might some gangly beast. The Persians, thinking he was an Underworld daemon or perhaps Hephaestus himself, refused to enter the smithy.

"First I've known my deformity to be a blessing," said Palaemon. "Still, it's no boon to remain untouched with your village in ruins and mistress Melaina, bright star of all Eleusis, missing."

Flames still rose from Myrrhine's home. The stone walls had been toppled from their foundations, gardens scorched, slaves gone. Melaina's chamber was strangely vacant, but there were no ashes of the ancient chest, no fused puddle of metal from the hidden cache of coins, no embers of rugs or robes. "The Persians plundered it," Myrrhine said.

Charred remains filled her own chamber, flames still flickering and coals aglow. She stood inside the entry, though the heat flushed her cheeks and smoke burned her eyes and throat. All her possessions, including her dowry, were in ashes. She scraped free pieces of her sacred robes, still wondering at the ashes in her chamber but none in Melaina's.

They hurried to the Telesterion where the columns had been pulled down. The large beams of the collapsed roof still smoldered. Picking apart rubble, Sophocles and Aeschylus went before her to the Anaktoron, Holiest of Holies. It was flattened to the floor and contained no sign of the Sacred Objects so crucial to the Mysteries. They found the smoldering bones of Myrrhine's father with charred pieces of his robe.

"He made his stand here," said Aeschylus.

"As I knew he would," she said. "He'd never allow the Sacred Objects in the hands of barbarians while still alive."

They crossed the Sacred Way to the grass-covered fields where Melaina and her girls had sat encircled beneath the plane tree. There she found the lone traces of her daughter, Melaina's sandals. She grabbed them and held them to her breast. She showed Agido.

Agido cried, grabbed Myrrhine and buried her face in her breast. She spoke her first words. "I ran, but she couldn't. I'm so ashamed!"

"Oh, little Agido!" Myrrhine squeezed her, looked into her eyes. Swift-footed Agido was the only girl of Melaina's circle to reach safety. "If you'd stayed behind, you couldn't have helped her and would've only been taken yourself,."

Myrrhine turned to Aeschylus. "Is Melaina still alive?"

"If they know who she is. She'll make some rich Persian a prestigious concubine; her child will become a valuable slave. She may already be on the way to Sardis or Susa."

"Retrieve her! She must be saved." But she realized that Sardis was deep in Asia, Susa in Persia, close to the world's edge.

Aeschylus threw up his arms. "Your husband has been dead ten years at the hands of Persians, your father freshly killed because of his own idiocy, and you want me to charge into the jaws of death." He walked off.

"She's your brother's daughter."

"I must return to Athens, assess the damage to my residence there, and relocate my family from Salamis. Turn to those who had the sense to evacuate." He walked off muttering to himself, "Chase after Persians? Incurably foolish!"

Sophocles made no move to go with him.

Aeschylus looked back. "Coming?"

Sophocles spoke to Myrrhine. "I too must go. My invalid father should be taken home to Kolonus. His health weighs heavily on me."

"Thank you, Sophocles. You saved my life and have always been a true friend to Melaina."

"Would that I'd been here to save her."

Myrrhine panicked at the sight of them leaving. She missed Kynegeiros terribly. "Oh for a husband!" she shouted after them.

Myrrhine calmed a bit, realizing that Aeschylus leaving was for the best. He would only stop her from doing what she must. Somewhere within Greece, Melaina was still alive. She could believe nothing else. As the hurt found new strength, she fiercely held Agido to her and planned to retrieve Melaina herself.

She'd turn to the one man who'd be safe in the Persian camp.

CHAPTER 2: IN THE PERSIAN CAMP

Myrrhine again entered the ruins of the Telesterion, where she and Agido collected the Hierophant's relics. They would have to be buried, but she hadn't time now. She stuffed them in a sarcophagus beside her husband's tomb and said a prayer over them while worrying Melaina's epilepsy. Would her captors put Melaina to the knife if she had a seizure?

Myrrhine heard the laments of others returning from Salamis to sort through the dead and prepare funeral pyres. She took Agido to her burned-out home. One of the deceased was Agido's father, the sight of whose remains sent Agido into a new fit of hysteria. Agido had always been tied to her mother, and her only time away from home had been spent with Melaina. Now Agido's mother was missing and her father dead. The girl wrapped her arms around Myrrhine's neck in a death grip. Myrrhine hated to leave her in the hands of others at such a time. "I'll make it up to you later," she said.

She found the blacksmith, not at his bellows and anvil, but alone in his chamber, head between his knees. When she spoke to him, he came alert although she could tell he'd been crying.

Palaemon asked, "Any word of the little mistress?"

"Nothing."

"But for these withered limbs.... The gods have turned all Attica into a smelter. With this purification great things must follow. But oh, the misery!"

Myrrhine had never actually taken note of his deformity. She'd always thought that his legs were weak, but now realized that though they were small, they were perfect in form. Still, she wondered why his mother hadn't exposed him at birth as was customary with a deformed child.

"I've come to ask a favor," she said. "Take me to the Persian camp."

"Oh great Zeus! That'll not be safe for you, priestess. I could never defend you. Aeschylus is a great warrior. He could raise an army."

"No one could protect me behind enemy lines. I'll be honest with you. I've heard that the Persians fear your shape. In this instance, no army would be as powerful and provide safety as well as would your deformity. We'll bring back Melaina."

At this, he again dropped his head. Myrrhine watched large tears splash mud on the powdery floor. He said, "We'll take Akmon and Damnameneus."

She wasn't particularly excited about leaving behind his two giant workmen herself. In fact, she felt her first affinity for the brutes, but she knew their presence could spell death. "No. We must project weakness. They'd be provocative."

"If these spindly legs can be of use in such an undertaking, the years enduring them will have been worth it."

"The longer we wait, the less our chances of finding Melaina," she said. She remembered the hard thoughts her father had toward the Persian general. "Let's find out who this Mardonius really is, man or monster."

Myrrhine loaded the wagon with what food she could find in the rubble heaps while he harnessed the mules. She salvaged a sacred robe with one singed cuff that smelled ferociously of smoke. She decided, the better for effect.

Myrrhine spoke to scouts who were passing through Eleusis on their way the Isthmus with reconnaissance for the Spartan generals, and learned that Mardonius was evacuating Attica for Boeotia. She'd originally thought they'd find him in Athens but now knew the entire Persian army was retreating east, circling Mt. Parnes, and would eventually turn north to seek a strategic position for the coming land battle. She and the blacksmith would take the shortcut north along the foothills of Mt. Pateras and through the pass in the spurs of Kithaeron to hated Thebes. Traitorous Thebes would be the Persian stronghold.

As the sun once again dipped toward the horizon, they set off, Palaemon at the reins of the two mules, Myrrhine beside him in the wagon. They wouldn't get far before nightfall, but time was precious. They stopped at the first village in the foothills, on the banks of a branch of the Kephisos River. It appeared deserted at first, residents huddled in their homes and afraid to come forward until they knew the strangers were not Persian. Myrrhine took a room with a family, but the smith bedded down in the wagon.

That evening before sleep, Myrrhine stood outside in the dark watching the smoldering fires south at Eleusis and east at Athens, wondering where her daughter was spending the night, if she was alive. She worried over Melaina's pregnancy, the epilepsy. The gods have taken everything from me, Myrrhine thought, every joy turned to pain. Her husband had been killed at Marathon, and her father's charred remains were now in an undistinguished sarcophagus. The Mysteries could no longer be held. The sacred officials were dead, the Telesterion destroyed. Was it possible for Greece to survive without the Mysteries? She dipped her head and returned inside.

★

Long before sunrise, Myrrhine rose sleepless, dressed, and went to the wagon where she found Palaemon already harnessing the mules. All morning they negotiated the undulating hills until they crossed another shallow tributary of the Kephisos. They started the ascent of the spur of Kithaeron toward Eleutherai, the last settlement before the pass. On the other side they'd be in Boeotia, enemy territory.

The road was rough and devoid of travelers. Word of Persian bands on the loose had sent the entire countryside into hiding. The wagon started quaking when one spindle loosened and the wheel wobbled. Palaemon did what he could, and they limped on into Eleutherai, arriving in late afternoon.

The fort at Eleutherai was heavily manned and crowded with refugees. At one time, it had been on the boarder between Boeotia and Attica, but hatred of Thebes drove the inhabitants to align with Athens. Myrrhine spent the night in the temple of Hera while Palaemon worked on the wheel spindles at the local blacksmith's and then slept in the wagon.

That evening, Myrrhine stood atop the city walls listening to wild screams coming from the wooded hills. These were the slopes of Kithaeron, ancient abode of Dionysus, the twice-born god, where dark legends told of many infants who'd been exposed on its slopes. Baby Oedipus had been abandoned there but had been saved by a shepherd and returned years later to unknowingly kill his father and marry his mother. Female devotees of Dionysus, maenads, also roamed these slopes, engaging in orgiastic rituals during which they ripped apart live animals and devoured raw flesh.

Another scream sent a chill through her. Was it animal or human? Myrrhine returned to her chamber.

★

Early the next morning the blacksmith and priestess resumed their journey, mules laboring against the grade, digging in and straining against their harnesses. Finally, they rounded Oak Heads pass and pulled to the side of the roadway. From here, they could see along the road in both directions. To the south, they overlooked Eleusis and the Thriasian Plain, and saw smoke still rising from Attica, all friendly territory lying in the midst of its own decimation. Pale Mt. Hymettos loomed beyond Athens, where Myrrhine and Melaina were reunited at Kleito's home after Kallias had retrieved Melaina from Brauron. To the north, where they were headed, they overlooked the deme of Boeotia that had gone over to the Persians, including Thebes and Orchomenus, between which the Kopaic Basin, with its eel-infested swamplands, glinted in sunlight.

They descended the mountain, the smith applying the brake to the wagon wheel to restrain the mules from careening out of control. By mid-afternoon the terrain gradually flattened, and they could see across to the Asopus. There, to their surprise, the Persian army gathered. They'd not have to travel as far as Thebes after all. Mardonius had brought his troops west along the north bank, using the river for protection, and was now setting up camp between the river and Thebes. They passed the small villages of Erythrae and Hysiae, both of which had gone over to Persia. The residents of nearby Plataea to the west had fled to the hills rather than fight.

Myrrhine realized she was overlooking the field where the battle for all Greece would soon be fought. They'd be within the Persian camp by nightfall. Myrrhine had made up her mind to do whatever it took to retrieve her daughter. But first, she needed divine guidance.

Before they reached the river, she had Palaemon turn right onto a trail, and shortly, they came to an old temple of Eleusinian Demeter standing amongst a grove of trees: pine, mighty elms, pears, apples. Though it was late summer, a creek gushed down from the slopes of Kithaeron.

Palaemon pulled the wagon beside the creek and drew water. But Myrrhine refused to drink or freshen herself, pulled her fire-scarred robe about her, and entered the deserted temple. She wondered why it'd been abandoned. The wooden icon of Demeter had toppled to the floor and been shoved in a corner. It was now covered with dust and cobwebs.

Myrrhine sought the smith's help, and the two of them returned Demeter to her throne. The goddess was majestically draped in a double cloak with a mantle across her knees. She held poppies and wheat in her left hand, her right resting upon the arm of the throne. She wore a crown, and a veil draped the back of her head, falling upon her shoulders. Myrrhine recognized Demeter's characteristically benign brightness, the strong lines at the eyebrow, chin, and cheek, yet she seemed softer, gentler than Myrrhine had ever seen her. Myrrhine raised her arms before the icon.

"Demeter, greatly hail! Bountiful goddess who came to earth, I come to you in great need. Only you can understand my suffering. Never before have I fully comprehended your grief when Kore was ripped from your breast. Greatly I admonish myself for thinking I knew. My daughter, Melaina, has also disappeared, snatched from me by the same fell monsters, who burned your temple and destroyed your sacred Mysteries. Just beyond the Asopus, Persian hordes gather for even greater mischief. Give me strength to enter their camp and retrieve Melaina. In the past, you've come to my aid, returning Melaina to me when she was in great danger at Brauron. I beg you, see to her safe return once again, and never will I live on in safety while one of your temples burns."

Myrrhine returned to the wagon to find Palaemon waiting at the reins. They traveled back from where they'd come, rejoined the road north, and crossed Morea Bridge over the slow-flowing Asopus. Now they were on the main road to Thebes, with the sun falling behind Kithaeron, and casting a traveling shadow along the plains. The Persian cavalry met them, one man on a huge black horse wearing a hammered-bronze helmet.

"State your business," demanded the horseman in broken Greek.

Myrrhine was even more frightened than she'd imagined, being amongst the enemy's army. These were strange men indeed. They wore turbans, greaves and corselets, and carried bows of cornel wood, arrows without feathers. Some slung goatskins about their shoulders and wore hats stuck around with feathers. Others carried daggers and riphooks, practiced lasso throwing. She stiffened her resolve, knowing Melaina must be amongst them.

"Sacred business concerning Mardonius alone," Palaemon answered, rising from his seat to expose his deformity as he spoke. Those accompanying the horseman shouted in dismay and retreated a comfortable distance.

"And the woman?" asked the horseman.

"A sacred official from Eleusis."

The horseman called another alongside, and they spoke in a foreign tongue, then argued heatedly. The other retreated, and the horseman motioned for them to follow him.

They entered the Persian camp amidst great curiosity from the infantrymen, who were dressed in tiaras, embroidered tunics, and coats of fish-scale mail. These men carried light wicker shields, short spears, and powerful bows with quivers containing cane arrows. Daggers swung at their belts. Every man glittered with gold and had a covered carriage with his women and servants. Each had a donkey, horse, or camel.

Palaemon spoke quietly to Myrrhine. "Though they have great wealth and have all their comforts with them, Hellene armor is far superior. They've not made the breakthrough in forging tough metals. They must not even know how to beat a complete helmet from a single iron ingot. Look! They have wicker shields. Ours are bronze. It'll be no contest head-to-head."

The great multitude spread far into the distance. Torches, lamps, and campfires dotted hillsides. Myrrhine knew that most enemy troops had returned to Persia with Xerxes, yet it still looked, with this wide mixture of peoples, as though they'd brought their entire civilization. Shameless men-giants, turned tree haters, were everywhere within the nearby forests. With great double axes and hatchets, they rushed about Demeter's groves felling tall trees and laying waste all the shady glens in sight. Great stacks of timber lay about.

"Sacrilege!" Myrrhine said. "Have they no restraint?"

They were led past the slaughter area where men sacrificed camels, horses, oxen, asses, deer, and smaller animals: ostriches, geese, and cocks. Rivulets of blood flowed into earth's creases and stood in deep puddles.

They approached a congregation of large tents, outside of which bakers and cooks swarmed over a conflagration rising from the outdoor kitchen. As the two became visible in the great light of the cook's fire, the crowd, seeing Palaemon's misshapen form, stood aside. A guard stepped into their path, accosted their escort in the foreign tongue and then brushed him aside, and addressed the two directly.

Myrrhine spoke no Persian and wondered if this would be their undoing, but Palaemon spoke up, guttural sounds pouring so naturally from his mouth that it frightened Myrrhine. Then she remembered that he'd lived under Persian rule at Rhodes. But the guard grew angry, shouted at them, then cracked his mighty whip over the heads of the mules, sending them into panic.

Palaemon regained control of the beasts and drove them back from the crowd. Myrrhine feared that she and Palaemon would not even have the chance to request an audience with Mardonius. She climbed down from the wagon, took hold the reins of one mule, and walked the team back toward the center of camp.

Several men stood in her way. One stepped forward to shout in Greek, "Turn about or eat arrows!"

Myrrhine recognized clubfooted Hegesistratus, the diviner with Mys who'd waylaid them on the road to Epidaurus. After speaking, he turned his back to walk away. "Shoot them!" he said.

"Hegesistratus!" she called out, "do the gods taunt you with pain in your self-mutilated foot?"

He wheeled about to see who'd shouted his name, strained to see the face of the woman.

"Your hatred of Sparta drive you to traitorous acts?" she added.

"That and money. Mardonius pays well," he answered, but he was obviously confused and, by the slowness of his speech, Myrrhine knew he was trying to judge who would know so much of his history.

"Can he save you from Tartarus as well as poverty?"

"Who addresses me such? What woman speaks to any man so?"

"It is I, Myrrhine, priestess of Demeter at Eleusis, whom you met on the road to Epidaurus this past spring. You sought my daughter, who has the falling sickness. I've come to speak with

Mardonius."

Hegesistratus swung into action, slandered the commander, then ordered him inside the tent. Shortly the man returned at a fast gait. "Mardonius will see the woman. Separate her from the daemon at the reigns of the mules. He's to come no closer."

Myrrhine stepped forward to walk with Hegesistratus and saw horses eating from an all-bronze manger. What riches, she thought. As she got closer, she realized she'd come during their evening meal. Some dined out of doors in full sight, others inside. When she reached the tent entrance, she saw that even those inside didn't eat in the presence of Mardonius, for he had two separate rooms. His advisors ate in one, and he in another accompanied by a chorus of his concubines who played the lyre and sang. He had a throne of white marble, embroidered hangings, and gorgeous decorations of silver and gold, couches inlaid with precious metals. Myrrhine wondered if he had aspirations of filling Xerxes' shoes someday.

Mardonius himself was of no remarkable appearance save his flame-colored robe strewn with gold beads, that and his assurance of manner. Standing before this man, who'd caused the devastation of all Attica and burned her beloved Eleusis, she still, by virtue of her mission, stoutly refused to be intimidated. His attendant eunuchs smelled freshly bathed and were dressed in white. The tent floor was covered with beautifully designed carpets containing miniature figures of Persian heroes. Tables were furnished with cups and mixing bowls of silver and gold. Upon the fire burned the spine and gallbladder of some animal.

Mardonius left her standing alongside Hegesistratus and continued his meal, laughing over a lyric sung by one of his concubines. The table glistened under rays of high-swinging lamps that lit tempting lures for the palate: cruets of wine, snowy-topped barley-cakes, wheat loaves. She saw steaming kettles of what she supposed to be rich shark, stingray or squid, polyps with soft tentacles turned black by inky cuttlefish secretions, glistening eels.

While Myrrhine waited to be addressed by this great Persian, cousin and brother-in-law to Xerxes himself, his slaves served flower-leaved cakes and spiced confections, frosted puff-cakes. Last came slices of steaming tunny carved from the meaty belly, intestines of swine, and a rump with hot dumplings.

A slave finally brought a chair to the table and Mardonius motioned for her to sit, but Myrrhine stood silent as they partook of the meal. She'd not eaten since the Persians burned Eleusis and had vowed not to eat again until she found Melaina. She seemed to gain strength from her fast. Before the chair meant for her, the slave set meat-ends with skin-white ribs, snouts, feet, and tenderloin spiced with silphium, the split head of a kid, brain steaming. All of which she refused, still standing.

When Mardonius finished eating, slave boys removed the plates and bowls, then poured water over his hands. Hegesistratus walked to his side and mumbled in his ear. Mardonius looked toward Myrrhine, and surprisingly, addressed her in Greek.

"Declare your mission. If you won't eat, at least tell your mind."

Myrrhine had planned to fall at Mardonius' knees and beg him to return Melaina, but so offended was she at the sight of the felled trees and excesses in camp that she couldn't restrain her anger. It was immediately apparent to her that she'd never gain her daughter's freedom from a position of weakness, and resolved not to tell him her mission right off.

"All Boeotia is a great center for Demeter worship, yet you lay waste to her sacred glens. Persian axes dig into the pale flesh of tender trunks, leaving holy groves desolate. Turn back your woodcutters lest Lady Demeter send drought over the entire world. Yield in this sacrilege!"

Mardonius bristled, stood to shout back at her. "Yield? Yield yourself! Lest I have an ax fixed in your flesh. From these trees shall I build a great palisade to house my warriors while we plan the end of Hellas. Surely this isn't the triviality you've come before me to utter. I've offered the greatest restraint, desiring only to govern Hellas, not destroy it."

"Glutton! Having thieved the rest of the world of its wealth, you've come to rob Hellas of its poverty. You've not been initiated into the Mysteries, wherefore you are insatiable, whether for lumber or table dainties. Food disappears into your bottomless pit of a stomach, wine flows as if into the depths of a sea. It's the same with your great hoggishness for countries. Yea, build your palisade with this great orgy of tree cutting." Myrrhine had never been one for prophecy, but she now felt her own daughter's influence. "All you plan within those cut timbers shall go against you. There shall you reap your reward for crimes against the goddess."

"Twice I've taken Athens without losing a man. Hellene soldiers flee before us like women. We are the greatest race in the world. All will bow before Persia."

"I see your love of mischief and adventure, your great arrogance. You surround yourself with flatterers, worms that bore into a man of simple character. Your very nature offends the gods."

Mardonius belched a great smelly cloud. "I'll not hear more of this." He turned to Hegesistratus. "Why bring this raving wretch before me?"

"She's the daughter of the Hierophant at Eleusis and priestess of Demeter. The great Mysteries of Eleusis are measured by her days. I thought it unwise to ignore her request for counsel. Besides, the deformed creature that brought her causes great disruption in camp."

Mardonius turned back to her. "Why come shouting into my tent thus? If you have another request, make it. Lunatic ravings do little to further your cause."

"Your gluttony is only exceeded by your battle atrocities. You've slaughtered the Hierophant, my father, and taken my daughter. I've come to retrieve her, along with the other women of Eleusis you kidnapped. Perhaps you don't realize Demeter's daughter is Mistress of the Underworld. My daughter is forever in the goddess' protection. You'll not find her an asset. She descended to the Underworld to ensure your defeat at Salamis."

Mardonius spoke to one of his lieutenants, who rushed from

the room. He started to speak again but Myrrhine cut him off.

"To speak the name of the Mistress of the Underworld in public is forbidden, so we use Kore instead. If necessary, I'll speak it here in your camp to get my daughter back. Even if you've butchered her, I'll have the body."

Mardonius raised his hand to silence Myrrhine, but to no avail.

"Dear goddess of death, Persephone," she emphasized the name, drew out each syllable to its fullest length, "mother of the Furies, Queen of the Netherworld, within this camp lies the great corruption that offends you. Bend your thoughts to visions of death and spread terror for these troops. Harvest these souls who lie in great insolence among your temples."

Clubfooted Hegesistratus shouted, "Enough!" and turned to Mardonius. "Please! Silence this woman, sire. Oh, the evil this woman brings!"

Mardonius' lieutenant returned, speaking again in the foreign tongue. Mardonius turned to her.

"You shall have your women. We have no knowledge of your daughter, though she may be disguised among them. Neither would such a priestess have been slaughtered on the battlefield against my order, nor would have a Hierophant. In the chaos of war, families get separated. Have faith that your daughter is still alive. We'll return these women who are rightfully ours as the spoils of war. Be content with more than your share."

Myrrhine turned on him, her eyes flaming. "They are Demeter's daughters, not yours!" Deep hatred flavored her words. "Never, never will they be yours!"

He walked her outside to where the after-dinner leftovers were being served to the bodyguards and light-armed troops in attendance.

"These women are all we have," he told her, pointing to a small group huddled in the dark. "Since Hellas is already mine, they'll not be missed long. Now remove the beast with a man's head. His presence is a disruption to both warriors and horses."

Myrrhine scanned the captive women's faces and suffered a great disappointment. Melaina wasn't among them. She staggered under the blow but recovered. She couldn't believe they'd taken only six women. Anaktoria must be in camp but neither was she among them. Still, Myrrhine knew she shouldn't push her luck. "Demeter will punish you for holding the rest," she said, but couldn't resist a last appeal. "My daughter is heavy with child. I must have her."

Mardonius looked surprised. "Was she among a group of girls outside the city gates by the river?"

"Yes!" shouted Myrrhine. "It was she."

"I saw this girl! I led the charge on Eleusis myself from my white stallion. We bore down on the group of girls, but from nowhere swooped a chariot, one driven by a madman and pulled by four black horses. Never have I witnessed such daring. He snatched the pregnant girl from us as our grip tightened about her."

Oh! Such sweet words. Melaina alive and in Greek hands! Myrrhine's heart was secretly aglow with gratitude, but not only for this gift of hope. Amongst the women of Eleusis, she'd spotted Agido's mother holding her infant son.

And another thing. She realized Mardonius was doomed. Tied beside his tent was a great white stallion. Melaina's vision when she fell on the way to Epidaurus revealed the death of a man on such a white horse.

At the wagon, Myrrhine saw the dejected look on Palaemon's face but couldn't tell him the full story there. "Into the wagon," Myrrhine ordered the women, afraid to acknowledge them worth taking. She urged the blacksmith turn about in haste. "Get us out of here," she said.

CHAPTER 3: CONTENTION AMONG THE ASHES

Mid-day, the blacksmith's wagon, carrying Myrrhine and the newly retrieved women, approached Eleusis. From a distance, Myrrhine saw the Thriasian Plain swarming with Greek warriors. The city was abuzz with citizens who'd survived, many more than she'd thought. Word of Myrrhine's rescue of the women spread by loud shouts and screams.

Agido came running to her mother and smiled broadly at Myrrhine. "You told me when you left you'd make it up to me."

Already the resurrection of Eleusis was in progress. During the past four days, walls had been repaired and makeshift roofs put in place. Even Myrrhine's home showed signs of rebirth. Several slaves had survived and chose to stay rather than join the Persians. Melaina's handmaid and two male servants were among them.

She had to bury her father's bones, and entered the ruins of the temple to recover them. There she encountered Aeschylus. His disposition was grave, and she feared what news he might have brought.

"Don't worry about Melaina," he said. "Kallias saved her. She's with him in Athens."

Myrrhine fell to the ground before him, prayed to Demeter silently, then once again looked up at Aeschylus. "The power of Demeter is beyond imagining. All my prayers answered. When will she return?"

"She won't," Aeschylus said. "Kallias has married her."

Shock and dismay quieted her momentarily. Melaina had married Kallias? Her anger quickly flared. "How could this be? Only I can marry her off. Who raised the bridal torch?"

"Hipparete and I provided all that was proper. We returned to take you to Athens for the ceremony, but couldn't find you."

"Why the hurry? All in good time, pleases Hera."

"The full moon was right to give its blessing."

"There'd be another."

"Uncontrollable events force the pace of our lives."

"Kallias doesn't know her weakness." Myrrhine had meant the epilepsy but wished she'd said nothing, realizing Aeschylus didn't, and shouldn't, know.

"Kallias knows she's pregnant but has wanted her from the time she was born, when he was only fifteen. Kynegeiros agreed to the match before he died in battle ten years ago."

Myrrhine slumped on a blackened stone, glad he'd misinterpreted. "Why the secrecy?"

"The decision was made on the battlefield at Marathon, but Zakorus would never agree to it. Melaina has belonged to me since Kynegeiros' death. I only let you raise her as a favor to your father."

Mention of her father's resistance lit a fire in Myrryine's thoughts. She realized that Aeschylus couldn't answer her question. She knew what was up. "My father resisted for good reason. Kynegeiros would never have given Melaina to a Kerykes," she said. "That would put the Mysteries in charge of a single family, and reduce the Eumolpids to secondary status. Demeter herself would never allow it."

Aeschylus looked shocked. He stammered. "I needed to get this scandalous indiscretion out of the family."

Myrrhine's mind was a whirlwind of thoughts conjuring Kallias' recent actions. No wonder he'd been there at Brauron when Melaina needed him, and again when the Persian hoards descended on Eleusis.

"This is an outrage!" she shouted. "You've upset the balance of power in Eleusis. You're a Eumolpid, same as Melaina. Your own family will turn on you for this."

A messenger from the generals interrupted them. The commander wanted to talk to all the women who'd been in the Persian camp. Aeschylus, upon hearing this, quickly disappeared, leaving Myrrhine puzzled and confused over her daughter's marriage to a man that went against both custom and divine will. Aeschylus would pay for this.

The Greek forces were assembling for the drive north to intercept Mardonius. While others questioned the rest of the women, Myrrhine was taken directly to Pausanias, the Spartan general commanding the united armies. Aeschylus reappeared tagging along behind her.

Myrrhine was shocked at Pausanias' youthful appearance. He looked to be in his late twenties with scant beard.

"Where are the Persian troops positioned?" he asked.

"Spread out along the north bank of the Asopus," she told him, "as far as the eye can see in both directions. Just northeast of Morea Bridge, he's laid waste to Boeotia's forests to build a gigantic palisade."

"To whom did you speak?"

"Mardonius himself," she said, sending murmurs through the crowd.

Pausanias took a deep breath, relaxed. "What can you tell us of him?" he asked.

"Gluttony is his most obvious trait."

"Aha!" said Pausanias. "If they don't conserve supplies, they'll be starving in a week."

"He's also a man of great confidence on the surface, but if I read him rightly, questioning within."

"Hum. So, what do you think?" he asked, turning to Aeschylus, who'd stepped out from behind Myrrhine

"At the first sign of trouble, they'll scatter like mice."

"That's also how I read it. Speak to anyone else?" he asked Myrrhine.

"Only Hegesistratus, his diviner."

"Ho!" a man shouted, stepped forward from the crowd. "My countryman, one of the Telliadae clan." The man was short, thin, effeminate in manner. Myrrhine recognized him as Tisamenus, a seer from Elis, where the Olympic games were held and, therefore, with a reputation unexcelled for fairness. She'd heard of an oracle from Delphi saying that Tisamenus would lead the Spartans to five victories. The coming battle would be his first test.

"The clubfoot?" asked Pausanias.

"Yes," said Tisamenus.

"He's long been a Spartan enemy. We should have finished him when we had him in chains years ago. Tell me, does he still limp?"

"He makes do with his wood foot," answered Myrrhine.

Tisamenus' amusement over Hegesistratus' impediment got the better of him. "Half man, half tree!" he shouted. "They say he must keep moving or his foot sprouts roots." His laughter was a contagion among them.

Pausanias spoke again. "Anything else about Mardonius?"

"He's fearless of the gods."

"Yet he retains a Hellene seer. Interesting."

"The gods will send him false prophecies," said Tisamenus. "Hegesistratus will be worse than useless to him."

"You should also speak to Palaemon," she suggested. "He noticed a weakness in Persian armor."

Pausanias then called for the smith as the generals tossed about her news, but Myrrhine could tell they were just buying time. Something else worried them. The generals stood weaving their thoughts, each afraid to speak first. Finally, Pausanias turned to her again.

"We have another problem," he said, "a greater threat than the Persians. We have no trust among ourselves. We see cowardice on the battlefield, insubordination. In the past, we've turned on our allies as soon as a battle was won. I wish nothing more than for us to live in peace beyond the coming battle, but we are all violent, changeable men, not to be trusted. We need an oath. If the aged Hierophant was still among us, he'd administer it, but since he's no longer with us, who could better perform the ceremony than his daughter, priestess of the goddess dwelling in the ruins of this holy temple?"

"You would have a woman administer it?" questioned Aeschylus.

Myrrhine felt hatred for Aeschylus thinking again how he'd given away Melaina.

Tisamenus spoke up. "The goddess Iris is oathgiver to the gods, so let us have a woman, a priestess to bind us in this oath."

Thus, it was agreed, over Aeschylus' objection, and the lot of them walked through the ruins to the toppled icons of Demeter and Kore.

Myrrhine ordered the heralds, "Bring a black ewe for Demeter, a snow-white ram for Helios, and a third sheep for Zeus."

The heralds departed while the rest mixed gleaming bowls of wine and water, in which they rinsed the hands of the generals. When they returned, Pausanias drew his sword and gave it to Myrrhine, who cut curly locks from the lambs' heads and handed them to the generals, as had the ancient Achaians at Troy.

Myrrhine read the papyrus scroll containing the words for the oath. She caught her breath and turned to Pausanias.

"You can't possibly expect them to swear this."

"What's wrong? We made a mistake?"

"By all that's sacred, yes," she said, her eyes flashing across those of each of the men. Her daughter's influence had overcome her. "The temples must be rebuilt. We can't expect Demeter to sanctify an oath denying her a new temple. What will happen to the Mysteries?"

The generals went off to themselves to discuss the issue, but resented being questioned by a woman and quickly returned, stone-faced as ever. "The statement stands," Pausanias said, sheepishly.

"Stubbornness is not a virtue," she chided. "We must rebuild the Telesterion." How could this be happening? she wondered. Surely the gods must still value the Mysteries.

"Leave these matters to those in power. If you'll not give the oath, we'll find another though it not strengthen our cause."

Myrrhine hesitated, she just couldn't do this, then remembered Hermes, the divine master of oath taking, how he lived by the letter but violated the spirit of the oath. Only those taking it will be bound, she thought, and these men will not do the rebuilding. She made her decision.

"Alright," she said, "I'll do as you wish. Woe be unto those who go against their oath. All oaths are surrounded by Furies." She stood before the ruins of the Telesterion and on the feet of Demeter, the only part of the Goddess' image that remained, and the spot where the full-figured stone sculpture had stood just days before. Myrrhine seemed to become Demeter herself as she raised her arms and prayed aloud so that all could hear.

"Father Zeus, greatest and most glorious lord of lightning ruling from Ida's height; fire-faced Helios, who sees and hears all things; Earth's Furies, snake-haired phantoms who punish the dead for falsely swearing; all ye gods be witness to our solemn oath."

Having so spoken, she turned to the multitude and had them repeat after her.

"I will fight to the death. I will not cherish life more than liberty, nor will I desert the leaders, whether they be living or dead. I will bury all allies who perish in battle. If we overcome the barbarians, I will never help destroy any cities that fought for Hellas nor will I rebuild any of the ravaged sanctuaries but leave them as a reminder of barbarian impiety."

So they all spoke, the murmur spreading in a dull chorus. Myrrhine cut the lambs' throats with the pitiless bronze and laid them on the ground gasping away their lives, black blood flowing into a large vessel. The generals stepped forward to thrust their hands into the rich liquid. They then poured wine while praying to the immortals.

"Zeus, father of mortals and immortals, to all who keep this oath grant prosperous cities, fertile land, faithful wives, and blameless children; but for those who don't, O Furies and all gods who wreak vengeance, sack their cities, decimate their fields with drought, and give them deceiving wives who bear children in the likeness of their enemies."

Myrrhine wasn't fond of the remark about wives and children but knew it had been customary since the time of Agamemnon. Tisamenus then read the entrails, obtained a favorable sign, and the army dispersed. The great mass of men then set off north. As the long river of humanity snaked along the road north, Myrrhine noticed a quiet determination she'd not seen before in warriors.

She retired to bury her father's bones, still smarting over Melaina's marriage to Kallias. Myrrhine, with the help of one of her slaves, prepared for the Hierophant's funeral. The slave dug the grave in the sacred chamber not far from where the bones of Kynegeiros lay. She looked upon her deceased husband's grave and felt the shame of what had happen. "How I wish you were here, Kynegeiros," she whispered. "Aeschylus has given Melaina to Kallias. Regardless of what your brother says, you surely didn't do this."

Myrrhine retrieved the sarcophagus containing her father's partially burned relics, arranged the ashes first, then the charred feet bones, what was left of the arms, spine, and finally the skull. The fire had consumed the fine bones of the hands. Yet, the skeleton seemed too small. They always did.

★

The next morning, as dawn's pink glow became visible in the east, she placed the sarcophagus inside the grave, covered it with dirt, and ordered a slave to place a large stone slab over it. She brought forward a cock, placed its head on the slab and cleaved it with one swift stroke, a sacrifice to Asklepios, god of resurrection. The wings flapped violently, sending huge gusts of wind about her and blood pumping from the wound. Myrrhine raised her hands. "Mother Earth, all mortals' Final Receiver, take this man, my father, into thy bosom for all eternity. I offer only this small fowl that his soul may be renewed in the Afterlife and taken directly to the Elysian Fields. Dear Hermes, guide of souls in the

Underworld, see to his swift voyage across the Styx, and let him not drink from the waters of the Lethe. Instead, take him directly to Kore, so that she may rest his cares. He was a great man, sending you many mortal souls. I know you must share my love for him, for you have seen fit to sacrifice all Eleusis as his funeral pyre. Care for him now. Never has the world seen the like of him."

Myrrhine returned to her own chamber of ashes. The fire had gone from the hearth of Hestia and from Myrrhine's world as well. When will I ever see my daughter again? she wondered. She retraced Demeter's steps after the goddess had lost her own daughter and had come to Eleusis after abandoning her search. Though she was hungry, Myrrhine sat without eating at the Kallichoron Well, where in the past, initiates had danced and twirled during the Mysteries. But now the well was crowded with old men trying to clean it of debris the Persians had dumped into it. She entered the sanctuary to the Mirthless Rock, where Demeter had sat mourning Kore's absence. Myrrhine spent the rest of the day there, and at the nearby Cave of Hades, wasting and waiting. The gates had been ripped from their hinges and the altar defiled.

At sundown, Myrrhine heard horse hooves on the cobblestone streets, and shortly, Aeschylus once again stood before her, this time with a nervous smile.

"Some time ago," Aeschylus said, "the generals received an oracle from Delphi saying that if we fight before a temple of Eleusinian Demeter, Hellas will be victorious. But since the Persians fled the Thriasian Plane for Boeotia, this has been thought impossible. It appeared all was lost, but last night the Plataean general Arimnestus dreamed that Zeus told him all the temples mentioned in the oracle are in Plataea. A frantic search has turned up nothing. I wonder if perhaps you know of a temple in Boeotia that might satisfy Delphi."

Myrrhine answered, "I was at that sanctuary a few days ago, but the goddess no longer resides there. The Boeotians abandoned her and her temple years ago."

"Then return with me. Show us the temple and ensure the

goddess' presence to bolster our cause. Bid her return."

"Let us examine this request," she said, turning to stare him down as she'd seen Melaina do in one of her most lax moments. "You've taken my daughter without permission, married her off to the biggest thief in Athens, not even allowing me my due at her wedding. Demeter's temple here in Eleusis is in ashes, and the generals have vowed not to rebuild it. Now you expect me to go into the war zone to resurrect another of Demeter's desecrated temples. All to save your stinking hide?"

"Stay then, but tell the location of the temple," he countered.

"Never!" she shouted.

Aeschylus shouted back, "We are not fighting Persia for me. Loose not your wrath upon all Hellas. We fight for our people-owned state."

"Bring Melaina. Let's talk of ending this marriage. Never will I believe this is the wish of your brother." She turned her back and walked away.

★

Myrrhine spent her days sifting ashes. She still went without food or washing, clothes tattered and blackened with soot, pulling her dark robe about her. Even in the presence of women, she lowered her veil. She took no interest in the constant stream of warriors from the east and west as they converged at Eleusis before turning north along the road over Oak Heads Pass and then continued on past the dark feet of Kithaeron to where the battle would be fought on the grassy banks of the Asopus. All her thoughts were of her dead father and Melaina, her pregnant daughter, now the caretaker of the home of the richest man in Athens.

Early one morning, Myrrhine dug herself out of her new sleeping quarters, a lean-to in the Cave of Hades where she'd taken to spending nights. She'd heard familiar voices and now saw young Sophocles coming toward her. Her old friend Kleito, messenger of mercy, was with him as well as Kleito's ever-present child Euripides, his hands already blackened with ashes.

"Oh, Myrrhine!" said Kleito, "how you've wasted away! You mustn't indulge in such fruitless grief."

"How can I live without Melaina? My father is dead. I have no one."

Myrrhine collapsed into Kleito's arms and cried the long hard tears she hadn't allowed herself. She still refused to eat, even refused a cup of wine. Kleito mixed a sacred drink, the kykeon: water, barley meal, and pennyroyal, which the initiates to the Mysteries took to break their fast.

"I saw Melaina a short while before she and Kallias left for Athens," said Kleito. "She was marvelously well, spirits high. In no more than a month, you'll be a grandmother."

"Oh Kleito!" cried Myrrhine, "I feel as though I've been sheltered all my days and now, finally, initiated into life itself. These painful gifts of the gods are too much to bear. The Mysteries have fallen into the hands of the Kerykes. The yoke about my neck is too heavy."

"Still, you can be glad for Melaina. There's no better bridegroom in all Hellas. Plouton, god of wealth himself, could offer no more."

Myrrhine wasn't consoled. "I must see her, Kleito. This marriage cannot be."

★

Two days later, Kallias showed his face for the first time since Eleusis burned. He didn't call Myrrhine to his home, but had come to her, entering the ashes of the cave looking tentative, guilt weighing heavily on his shoulders, and Aeschylus trailing behind. Melaina wasn't with them.

The mere sight of Kallias softened Myrrhine's heart. She'd coveted him for her own bed, and didn't really believe he was a thief, until now. She'd have to make peace with this man if she'd ever get to see her daughter, though she still hated him for what he'd done to the Eumolpids.

"Mardonius tells me you snatched Melaina from his very grip. An act of extraordinary courage."

"The prize was worth the risk," Kallias said.

"That man hiding behind you also tells me that you've finally snatched the Mysteries from the Eumolpids."

He would not meet her eyes and looked away, and Aeschylus stayed in the background.

"Kynegeiros would never have given Melaina to you. We both know that. Rest assured this is not over."

"What does a woman know of battlefield promises? Besides, what's done cannot be undone."

"Twice you've saved Melaina. Kynegeiros would be grateful. I'll not trouble you with a mother's disappointment at being absent from her own daughter's wedding, just a request. I must see her."

"In due time. Divine Justice weighs our fate against Persian greed, and all must seek their rightful place in our salvation."

"You'll not take me to her?" Myrrhine realized now that he'd been gentle with her in the past only because of Melaina.

"Some will fight at Plataea, others to protect Hellas from another attack by sea. Already I'm late to assume command aboard a trireme."

"Return when you have something to offer," she said.

Kallias maintained a silent stare, then relaxed. "Perhaps I have a solution. I maintain a home here in Eleusis. After all, I am the Dadouchos. I'll go this far. You help the generals at Plataea, show them the temple, pray Demeter's allegiance, and I'll see to it that Melaina spends two-thirds of the year here in Eleusis. I'll not stand in her way if she chooses to officiate at the Mysteries."

"As a Eumolpid or a Keyrkes?" she asked. Myrrhine was still angry and not able to force herself to voice acceptance. "The Mysteries are no more," she said. "The oath the generals took has relegated them to the past."

"Your daughter is well," he countered. "If you have words for my wife, I'll relay them."

When she made no reply, he quickly vanished, leaving Aeschylus standing before her.

"Would that the Hierophant had lived," he said.

"No doubt he'd have been able to stop Melaina's marriage and been more sympathetic to your request." She turned her back to him, walked away as she knew no woman should ever treat a man. But she'd done so to Kallias and was beginning to enjoy it.

"This people's republic has sprouted only a few years here in Hellas and is but a young sapling," Aeschylus said to her back. "It's the greatest gift any civilization has ever given humanity. If cut down now, it may disappear forever. Don't let it die on the battlefield at Plataea."

Myrrhine realized that he spoke the truth. She remembered her daughter's love of freedom. Devotion to her daughter changed her mind. She turned toward him. "The Hierophant could never have spoken for Demeter, anyway," she said, "but I can. Yes, I'll do this, Demeter willing."

CHAPTER 4: THE BATTLE OF PLATAEA

This time they reached Oak Heads Pass in half a day, Myrrhine astride a horse behind Sophocles, having refused to ride with Aeschylus. Riding for the first time was a frightening experience, and she clung desperately to the young man, her arms about his waist and embarrassment in her heart. They thundered past pack animals and foot soldiers going to reinforce those already at the battlefront.

At the narrow pass where rocky cliffs bordered each side of the road, a soldier commanding a squadron of Greek soldiers stepped into the road with his arm raised. Supply wagons crowded the side of the road. "Three nights ago," said the man blocking the way, "Persians waylaid a convoy of five-hundred wagons loaded with supplies. Only troops who can defend themselves are allowed through."

Aeschylus, Sophocles, and Myrrhine dismounted to stand beneath the towering crags, staring out over the spurs of Kithaeron that humped downward to a broken range of low rolling hills with the Asopus beyond. This was Boeotia, spread like a patchwork quilt. They saw Mardonius' army encamped on the far side of the thin ribbon of river, the bright sun revealing wispy outlines of the newly built palisade.

Aeschylus stood before the soldier. "We come at the order of Pausanias himself. Provide an escort. We must get through."

They waited while the soldiers argued and cursed. Finally, three unwilling horsemen with breastplates and iron helmets mounted. "They are all we can spare," the commander said.

On horseback once again, they plunged down the steep slope into the valley with the three mounted soldiers going before them. They rounded a hilltop and abruptly came upon a slaughter field. Bodies were strewn about, some lying in the road, others among shrubs and tender sprouts of fall grass. Two arrows were unleashed in their direction before they could arrest their charging pace and take to the brush themselves.

"Identify yourself," called a shaky voice.

Myrrhine slunk down behind Sophocles, felt herself tremble.

Aeschylus shouted back, "We're on a mission for Pausanias. We escort the priestess from Eleusis."

"Come forward slowly," said a shaky soldier stepping out of the bushes. "Proceed," he said. "We expected you yesterday."

Both Greek and Persian casualties of the recent battle lay beside the road and in the bushes, some dead, some in wounded agony. Several horses, bridled but riderless, stood nearby. "We've been harassed by Persian cavalry, called women," said one warrior. "What a grievous insult. The battle was very bloody." Several others came to the side of the road to watch them pass.

Myrrhine hid her face against Sophocles' back.

Before reaching the Asopus, Myrrhine motioned them off the main road toward Demeter's temple on a gentle swell of land where she and the blacksmith had been only days before. The temple was still abandoned and the softly rounded hills still covered by unspoiled grain. Breezes swept through wheat, the rich hair of the bountiful goddess, in this the most fertile plain of Boeotia.

As soon as he'd scouted the area, Aeschylus rode off in a cloud of dust. Myrrhine and Sophocles attended the icons of Demeter and Kore, clearing loose stones from the temple and propping the roof. She stood back and observed Demeter on her throne, set Kore standing straight on her pedestal alongside her mother. Long and hard she prayed that the goddesses return to the temple. She made excuses for the neglect shown Demeter's temple in recent years and promised her a great bounty for her support.

From the temple gate, Myrrhine stood with young Sophocles viewing the distant line of trees along the Asopus and Mardonius'

Palisade on the far shore. Since Myrrhine's little group had successfully crossed over Oak Heads pass, men and supplies streamed
along Kithaeron's spurs. The mountain was deep in shadow. Myrrhine heard Kithaeron and felt it as a great presence looming over
the sanctuary. Many considered Kithaeron Hera's mountain because she and Zeus were married on its summit. Myrrhine heard
the mountain's moan, sweet whispers in the late summer breeze.
It had been mother and nurse to newborns exposed on its slopes
since the days of Oedipus.

Aeschylus returned with three generals: Pausanias of Sparta,
commander of the united Greek forces; Aristides, general of the
Athenians; and Arimnestus, general of the Plataeans in whose
deme the temple of Demeter stood.

"This district is Argiopium," said Arimnestus. "We asked all
our eldest countrymen about the temple of Demeter, but no one
knew of it."

Myrrhine said, "Plataea has too long neglected Demeter in favor of male gods. Her temple here has been abandoned for many
years. Now you will have an opportunity to correct the injustice.
I've prayed to the goddess, but can't guarantee I've erased all her
anger at the neglect."

Arimnestus spoke to the other generals. "The foothills here at
Kithaeron's feet are full of ridges, hollows, and concealed potholes.
This makes it unsuitable for horses but good for foot soldiers.
Thus, it will be to our advantage in battle. Within this thickly
shaded grove stands the fane of Androcrates, another requirement
of the oracle. Thus all elements are satisfied."

"No! One remains," said Aristides. "The land belongs to Plataea, not Athens. The oracle stated that we Athenians must fight
on our own soil."

"That's critical," said Myrrhine. "Delphi's reasoning is sound.
Plataea must give this land to Athens, so that Athena will protect
it and all its allies. It is the goddesses who will save Hellas."

Arimnestus looked daggers at Myrrhine. "I'd be interested in
knowing more about why this is so. This controversy puts us at

odds with Athens."

"Thebes is the land of Ares, god of war. Its people are his descendants. Because of this, Ares will be on the side of Thebes and Persia in the coming battle."

"How can we hope for victory if Ares is against us?"

"Athena is always more fearsome in armed conflict than is Ares. She wounded Ares herself during the Trojan War."

"Eyie!" cried Arimnestus. "The priestess is correct. Plataea has a great dilemma. We must give our land to Athens or lose it to Persia."

Aristides said, "We're all Hellene, Arimnestus. Athens is a good friend."

"All right, Aristides. The oracle must be fulfilled. Although we prize our independence more than any other people, we'll remove our boundary stones."

"This is a great act of patriotism," said Aristides. "Plataea will live forever as the supreme example of nobility and magnanimity."

Myrrhine added, "Let it be known throughout the army that the battle for Hellas will be won and lost here, before Demeter's temple."

Myrrhine's words evaporated in the noise of sheep, goats, and pigs descending on the sanctuary. It seemed an invasion of the four-footed. Soon she saw that shepherds drove the animals. A chariot drawn by four white horses followed them closely. At the reins was a female charioteer, the first Myrrhine had ever seen. Beside the woman, Myrrhine recognized, having seen him only recently at Eleusis, short, thin Tisamenus, the seer. No sooner did Tisamenus dismount the carriage than four more men arrived. Myrrhine took them to be assistants and students of the great seer.

Myrrhine couldn't help staring at the woman charioteer. She was so beautiful. She wore the normal chiton belted at the waist, but over it, a long black mantle fastened with buttons at the shoulders. Her hair was the most brilliant gold Myrrhine had ever seen, Helios himself seemingly shining from within. The woman wore her hair parted in the middle, brought low down the sides of her face, and pulled to the back in a braid so long that it fell all the way to her feet. It was tied-off by a black tassel. Myrrhine tried to talk to the woman, but found that they had no common language.

The generals left, slapping their horses' flanks for more speed, and Tisamenus quickly set to work, shouting his assistants into action. First, in the courtyard before the icons of Demeter and Kore, he put up a large slaughter stone and dug a roasting pit where his helpers stacked firewood. Then he pulled a table from the carriage and, on the ground beside it, placed another large stone. He placed his left foot on the stone and leaned forward, resting his left arm on his knee. Again and again, he assumed the position, gauged the table's distance, pushing it away, then pulling it closer. Once satisfied, he ordered the sacred animals placed in pens, the sheep and goats separated, the swine isolated.

Several other seers and their assistants also appeared, but Tisamenus drove them a stone's throw away while mumbling to himself, "Charlatans and the feebleminded. What a worthless lot we seers are."

When all was in place, Tisamenus unlaced his sandals, discarded them, and dressed himself in seer's clothes. The liver scrutinizer wore a short-sleeved undergarment closed at the neck, and over it a knee-length, pleated cloak held together at the breast by a golden clasp. Upon his curly head, he wore a hat rising to a high, narrow, conical top, held fast by bands down the sides of the face and knotted under the chin. He remained barefooted.

Myrrhine took the woman's hand, and led her back from the men. She seemed afraid, but Myrrhine appreciated her presence, the two of them the sole feminine presence in this world of men. She wore a diadem, which marked her as royalty. "Who is this woman," she asked of Tisamenus.

"She's an Etruscan Priestess of the Dawn," he answered. "She's also my wife, Auroriana, and not very pleased with me bring her here." He adjusted his cloak that seemed a bit large for his thin frame, told Auroriana something in a tongue Myrrhine did not know.

Auroriana hugged Myrrhine than held both her hands in front of her, smiled.

Tisamenus said, "She's pleased you're a priestess. Look after her, if you don't mind. She's lacking in your battlefield courage, though she can drive a chariot like a madman."

What battlefield courage? thought Myrrhine. She let go of the woman's hands and looked back at Tisamenus, who'd finished dressing. Not only was Tisamenus small in stature but also small-boned. His fingers were long, supple, and delicate. The hands of a woman, Myrrhine thought, and felt jealous of the smooth, soft look of his skin.

"You approve of my uniform?" Tisamenus asked.

"It's not my place to approve or disapprove," Myrrhine answered.

"Still, you have an opinion."

"I'm curious of its origin."

"Also from Etruria," he said, "the city of Tarquinia, northwest of Rome. I learned seercraft from the Etruscans, and they let me take a wife. You may have heard Hellenes call them Tyrrhenians. I'm one of the few to read from the Disciplina Etrusca of Tages, grandson of Tinia, greatest of all gods. There I'm known as a haruspex."

Myrrhine was familiar with the myth of Tages, a gray-haired infant who was supposed to have been unearthed by a peasant plowing with a bronze-tipped blade. The divine child sprang out of the soil chanting ancient texts from which came Etruscan knowledge of prophecy. The Etruscans were known as the most religious people in all the world. She wondered why a Greek had been given such distinction, then remembered that Delphi had foretold that Tisamenus would one day guide Sparta to five victories in battle. Even the Etruscans respected Delphi.

Aeschylus returned along with several more generals, and Myrrhine watched as the Greek army strategically repositioned about the temple. Shortly the grove came alive with men of war and their assistants. Wagons loaded with supplies and armor came alongside them.

Myrrhine stood beside Auroriana, out of Tisamenus' way, as she knew a woman's unrequested presence during a sacrifice wasn't appreciated. The generals hovered about in the failing light like lost souls in the Underworld while Tisamenus prepared to perform his entrails-reading at the table lit by torches and oil lamps. His assistants gathered about, two of them removing their tunics, to Myrrhine's great surprise. She turned her head a walked away.

Just to Tisamenus' left stood a powerfully built naked but bearded man with a spear. On the other side of the seer, opposite the naked spear-carrier, stood an older man, also in haruspex dress and leaning on a staff. To this man's right stood another naked man holding an olive branch. Tisamenus draped a cloak about the man's shoulders.

Tisamenus called Auroriana to her horses and then turned to Myrrhine, entreating her to stand behind the two seers.

"Surely not among naked men," she answered.

"They serve the ritual. We can't do it without another woman."

Slowly, she crept around to the place Tisamenus designated.

"Stand here," he said. "Face forward and keep your eyes intent upon the entrails. She peered between them at the liver on the table as Tisamenus examined it. She hoped he didn't expect her to voice an opinion for she had little knowledge of reading entrails. She wished she'd been party to her daughter's teaching by blind Udaeüs at Epidaurus.

All the masculinity around her overcame Myrrhine. She'd never been this close to a group of male relatives, much less so many strangers, and naked at that! Her heart raced wildly in spite of herself. She felt an uncommon sense of purpose and dignity among them. After they all fell into position, Auroriana led forward the four white horses by their bridles and stood behind Myrrhine and Tisamenus. So close was she to Myrrhine, she could smell the marjoram in the girl's hair and feel horses' breath ruffling her skirt.

Tisamenus turned to the generals. "Your question for the gods?"

The generals argued among themselves for a moment before Pausanias gave an answer. "Ask them under what conditions we'll win the battle against the Persians."

Tisamenus stepped from his carefully positioned compatriots to stand before Pausanias. "Idiot! You expect I'll extract a scroll from within the animal? Perhaps I should ask for a discourse on the meaning of the universe? Formulate a question with a 'yes' or 'no' answer, otherwise I'll retire to tend the flocks."

Pausanias, though young, was a large man standing before small Tisamenus, and the heated reprimand appeared as though it came from a child. Again, Pausanias consulted the generals while Tisamenus set fire to the timber in the roasting pit. Shortly Pausanias and the other generals came to him again. "Will we defeat the Persians if we force the attack?"

Satisfied with the question, Tisamenus brought the first sheep forward and slit its throat on the slaughter stone, couching the question within unintelligible words and waiting for blood to drain into the pit. When the animal stopped kicking, he slit the underside from stem to stern, broke open the ribcage with a crunch, and extracted the entrails: the still-beating heart, lungs, windpipe, and liver, all of which he laid on the table before him as he reassumed his position within the group. He performed a superficial examination of the heart, lungs, and windpipe, finally pronouncing, "The animal is healthy."

Picking up the liver, Tisamenus placed his left foot on the stone and turned his right foot perpendicular to it but flat on the ground. He held the liver in the hollow of his left hand, the large lobes hanging like pouches, making the liver's details distinct but dripping both blood and green bile. The back of the wrist of the holding hand rested on the bent knee of the left leg. Fingers of the right hand gently, sensually stroked and alternately played along the liver's wet surface as though he was plucking the strings of a lyre. All the while, Tisamenus chanted in a foreign tongue and complained of the liver's condition and color. Finally, he stopped.

"No!" he shouted, and Myrrhine jumped, so close was she to him and so loud his response. "The god's answer is, 'No!'"

Myrrhine stepped away from the group, assuming they were finished, but Tisamenus called her back. While Tisamenus put the entrails on the fire and called a slave to finish carving the animal for roasting, the generals again consulted, then put a new question to him. "Ask if we'll be defeated if we force the attack."

"Never ask a question so a favorable result means your doom. You can't trick the gods into the answer you desire."

"Then put it this way: Will we win if we let the Persians force the attack?"

A second sacrificial lamb was brought forward.

Myrrhine had witnessed seers at work before, but Tisamenus had an aura about him. She'd also not seen one so deliberate in his actions or mindful of his assistants. He demanded that the position of each remain the same as when he'd read the previous liver. She finally realized that their motions and posture were not at all spontaneous but repetition, ritual. He's recreating some scene from Tages ancient text, she thought. The magic of the setting must provoke the presence of the gods, causing them to impress their intentions upon the animal's liver. She'd never seen so much blood.

Again the rite was performed, another lamb slaughtered, and this time the answer came back "yes." The generals had confirmation that they must wait until the Persians crossed the river.

Yet not all the generals were so impressed, as not all believed in divination. "What a petty trifle augury is," said one. "I've seen it all before. What if two lambs are sacrificed simultaneously, but in one the liver is smooth and full and the other rough and shrunken? What ambivalent divinity then sent the condition and color? All these contrivances are but a joke sent by Zeus. The troops are starving to death. We must engage the enemy soon or they'll have no strength to fight."

Pausanias argued his support for Tisamenus. "My blood has not turned cold but boils for battle also. Although I'm young, I've learned respect for the will of the gods. I'm aware of our need for provisions," he said. "Losing the caravan a few nights ago cost us dearly. But going against the gods would prove disastrous. Patience, my friends, patience."

The men wouldn't let it rest. "Zeus speaks to us through lightning and thunder. Read those signs also."

"I'm a haruspex," said Tisamenus. "If you desire a fulguriator, seek another diviner. Look!" His arm swept their surroundings. "Local seers are thick as the trees of this sacred glen. Use one of them."

Thus the generals did consult with the uncommissioned seers gathered on the outskirts of the temple, but all the omens came back the same. Still, some complained that the generals didn't want to fight and had influenced the seers toward negative results.

Tisamenus was outraged. "Soldiers!" he shouted. "The sacrifices are not favorable for good reason. Remember, Delphi also said to honor patience until the Persians charge across the Asopus."

Since none of the victims proved favorable for an attack, the generals suspended the offerings. Tisamenus and Auroriana retired to their tent, he pulling the woman from Myrrhine's arms, neither wanting to be separated. The generals argued well into the night. Some championed attacking at dawn no matter what, others favored waiting until the augury changed. The two groups hammered at each other with all the arguments. Finally, the generals rose to their feet with a roar. No decision! Wanting it both ways.

Myrrhine was expecting the warriors to turn upon each other, when a shout went up from outside the sacred quarter. A lone horseman had entered the outskirts of camp and requested audience with "Aristides the Just."

Aristides talked with him outside torchlight, the horseman holding the reins in one hand and gesticulating wildly with the other. Presently, he mounted and rode back in the direction he'd come. Aristides returned, heading directly for Pausanias' tent. The two then entered the temple, fearing they'd be overheard, but took little notice of Aeschylus, Sophocles, and Myrrhine.

"Our visitor was King Alexander of Macedonia," she heard Aristides say to Pausanias. "He tells a strange story, insisting I tell you but no other. Mardonius has decided to attack at dawn, no matter the omens. Myrrhine was right about Mardonius. He doesn't fear the gods, or if he does, doesn't fear them as much as he does the reinforcements joining us daily. Hegesistratus' entrails readings have also been against the Persians carrying out an assault, but Mardonius has chosen to ignore them. The Persians are running out of food."

"Mardonius is indeed foolish," said Pausanias. "The one who crosses the Asopus will lose the war. What great news! Does Alexander want something in return?"

"He's obviously playing both sides. Since Mardonius occupies his country, Alexander must support him but, being Hellene, wishes us well tomorrow and asks that we remember the great risk he's taken coming here. He wants us to do something about freedom for Macedonia should we prevail."

Myrrhine searched for a place to put a bed where she'd be away from Aeschylus and Sophocles. She wished Auroriana hadn't gone with her husband and would have stayed with her. She heard the generals discuss shuffling their forces to resist the Persian assault. The Athenians had successfully fought the Persians at Marathon; therefore, they'd line up opposite them. Since the Spartans had fought the Boeotians many times, they would try their luck with them again.

Myrrhine put out the torches in the temple, hoping to sleep a little before dawn. Aeschylus and Sophocles stood guard and talked softly at the entrance. As she laid a bearskin on the hard ground, thoughts of Melaina returned. Kallias had mentioned joining the fleet in the Aegean. Would Melaina be left alone? Who would take care of her? The baby could come at anytime.

At sunrise the next morning, Myrrhine woke hearing Auroriana praying to Thesan, Goddess of the Dawn, and she rose herself to see what the generals were up to. Mardonius, instead of attacking, sent a herald across the river to propose that the Spartans and Persians fight a single battle to determine the victor. The herald insulted the Spartans, calling them cowards for letting the Athenians line up opposite them. When the herald received no answer, he returned. Shortly, the Persian cavalry engaged the Greeks in skirmish after skirmish, but Persian ground forces stayed north of the river. All day the raids continued, ceasing only because of darkness. The assault about which King Alexander had warned never came. And apparently, all had been done in hopes that the Greeks could be provoked into crossing the Asopus to attack first.

That night, the Greeks again shifted their positions all along the front, seeking a location with more water. Persian cavalry had defiled the best source. Tisamenus was missing from camp, and Auroriana came to stay with Myrrhine, the two of them fashioning a makeshift bed next to Demeter's statue. Myrrhine heard Auroriana's soft-whispered breaths of sleep but could not slumber herself. She heard the generals arguing well past midnight.

★

The rattle of armor woke Myrrhine well before Auroriana rose to start her prayers to Thesan. Tisamenus also stalked about, rounding up sacrificial victims and grumbling of an apparent shortage. Some had been stolen for food during the night. When Tisamenus took to sacrificing again, the generals, along with thousands from the Spartan army, flocked around the altar, a great herd of humanity, each man weighing his own fate in the outcome of the sacred rite.

Myrrhine, Auroriana and the rest of Tisamenus' little group fell into place. The beautiful woman brought forward the four white horses, and the sacrificial victims' blood flowed. Cries of dismay erupted when the omens again showed unfavorable. Again and again sacrificial animals were brought forward, black blood flowed upon the slaughter stone, thirsty earth drank life's sap, and all for naught.

Came the sun, and with a great cry, the Persian infantry finally crossed the Asopus and began mustering for a full assault. Pausanias, desperate that the gods let him repel the attack, pushed the seer mercilessly for favorable omens. Still, the gods forbade the Greeks to fight. Pausanias ordered the army to sit on its shields and offer no resistance. This, the men accepted grudgingly as barbarian horsemen charged their position and whistling arrows decimated their ranks.

Sacrifices came as fast as Persian horses, with Pausanias in the middle of Tisamenus, and Tisamenus himself struggling, now breaking open a trembling carcass, now standing one foot upon his stone and fingering the shimmering translator of the gods' will, the liver.

"Perhaps the other entrails," suggested Pausanias. "How about the lungs?"

Tisamenus, his eyes revealing a mind in a whir, hadn't heard the commander. "We're out of animals," he said, eyes wide with terror.

Pausanias flew into a frenzy, words but no sense coming from his lips as he raged wildly among the trees, imprecating unholy curses. He stopped all of a sudden having noticed Auroriana's four white horses used in the ceremony.

"Four hoofed entrails there," he said.

Auroriana screamed in protest, as if she'd understood him.

"No!" shouted Tisamenus, "never could we violate the sacred ceremony they serve." He pushed Pausanias back from them.

"By Zeus! Extract your own then and read them." Pausanias stood before Tisamenus as if he'd filet the seer himself, misfortune had so unhinged him. He spotted an ox yoked to a wagon. "The beast of burden!" he cried, dragging it forward, the ox bellowing protest.

"The victim must be pure in body and soul, uncorrupted. Next you'll have me read entrails of rats and lizards." But Tisamenus relented, tried to feed the ox a handful of grain, but it bellowed and took no notice. "The animal is not healthy!" he shouted.

But Pausanias wouldn't take no for an answer. Soon, the gigantic liver was laid out on the table, and when the seer positioned himself, eyes feasting as if never having seen so much victual for scrutiny, he had to use both hands to lift it.

Pausanias loomed over him, helping along the reading.

"Stand back!" Tisamenus said. "You're a disruption."

Pausanias didn't budge. "There, the hue is deepest next the gallbladder," he said.

"The broad lobe carries the greatest import," countered Tisamenus. "Zeus' influence is there. But look! The liver's head is wanting. The answer is 'no.' The omens taunt us still."

Over Tisamenus' protest, they brought another ox, felling it without bothering to remove the yoke. As the seer leaned forward to read the new behemoth liver, the roar of Persian menace rose among them. Enemy horses entered the sacred glen, and Myrrhine fell back inside the temple as Aeschylus and Sophocles rushed into the fray. Auroriana abandoned her horses to stand behind her. Myrrhine watched as Persians on horseback scattered the sacrifice and neared the temple entrance. Pausanias and the other generals, even without actual weapons, drove the horsemen off with staves and whips.

But the chaos had rousted a sacred swine refuged amongst the bushes. Tisamenus, his little group scattered and the four horses nowhere to be seen, fell upon it and dragged it to the slaughter stone, threw a little holy water at it, slit its throat.

"This is indeed a good omen," said Myrrhine. "You've been sacrificing to the wrong god. Swine is the proper sacrifice for Demeter. It's she who'll save Hellas."

"But Hera's area of the liver overlaps that of Demeter. Who can tell the difference?" Tisamenus appeared disillusioned himself.

"Perhaps Hera's jealousy is interfering. Ever she bemoans Zeus siring Kore by Demeter," suggested Myrrhine.

"Yes!" shouted Pausanias, "the mother of us all is against us.

'Tis hopeless!" While Tisamenus remained bent over the liver, young Pausanias turned his back on the whole affair. Greatly depressed, he looked towards Kithaeron with tears in his eyes and shouted a prayer.

"Glorious Hera, greatest of all goddesses, high upon the tip of Kithaeron's darksome hollows where you and almighty Zeus were married, peer down upon us here on its slopes where Greeks now die at the hands of Persians. Listen to this prayer of desperation. If it's not our fate to win victory, at least let us not perish to Persian might without performing some great act. Let the enemy know they've waged war with courageous warriors and not cowards. Come to us in this hour of doom, rescue us from disgrace and forever we'll sacrifice glistening fat and succulent thigh pieces in your honor."

While Pausanias prayed, so Tisamenus read the last entrails, ignoring the portents of Zeus and relying exclusively on those from Demeter. Thus the soothsayer called out, "Yes! Victory is at hand! Loose the troops upon the battlefield."

Pausanias charged from the shady glen into the bright sunlight, his face relaxed and joy in his voice as he shouted the news. Aeschylus followed, but Myrrhine and Sophocles went only a short distance beyond the temple gate. Auroriana, having abandoned her horses, trailed along behind them. The Persian cavalry had broken off contact, but the enemy army, now fully mustered for a full frontal assault, began to move forward. Pausanias drew himself upon a wagon, and Myrrhine heard him address the troops of the phalanx as they donned battle garb.

"Mardonius hastens toward two evils, loss of valor and death. Therefore, welcome Persia! Bring your arrows, swords! Harness your steeds. Fill the plain with the clangor of shields. Great warriors of Sparta! Finally, we go to battle and grave danger. Even the most gallant feels fear, so if you see someone faint of heart, bethink you this: we are all that stands between Hellas and ruin. Summon to glory one another by name. Pursuit creates courage even in cowards. Sweet are the memories of a gallant victory."

Myrrhine watched heavily armed hoplites slip on bronze helmets and tighten their bony cuirasses about their chests, fasten greaves about their shins. Each lightly armed assistant nervously performed the motions of dressing his hoplite, holding his master's shield with its large 'Α' in the center, the Spartans their 'Λ,' handing him his long spear as the trumpets sounded for all to fall into phalanx formation. Officers ran down the ranks shouting for a tighter formation. Soldiers, eight rows deep, stretched into the distance as far as Myrrhine could see.

Aeschylus ran off to join the phalanx, and as she watched him leave, she couldn't help wishing some Persian would kill him. She stopped her vengeful thoughts and chidden herself. "Forgive me, Kynegeiros," she said softly. "Don't punish me for the runaway anger."

Sophocles had stayed behind, and now he climbed to the top of the temple wall and called to Myrrhine. "Stretch out your hand," he said. "I'll help you mount the stairs. Look before us! We've a fortunate position here. The Persian host is clearly visible." Myrrhine helped Auroriana up the wall. Once there, Myrrhine saw the field ablaze with bronze, the fiery glint of polished iron, shield blazons.

"Look, priestess, a white horse," said Sophocles.

"It's the cousin of King Xerxes, Mardonius himself, come to lead the charge. I spoke with him only a few days ago."

Pausanias, at the right corner of the phalanx, shouted the order to march as long lines of red-and-blue plumes began to nod rhythmically. He cued the corps of auletes, the pipers, to toot the beat, and it moved forward, increasing the rhythm to move quickly past the zone of arrows as the rumble of their feet shook the ground. The unerring marksmen finally let loose their deadly darts. At that range, any man could die without encountering the enemy and without the opportunity of at least winning a glorious death.

With the Persian war cry, the Greeks broke out in song and struck up the paean, the great chorus of tuned voices raising the battle shout. Warriors couched their spears, the song heating every faint heart's blood to battle fever. As they marched, so they came closer to the Persian line and the louder they sang.

"Hie! Hie! Paean! To him we cry! Oh joy! Oh joy! May you never leave us. Cast out pestilence and bring valor and victory! Oh joy! Paean. Oh joy! Hie! Hie! Paean!" The force of their voices charged them forward, with the aulete piping the rhythm and melody.

"The crowd of Persians comes in full panoply," said Myrrhine. "It's my place to brace the temple gate. Eleusis was the last of Demeter's temples they'll desecrate."

Myrrhine descended the stairs, heart racing with fear. Did she have the courage? She assumed her station with young Sophocles at her side. She heard the unearthly clash of steel as the two forces collided, shrill cries telling of the wounded and maimed, the dying. The paean dissipated in the thud of battle. Spear met javelin, sword rung against dagger, as the two phalanxes thrust and writhed together in a grotesque deadlock dance. Desperate Persians took to catching Greek spears with their hands and breaking off the tips. Myrrhine was glad the battle raged at a distance.

Just as it appeared the two forces were headed for mutual annihilation, the formations broke, lines shattered, and warriors fell into lumps of agonizing, cursing humanity. The light-armed troops piled into the fray, and the blood-spilling masses drifted about the battlefield until they came directly before the temple of Demeter. A Persian spear hit the ground flat at Myrrhine's feet and scooted all the way to the temple wall. Arrows whistled overhead.

Myrrhine took a step back, her courage faltering, and bumped into Sophocles. Where would she muster the spirit to perform her task? She couldn't imagine the courage it took for the men to stand their ground against such odds. Her own husband had died in such a battle. What a man he must have been, the bravest of the brave, everyone called him.

Myrrhine stood facing the battling forces. Dressed in white, she was a stark presence glowing in sunlight amid the sacred glen's shadows. She raised her left hand to lift a lapel of her mantle, her long curls falling to her shoulders. About her head was a stephane of myrtle. To find strength, she prayed, her words cascading over the battlefield.

"O great goddess Demeter, bringer of seasons, she who causes seed to sprout from fertile fields so the whole of broad Earth teems with leaves and flowers, she whose holy rites bless those who have seen them, terrorize these barbarians, send your maelstrom of malevolent ecstasy, bring holy horror upon those who defiled your temple at Eleusis, punish…"

In the midst of her prayer, Auroriana came up behind her, using Myrrhine as her own human shield. Auroriana pointed off to the right. So it was that the man on the white horse came screaming into battle: Mardonius surrounded by his best thousand troops, flower of the Persian army. At the edge of a crag, a lone Greek crawled to its summit, raised a stone. As horse and rider passed beneath, he smote the general square upon the skull.

Myrrhine's prayer echoed among the din of war as the force knocked Mardonius from the white charger, laid bare the warm brain steaming. Mardonius crumpled into dust, flung wide his arms and panted away his life.

Still the battle raged, a victor nowhere in sight.

CHAPTER 5: EXILE

Kallias flogged the four black horses drawing the chariot, his concentration broken only as he shouted to all they encountered, "Persians! Persians!" Along the bay he fled with Melaina, out of Eleusis with the open sea to their left and sunset turning from bright orange to dull gray before them. Melaina wondered if he'd run the horses to death. Great beasts they seemed, harbingers of the death from which they fled. She feared the child within her would be shaken from her womb.

Not until they entered the outskirts of Megara did Kallias let up to negotiate the shadowed city streets along the waterfront. He reined in the stallions at the ferry to Salamis and drove the chariot aboard the two-oared skiff without consulting the ferryman.

"Get us out of here!" Kallias shouted.

The aged ferryman stood sullen, unresponsive. A soiled garb hung by a knot round his shoulders, his hand upon the boatman's pole. His chin was an untrimmed grizzle, his eyes orbs of staring fire.

"Persians!" shouted Kallias walking among the horses trying to quiet them, and them blenching at his bellow. The horses were all eyes and trembling, nostrils flared, soapy foam soaking their flanks.

Melaina was glad to be aboard the ferry and stepped from the carriage realizing she was barefooted. She took the reins and tried to quiet the horses, huge gusts of breath coming from their nostrils.

The ferryman refused a sack of gold Kallias thrust on him. "Patience," the man said, "never does the ferry leave dock before time."

The dusky barge swelled with shouting passengers: matrons, boys and maidens, mothers panting pink from the run. As birds flock south when the fall chill fills the air, so Megarians came before the Persian flood, a migration seeking safety afloat the ferry.

Melaina looked along the coast to the bright flames rising above Eleusis wondering if her mother and grandfather had met their fate. And what of her companions? Tears streaked her cheeks as she thought of little Agido and Anaktoria. Everything had happened so fast that she could hardly believe she was alive herself. She owed her own safety a second time, plus that of her child, to Kallias.

The ferryman called out his destinations. "Who's for Salamis' westward tip? Who for Kerberia or Lethe's plain?" Melaina recognized the last two as references to the Underworld and thought it a grim joke.

Kallias left the reins with Melaina and chased after the ferryman, spouting a stream of oaths. "You pus bucket. I'm the Dadouchos with a priestess of the Mysteries to protect. Get us out of here!"

But the ferryman went about his business collecting fees and apportioning the deck to old men and mothers with children, refusing a herd of goats, one of sheep. Finally, he unfurled the small sail, loosed the tie lines, and signaled to the man at the poles. "Heave ahoy!" he shouted.

At the last moment, a runner carrying a torch jumped onboard. "Delphic fire!" the man shouted, "by order of the Archon Basileus."

They pushed off, two men at the stern alternately pushing and pulling at the handle, plying the long sweep-oar propelling the craft. Gradually, they moved away from dock into the black night. A torch at each end of the ferry cast an eerie glow onboard, but black water surrounded them. Flames spread along the coast as the Persians loosed wildfire on buildings, orchards, wheat fields. As the ferry crossed the Strait of Megara, the torches on dock at Salamis gradually emerged.

"Slow down! Easy!" shouted the ferryman as he loosened the halyards. "Push her to." They crunched into the dock, sending a shudder through the crowd and shaking the horses so they stumbled about and whinnied nervously.

Once offloaded, Kallias ushered Melaina quickly into the chariot and once again drove the horses with the whip, although the stallions' eagerness equaled his. The previous year, when he'd brought Melaina home from Brauron, they'd had young Sophocles to light the way, but now they charged blindly though the perilous night, courting disaster at every turn. Once off the peninsula, the surface improved and lights of small villages cast a dim glow across their path. A bay cut deeply through the island to the right of the road, and they entered a town at its edge, but Kallias kept the whip cracking.

When she saw refugees' tents dotting the roadside, Melaina knew they were approaching Samos Town. She'd seen it all last year. Kallias then slowed, picking his way through the crowds to the far shore and to the hill on the promontory from which Melaina had fallen during the battle of Salamis. He pulled up at water's edge. Here they needed no torches, for across the channel, all Athens was flame atop flame, lapping darkness from the firmament. Melaina remembered her mother's words that fire was the coinage between mortals and immortals. Melaina wondered if the gods had felt cheated by their puny sacrifices and wanted Athens and the whole of Attica sent to the Realm of the Divine. She could feel the heat and feared the earth and water themselves would catch fire, the world burn.

Kallias was quiet, staring off into the distant flames. Melaina wondered whether he viewed the fire only as a spectacle or truly sensed the loss. She glanced out the corner of her eye, knowing it was not proper to take in his presence fully. She saw the red glow reflected on his wet cheek, thought it glistening sweat, then realized the truth of it. Kallias was crying.

"Will you take me to Kleito, please?" she asked.

As they entered the women's quarters at Mnesarchides' home,

Melaina heard loud voices and saw a distraught, fist-shaking Kleito standing before her husband. Kleito stabbed a finger at him while holding her truant son, Euripides, by the ear.

Little Euripides saw Melaina first and struggled from his mother's clasp, sacrificing his ear for the comfort of Melaina's arms. "I haven't the strength to lift you now, Euri," she said.

Seeing Melaina, Kleito screamed and rushed to her as if the rest of the world, husband included, had evaporated. She threw her arms around the girl. "We thought you were all dead. Your mother! Are you here without Myrrhine? And barefooted?"

Melaina told her of the narrow escape in Kallias' chariot and that they knew nothing of her mother's fate.

Kleito noticed Melaina's swollen abdomen. "I doubt anyone in Hellas doesn't know that the maid who gave the prayer the night before the battle of Salamis is pregnant by a god. The priests of Epidaurus claim you conceived there in the Abaton."

Kleito led Melaina to the hearth, piling on wood for light and heat. She locked the double doors to the women's quarters and ordered the maids to bring a chair and cover it with a heavy fleece. Kleito insisted upon examining Melaina, stripping the chiton with a force Melaina was powerless to resist. Kleito slackened the breastbands and let them slip free.

"You appear healthy enough, but signs indicating the baby's sex are confusing. You've excellent color and your right breast is enlarged, firm and full, as one would expect with a male child. But your left breast is equally large, perhaps even fuller, the nipple more swelled as with a female. Still, you're without the pallor. Is the baby's movement notable?"

"Vigorous at times. Slow, even sluggish at others."

"Strange. I've not seen all this except with twins, but signs are never certain. How's your movement?"

"Oh! Slow. I'm a cow!" She noted Kleito had adopted the mannerisms of the physician who examined her at Eleusis, his clipped questioning.

"Another sign of a female. What a bag of contradictions!

You're past your eighth month, not a time to be jostled about in a chariot. I'm surprised you and the child survived intact."

It was late, and Melaina wanted to sleep, but Kleito wasn't about to let her rest. The woman pushed and poked at her abdomen until Melaina thought surely she'd injure the baby. Even the personal regions weren't beyond Kleito's scrutiny. Melaina had never seen such fuss even from a midwife. Kleito went to her chamber, and when she returned, held two white lumps. "Vaginal suppositories," Kleito said.

Melaina was vexed, blushed crimson. "But why?" she whined.

"Goose fat and marrow to relax the womb," added Kleito. With that, she spread Melaina's knees, felt the cleft with her fat warm hand and inserted the cold lumps, fidgeting as if something were wrong. "The vaginal covering is still partially intact. Astounding, considering your condition!" She pushed the suppositories home and proceeded inside to the orifice of the uterus, anointing it with her finger.

Melaina squinted and winced with pain. "The priest at Epidaurus told me no such membrane exists."

"Women's truth and what men think they know of it are two different things." Kleito sat beside her, content to stare at Melaina's face. "Some immortal certainly set your cheeks aglow." Kleito jumped into action again. "You sag!"

Kleito's head disappeared inside a chest but quickly reappeared with a broad linen bandage. She placed the middle under the bulk of child-filled abdomen, brought both ends round the sides, crossed them, laid them over Melaina's shoulders and fastened them in front on the encircling band. The contraption reminded Melaina of that she'd used on her grandfather following his ordeal with the irons. Kleito anointed the protruding abdomen with a cerate of green-olive oil and myrtle. "Toned skin doesn't break or wrinkle," she offered.

Finally, Melaina was laid down to sleep. A guarding maid sat at her bedside.

★

Next morning, Kleito found a pair of sandals for her, and Melaina paced, awaiting any word from Eleusis. Kallias stalked in the background, a dark shadow among stone walls outside the women's chamber. Kleito's maids hovered around Melaina. Midmorning they heard a great flurry of activity from the slaves and the shouts of approaching men as Aeschylus entered the courtyard.

Aeschylus was more surprised at Melaina's presence on Salamis than she at his, and very pleased. "I thought the Persians had you for sure."

"My mother!" she cried. "Tell me of my mother."

"Safe!"

"Oh, what relief! Yet, your eyes betray some catastrophe."

"A tale to slaughter the heart."

"Oh, do tell me it's not Grandfather."

"Perished defending the Holiest of Holies. Cremated by its timbers."

She turned away. "And he'd just regained his health at such a terrible price. The others? Palaemon, my girlfriends? What of stout-hearted Sophocles?"

"The blacksmith and his slaves weathered Persian wrath. Sophocles saved your mother."

"My friends?"

"Agido, saved herself, her swift feet."

"Oh, the comforts amid such sorrow! Agido alive! But Anaktoria?"

"No word."

With that, Kallias drew Aeschylus aside and walked him back to the men's quarters, where they remained for sometime.

"War plans," Kleito said. "Carnage forever occupies men's minds."

When the men returned, Melaina approached her uncle. "Please. Return me to Eleusis. My mother mustn't go through this alone."

Aeschylus stared at her before answering, his great black eyebrows twitching. "You and your mother must go separate ways. Henceforth, you'll be with me."

"But my mother needs me, and I her. It's but a short distance by boat. Surely someone, a slave, could return me."

"You're no longer in your mother's care."

"I belong to my mother. Nature demands it."

"No. You were your father's daughter. At his death, you became mine."

"But surely I'm of no use. I'm always in the way. You know the trouble I cause. Aunt Philokleia, why she'd flog you herself for bringing me."

Aeschylus laughed. "You won't be long with us. I'm giving you to Kallias."

"What travesty is this? Enslaved within my own country? Is that the punishment I suffer for an unwanted pregnancy?"

"Not a matter of slavery but marriage. Your father willed it so on the battlefield, before his death."

Oh, no! she thought. She felt dizzy and wondered if she was to have a seizure. No wonder Kallias has always been there to pull me from death's clutches. "But he doesn't even like me." She saw a wry smile cross Kallias' face. "Besides…." She could never voice the fact that she herself didn't care for the man. "I'm to be exiled from Eleusis?"

"Not exile. Given a new life."

"I have no dowry. All I own is in ashes at Eleusis."

Kallias stepped forward. "I've seen to your dowry. That I was close to you when the Persians charged was no accident. You were being evacuated when they struck. My slave confiscated all the belongings in your chamber."

Melaina felt her face flush with rage. How dare he invade my privacy! she thought. How can I live with this man? Bear his children? She considered telling them of her epilepsy but knew that would mean disaster for her and the child. If what her mother told her were true, he'd never put up with such a defect. Anyway, if she'd been cured at Epidaurus, it was a useless argument.

Kleito took her hand. "I'll go to Myrrhine. But this news will greatly upset her. Not a burden she'll carry well along with the death of her father."

Melaina remembered her covenant with her father and felt shame that she'd tried to go against his command of marriage. Somehow, I'll have to swallow my pride and deal with this new, unimaginable circumstance.

Aeschylus spoke to Kallias. "Mardonius has retreated from Athens and Attica to move farther north and prepare for the final engagement. Hellene forces will muster at Eleusis before traveling north through the foothills of Kithaeron into Boeotia. If Mardonius does in fact pull all his troops out of Attica, we'll return to Athens immediately."

★

That afternoon, a squadron of Hoplites boarded boats and sailed the strait to Phaleron, Athens' seaport. They encountered no resistance among the city's smoldering ruins and sent back word, all was clear. The Greeks took back all of Attica without a blow. Families prepared to return to what was left of their homes. Kallias owned a commercial galley that was quickly loaded with household goods and shipped across the channel the following day. The refugees' migration home had begun.

Melaina said her good-byes to Kleito and little Euripides, bid Kleito tell her mother not to worry. When aboard ship, Melaina looked longingly to the north at the wisps of smoke drifting skyward above Eleusis. When would she ever see her mother again?

As the sea breeze chilled her cheeks, Melaina sensed the onset of another seizure. I've not been cured, she thought. She knew not when the frenzy would take her, only that it was a hidden, stalking presence. And when it did come, she'd be in the hands of those who knew nothing of her illness. Should she tell them? What if she was wrong, and this only some minor illness, perhaps the sniffles?

From the docks, Aeschylus and his family, now including Melaina, walked through the ashes of Phaleron and along the footpath to Athens, wails of returning residents growing with each step. Aeschylus put Melaina aboard an ox-drawn cart. As they traversed the ruins, Melaina fell to self-pity and tried to take stock of what had happened to her. I love freedom so much, she thought, and yet have not only been stripped of it, but also of my internal sovereignty. The gods have stolen my body and given my mind over to frenzy. Aphrodite has taken my heart and given it to Sophocles. Uncle Aeschylus has stolen me from my mother and given me to Kallias, and I'll spend the rest of my life in terrible Athens. What else can they take from me?

On they went, Melaina's despair growing with every step. Despondent old men, women and dogs, who'd been left behind during the evacuation and had survived, came to the side of the road to witness the return. Smoke trailed overhead and coals glowed in dark places. A chorus of dog howls filled the ruins.

In Athens, her uncle Aeschylus found his home without a roof and the stone walls pulled down, all but two rooms scorched. In these, Philokleia set up housekeeping although she screeched and raved. Slaves set to silently rebuilding. Miraculously, Kallias' home had been spared. The Persian generals had used it for their headquarters and left too quickly to have had time to work mischief on it.

A runner arrived, bearing a torch from the Archon Basileus, who'd decreed all sacred hearths extinguished to purge the city of Persian pollution and relit with Delphic fire. Melaina remembered the torch brought aboard the ferry at Megara. Runners with flame from that torch would now relight all Athens' sacred hearths.

While slaves unloaded household goods, Aunt Philokleia and her handmaids tried to salvage as much as possible. Though many slaves had evacuated with Aeschylus' household to Salamis, several had run off. Philokleia complained of having to set up housekeeping shorthanded. Melaina refused to enter her uncle's home. The flame inside her had also been extinguished. Where would she ever find a source to relight it?

CHAPTER 6: A Mistress for the Dadouchos

Melaina remained in the wagon outside, lapsing into a state of silent desperation. She was now in the hands of Aunt Philokleia, wife of her most vocal critic, her Uncle Aeschylus. She wished the Persians had captured her. She felt exiled, forced to take up unwanted residence on foreign soil. Athens is not my home, Melaina thought, nothing will ever make it home. Sitting alone in the wagon, she prayed against Kallias. "Oh most glorious Hera, grant not the dark wishes of a cruel heart."

Aeschylus returned, scooped Melaina into his arms and carried her inside. "You'll not be allowed to mope while the rest of us re-light the hearth," he said. "Your self-indulgent life is over."

After the slaves had cleared debris from Hestia's habitation, Aeschylus slaughtered a goat, prayed first to the hearth goddess for prosperity and happiness, and then to his ancestors to receive Melaina into their care as a new household member. He also asked divine Dionysus to provide guidance for her during the coming days.

Melaina's family ancestors were much the same as at Eleusis, her father being Aeschylus' brother, but she hadn't anticipated the loneliness she felt at no longer being in the care of Demeter and Kore. She hadn't thought much about her uncle's devotion to Dionysus, although it made sense. Dionysus was the patron god of theatre, and Uncle Aeschylus the most famous playwright in all Greece. Melaina had shied away from Dionysus, god of frenzy, wondering at times if he wasn't behind her epilepsy. Now I end up in a home where he's worshiped as the first god, she thought. She remembered her uncle's strange story of Dionysus coming to him in a dream and telling him to write tragedies.

Melaina took a deep breath and reassessed her situation. Since Athens had its own temple of Artemis Brauronia on the Akropolis as well as a school for girls, she wasn't needed as she'd been in Eleusis. But all was not lamentable. Her baby would now have a father. Provided Kallias would accept the child.

The longer she thought about it, the more Melaina wondered if her predisposition against Kallias clouded her reasoning. Let me take heart with my misfortune as might a philosopher, she thought. My soul, by its own nature, often adds heaviness to circumstance. Oh, if I only had my mother's pleasant disposition. Why be a lover of grief and fault-finding? Evenhanded Zeus doesn't administer misery to some in a gentle, well-tempered flow, and unleash on others an undiluted stream. I count upon myself only the worst of my lot. Kallias is the wealthiest man in Athens and will care for me with great extravagance.

Melaina hoped the marriage would take place in Gamelion, Hera's sacred month in the dead of winter and five months hence, as did most. But Kallias wouldn't let it rest, saying, "At the full moon." He would not tolerate the childs' arrival before they were joined.

"Tell my mother, so she'll be here to carry the torch," said Melaina.

"We'll see," said her uncle.

Reluctantly, Aunt Philokleia prepared for Melaina's wedding before they had the ashes scraped off the floors. Philokleia scoffed at the thought that Melaina was carrying a divine child. "Simple promiscuity," she said. She pumped Melaina for the name of the father. "Tell me!" she ordered. "We both know he's around here somewhere."

Melaina fell to crying and prayed that her mother might rescue her.

The evening before the marriage, Aeschylus and Philokleia took Melaina to the Akropolis, where they mounted the hill through the propylaea to the temple of Artemis Brauronia, badly desecrated by the Persians. Melaina had brought her childhood toys and deposited them at the altar: clay animals, dolls, noisemakers, knucklebones. Kallias had brought so many of her possessions, including all her trinkets, that she wondered if he'd scooped the dust from the floor. Kallias and his mother, Lady Hipparete, met them at the temple for the marriage preludes.

Melaina knew this would be her last chance, so she ran to Kallias. "Tell me of my father's promise," she said. "I must know his exact words when he give me to you."

Kallias stopped short and stared at her as though he'd like to smack her into the ground. But unaccountably, his glare softened. Still with considerable irritation, he spoke. "We'd pulled him from the Persian boat where he suffered the loss of his hand. He was in the physician's tent, very weak, and no one could stop the bleeding. I'd seen you only a few days before and knew what I beauty you'd one day be. I went to him even though the others had left him to his death. 'Give Melaina to me, Kynegeiros,' I said, 'and forever you can trust that I'll be there when she needs you.' At first I thought he'd already died, but then his head turned slowly toward me. 'Take her, Kallias, when she comes of age. But if you mistreat her, I'll send a maelstrom of evils upon you from the Undergloom.' He then passed from us, and I shut his eyes."

Tears had filled her eyes during the telling. "Where were you the night I conceived this child?" she asked.

Kallias' face turned bright red, but he would not answer.

She shook her head at him but asked nothing more. They fell in with the rest and walked to the temple. As her father wished, so would she live.

As the sinking sun cast the giant shadow of the Akropolis across the group, Melaina stood before the altar, a dark veil pulled over her face, refusing to speak and tears rolling down her cheeks. The wind had kicked up, sending a scattering of ashes through the air. The temple, although in ruins, reminded her of that at Brauron and the terrible events of the previous year. Finally, Melaina steadied herself, dedicated her toys to Artemis, and stood ready to recite her prenuptial vows.

Except for one last thing.

Melaina looked down at her feet, the sandals Kleito had given her covered with ash. I can't do this, she thought, not without at least knowing how my child and I will be treated. She wished desperately to speak to Kallias alone. She took hold of his coat and pulled him aside. She thought, Holy Demeter, he really is a large man, all those muscles. "This business is troubling, Lord Kallias," she said. "What'll be my role in your home? How will my child be treated? Shall we be prisoners, slaves to those running it?"

"Oh no, my love!" A look of outrage flashed across his face. He smiled a little. "You'll be mistress of everyone living there. Your honor among Athenians will be the greatest and those who wrong you punished unless they propitiate forgiveness. You are a priestess and the daughter of Kynegeiros, hero of the battle of Marathon. You'll bring prestige to my household."

Melaina had never imagined any fate for herself, save as appendage to his mother. He called me, 'my love'? "What will be the role of my child in your home?" Again the thought crossed her mind that she had but to tell him of the epilepsy to end this. But she knew the consequences could be disastrous.

"Our home," reminded Kallias, "and our child." He pulled her even farther from the others. "Do not question my allegiance to this child, for its fathering is no mystery to me."

Melaina was astonished. "You know how I came by the child?"

At first, he looked bewildered, as if he didn't understand her. "I know of the fathering of divine children…" He stopped in mid sentence, unsure of his ground, then tilted his head back in a gesture of reassurance. "Then let me tell you something that will satisfy you, I'm sure, a story of my family, the Kerykes. We descend from Hermes. Hermes was also the sire of Odysseus' grandfather, Autolykos. Odysseus was my distant cousin. Laertes didn't sire Odysseus though he loved him dearly. It was cunning Sisyphus of Corinth who first lay in shameful promiscuity with Autolykos' daughter, Anticlea. Yet Laertes took the pregnant woman to wife and accepted the child, Odysseus, as his own. No one will blame me for doing so with our child. The question of the child's father is not a liability but an asset. Speculation runs rampant concerning which god fathered it. What man, who fears the gods, would deny shelter and parentage to a divine child, such as yours, ours."

Somehow this news disappointed Melaina. She'd hoped he'd give her an excuse to end this. But her heart now softened toward him, and she realized her dreams were gone. "Forgive my questioning, Lord. I'll not be so difficult henceforth."

The two rejoined the others.

Melaina took a deep breath and recited her prenuptial vow. "I earnestly swear to behave myself," she said, a note of irrepressible irritation flavoring her words, "to obey my husband and stay indoors, to dress as befits modesty and hold my tongue in public and private." She bitterly resented the staying indoors part. She so loved Helios' bright rays. Her one consolation was that she'd finally get to see her mother.

★

The following day, Melaina went with Aunt Philokleia and the maids, who seemed somehow afraid of her, to draw her nuptial bath from the Well of Nine Springs. After swearing to stay indoors, she longed to get into the open. She and the maids passed outside the city walls and along the grassy banks of the Ilissos, where Melaina slipped off her sandals, breathed deeply and sat cooling her feet in the quiet, shaded stream beneath an oak tree. The maids drew water while they whispered about her.

Melaina was familiar with the area because it was here that the lesser Mysteries were performed every year. Her mother always participated and brought Melaina. Initiates who wished to attend the greater Mysteries of Eleusis, but who'd committed murder or were otherwise in need of purification, first attended the lesser Mysteries. Melaina listened to the shrill voices of cicadas while resting her head on the soft grass. She felt the baby move. It had been unusually active the last few days, and she wondered if the chariot ride had upset it.

Today was Melaina's last as a free woman. She regretted having never been on her own, never experiencing her dream of living free as did Keladeine. She wondered why she hadn't heard from the young priestess. Melaina had sent the letter months ago.

After returning with the sacred water, Aunt Philokleia bid the bath-maids set a kettle on the fire and wash Melaina's feet. When the girls hesitated, she added, "Don't be afraid. She's not divine." She told another, "Pour a bath in the tub."

Melaina watched as the maids filled a bronze basin, first with cold, then hot water that glittered in firelight. She dipped her toes into the wet warmth. One maid loosed Melaina's long hair, handling it gently, and another scrubbed her feet, then helped her into the shallow tub. The bath-maids scrubbed her back and thighs with a tickly brush, laid her head back, and ran warm liquid through her silky hair. They stretched a fresh fleece for her to sit on, dried her with soft linen, and anointed her with golden olive oil.

Finally, the maids dressed Melaina for the ceremony. They brought forth a new white chiton with the midriff dyed purple from the blood of a murex snail. Over the chiton, she wore a himation that passed from the left shoulder under the right arm, the hem folded back over the cross strap to fall in zigzag folds. The rest of the garment hung over her torso and left thigh. They arranged her golden hair in concentric, smooth ridges over the top of her head, leaving two rows of scalloped ridges across her forehead in vertical locks. Behind her ears, the hair formed long wavy, corrugated locks, four falling forward over each shoulder. Her light eyebrows were darkened and rendered as arching chevrons. Coordinated patterns of red and green wound round her stephane, on the seam of her chiton, down her right arm, and on the border of her himation. She wore disk earrings, a pearl necklace, silver and gold bracelets on both arms, and a crown woven of myrtle.

Melaina's breasts bulged obtrusively, as did her abdomen, yet she stood and, using her left hand, clasped the folds of her chiton to the edge of her thigh, smoothing the skirt across her legs. The girls laced her sandals, although Melaina couldn't see them below her protruding tummy. Her belt was tied with a double knot, veil draped over her head and shoulders.

"What an object of delight!" cried the handmaids.

"Beautiful as Pandora," pronounced her aunt. "What a waste."

Melaina ignored the insult though she cried inside. Pandora was the first woman, created by Hephaestus and dressed alluringly by Aphrodite as a snare to men.

That evening, Uncle Aeschylus' torch-lit home swarmed with guests. All day Melaina anticipated her mother joining them, but when all were assembled, Myrrhine still hadn't arrived.

"Where's my mother? You promised," she said to her uncle.

"We searched all Eleusis but couldn't find her."

"Postpone the wedding," she declared.

"No!" he cried. "We've a war to fight. No time for women's business after this evening."

Melaina sunk deeply within herself. What a travesty!

Uncle Aeschylus stood before the hearth of Hestia, Kallias beside him, and sacrificed to Hera. He slit the throat of a lamb, let it bleed over the slaughter stone, then removed the gallbladder and threw it to the dogs, thereby signifying that neither gall nor anger should play a part in the marriage. Aeschylus prayed. "Dear Hera, the cream of whose breasts lights the milky circle of stars spread across the heavens, goddess of the divine yoking of mortal couples, bring the fulfillment of every woman's destiny to Melaina, and sanctify this couple's marriage."

Melaina maintained her head and eyes downcast to connote modesty, shame, and submission, as she knew she must, all her bracelets rattling nervously.

Kallias stood tall beside her. As Dadouchos, torchbearer of the Mysteries, Kallias was dressed in priestly-garb, black wavy mane flowing down his back and bound at the temples by a strophion. His sleeveless chiton reached midway between knee and ankle, a row of embroidered red dots circling the hem. Over the chiton, he wore a heavier, sleeveless pullover, decorated with a scattering of blue circles, and bound at the waist by a green–chevroned sash. A stole–like military mantle, typical garb for horsemen, passed beneath the sash.

Such a splendid, regal–looking man, Melaina thought, how can I not love him? But she didn't. She preferred the striking image of young Sophocles astride his horse, torch in hand, as she'd seen him leading the way back from Brauron.

Aeschylus spoke words of transference. "I give Melaina over to you, Kallias, for the plowing and sowing of legitimate children."

The couple tipped cups of wine into flame and drank deeply.

Kallias reached toward Melaina, who lifted her left arm as if to ward off a blow. He grabbed her by the wrist in the customary ritual gesture of matrimonial possession. Melaina cried out, and the women accompanying her pretended to defend her, but Melaina wasn't kidding. She stared daggers through her veil, hot anger welling up inside her, and tried twice to jerk her wrist from Kallias grasp. Her hatred of him rekindled in one last flaming before being extinguished.

In the deep darkness outside, Kallias, his golden chariot hooked to the four handsome horses, hefted Melaina aboard, where she stood at his elbow, face still covered with the veil. He gave a flick to the horses, as they pranced with streaming manes through the labyrinthine streets. The dark ashes of Uncle Aeschylus' home disappeared behind as Kallias kept the harness shaking all the way. The nuptial torch preceded the car, and a chorus came behind singing hymns.

"Ho, Hymen! Ho, Hymen! Hymenaeos! Io!" So ran the refrain with aulos and lyre keeping up the tune. Aunt Philokleia, frowning but acting in Myrrhine's place, followed the procession holding a lighted torch in each hand. Women came streetside to stare at their passing.

At Kallias' home, his mother, Lady Hipparete, smiling and looking not much older than Melaina's own mother, greeted the couple at the threshold. Philokleia passed her the two torches. Melaina feared Hipparete greatly, knowing the woman would be living with them.

Melaina and Kallias stood before the door. An inscription above the lintel read, 'No evil enters here!'

"Pai! Pai!" called Kallias.

Melaina heard the clunk of bolts and bars, the groan of hinges as the doors swung inward. A foreign-born porter stood before them, a eunuch, who viewed them suspiciously, as if he didn't recognize his own master.

"Step aside, Pai," said Kallias.

As they came into the entryway, a cornucopia of dates, nuts, figs, and dried fruit was upended and showered over Melaina, whose face was protected by her veil. She was greeted by Kallias' dog, which had profusely-foaming jowls and a snakelike tail. The dog squinted at her through loose rolls of hanging skin. He licked Melaina's fingertips and then her toes through her sandals.

"Away, Argos!" shouted Kallias.

At his father's death, Kallias had inherited the family home and everything within, and he had become priest of the hearth. To become hearth priestess, Melaina had to sacrifice at his fire. Melaina had never seen more elaborate homage paid to Hestia. The hearthstone was of such size, it could only have been laid by a Cyclops. Flames roared within its confines.

Melaina hated herself for being in a house of plenty when so many throughout Athens were decimated.

Kallias said to her, "I realize Demeter and Kore have been your family gods, but in my home, we worship Hermes, from whom my family descended, and Hades, Lord of the Underworld."

Myrrhine felt a chill pass through her. "No one worships Hades. He deals not with the living."

Kallias at first looked hurt but recovered quickly. "We worship him as Plouton, the bringer of wealth."

Melaina felt like resisting further, but knew it was hopeless. Plouton was Kore's husband. She'd best keep her mouth shut or risk insulting the dark goddess. Besides, Kallias had been amply rewarded for his worship.

After she sacrificed a lamb to Plouton, Kallias dipped his fingertips in a bowl and sprinkled Melaina with lustral water while praying to Hermes as he held her hand over the flames until she felt as though the heat would singe her nails. Kallias closed his eyes and breathed deeply, but still held both their hands over the fire. He mumbled something she couldn't discern, then prayed aloud again, this time to Hades.

The company then gathered closely about for Melaina's unveiling. Finally, she'd be allowed to look Kallias in the eyes. This was the beginning of her disrobement and signified sexual submission, taming. She let out a sigh.

Melaina fingered the edge of her veil, pulling it up and back to expose her clustered curls and blushing cheeks, as she looked upward, her eyes meeting those of Kallias. She'd always heard of the emotion the wedded couple felt for each other at that instant, that the man felt Eros break his knees, as might those wounded in battle, since the bride's glance was supposed to be irresistibly erotic. Kallias' eyes were deep-black, pupilless pools, revealing an inner darkness of the soul that Melaina thought must link him directly to the Realm of the Dead.

Melaina felt nothing of the devastating effect of Eros, even caught herself about to laugh. She remembered the first time she'd looked into Sophocles' subtle-blue eyes and longed for that feeling. But Kallias was sweating. "Great Zeus," he said, "such penetrating blue I've never seen but in the depths of the Aegean. Long have I avoided your eyes, knowing your gaze would be fatal, as was the gaze of the Amazon queen Penthesilea, who overwhelmed Achilles even as his blade delivered the fatal blow."

Kallias and Melaina then shared a fertility cake of sesame seeds and honey, and she gave him a tunic she'd woven herself. From her dowry, which Kallias had brought from Eleusis, Melaina displayed her loom-work containing all the necessities of home: carpets, wall coverings, hangings, curtains, and embroideries for every surface. Melaina's skill and diligence would definitely add to the honor of the house.

Kallias' mistress of stores brought provisions of bread and wine along with victuals fit for kings. Now the feast would begin.

"Kallias," said Melaina, remembering the devastation she'd witnessed on the way from Salamis, "it's not right that we should eat while others starve. Have the slaves take some into the street and disperse it to those decimated by the war. We'll never miss it."

Kallias thought about this a moment and so ordered. "You've a kind heart to give up part of your marriage feast," he told her. In a wine bowl, Kallias mixed water with sweet red wine mellowed eleven years before his eunuch uncapped the jar. He poured his offering, prayed to Hera, daughter of royal Kronos. The others also made libation and drank deep.

When the festivities ended, all the company retired to their quarters, and Kallias and Melaina to their inner chamber. Melaina carried a blood-red pomegranate into the wedding chamber and ate from it, as had Kore when abducted into the Underworld by Hades. The eunuch stood guard at the door, gatekeeper to the marriage chamber. Girls were brought forward to stand outside it, singing wedding songs. Melaina cried at this because they should have been her closest friends, Agido and Anaktoria.

When Kallias asked about her sadness, she told him not to worry. She was only lamenting not knowing the fate of her friends.

"Melaina, you seem docile and sufficiently domesticated to carry on a conversation. Still, I realize you come to me barely fifteen, seeing, hearing and saying as little as possible. Such is the way girls are raised, so I won't expect much. Why, what could I expect of someone who knows nothing of camels?"

"I hope you won't forever hold the fell beast against me, my lord. But I would like to know what you do expect of me."

"Let me explain how marriage works," he said, seeming to take great pride in his role as teacher. "The gods, with divine discernment, have coupled together male and female in mutual service, adapting the woman's nature to the indoors and man's to outdoors. I have considerable land not far from here. I'll work at the open-air occupations: ploughing, sowing, and planting."

Melaina looked at him from the corners of her eyes, unable to imagine Kallias working the fields. This sounds like something he's memorized, she thought.

"You must work at things done under roof, nursing infants, baking bread, weaving. Your tasks resemble those of queen bee, staying in the hive without suffering idleness. Those who work outside, you'll send forth, and that which they bring in, you'll receive and apportion just shares. You'll preside over care of the little ones, and later, just like young bees duly reared, you'll send them forth to found new colonies."

"I'll do my best," she said, but still had to smile.

"I assure you, dear, you'll have pleasant duties rewarding the useful members of our household and punishing anyone revealed to be a rogue. Together, we'll have friends from all of Athens' great families."

"Sophocles and his father?" she asked.

"Sophocles? Forget him," he said, drawing his brows together. "His father has wealth, but Sophocles isn't an aristocrat, doesn't know how to throw his cloak over his shoulder from left to right."

Melaina yawned. "I'm tired. The baby weighs heavy upon me."

"To bed with us then. I'll strip off and work the land," he said removing his robe.

"My lord! Consider the child!" She reached for the sack of sneezing power the physician from Kos had given her. "It'll not suffer you entering my womb."

"What's a marriage without consummation?"

She inhaled the white powder, sneezed ferociously. "True," she admitted, then sneezed twice more. "Still, if you take me, it'll not be in the interest of the child."

"What is this fit that's come upon you? Are you sick?"

"Simply a precaution … something a physician gave … ." She didn't know what else to say. "Aids the development of the fetus," she lied.

"Disgusting." Kallias removed the nuptial blanket from their bed. "Then we'll not need this. I'd so hoped to weave our souls beneath this tapestry. But promise you'll not tell anyone that the marriage hasn't been consummated." He lay beside her, but presented his back. "Point your nose the other way. I'll not have you spraying me."

Melaina felt lonely and didn't want him angry with her. "Dear Kallias," she said, "don't sulk these few weeks until the baby comes. Still love me, and the anticipation will make future coupling that much the sweeter."

"You conjure limb-gnawing passion, then cast me aside."

But Kallias, son of Hipponicus, rolled over, caught her up in his arms, and they lay together, drawing the covers about them like a golden cloud. Melaina slept within the arms of her husband, the Dadouchos, torchbearer of the ancient Mysteries, her passion unaccountably stirred, and feeling in his arms a comfort she'd never thought possible.

★

Next morning before sunrise, Aeschylus rattled at the gate. Melaina heard the eunuch arguing with him at the front door and the dog, Argos, whining to see him. "Come in if you must," the eunuch finally said, "but you can't stay long."

Kallias rose quickly, and Melaina heard the men argue in the courtyard. Kallias then returned with wrinkles across his brow, but wouldn't tell the trouble. He left with Aeschylus, Argos nipping Aeschylus' heels until Kallias cuffed him. The hollow sound of horses' hooves faded into the distance.

Melaina took the opportunity to survey her new home. She'd never seen one kept so dark. Out back, she saw orchards enclosed by stone walls, two hectares of trees weighted down for picking: pears, pomegranates, brilliant apples, luscious figs. Water channels ran from a clear fountain, while another gushed under the courtyard entrance. What luck, the Persians hadn't defiled any of it.

Lady Hipparete came from her chamber sleepy-eyed to greet Melaina. She wore a pleasant smile but wrinkled brow, definitely without the spark she'd exhibited last night. Perhaps she's not pleased to have me as daughter-in-law, Melaina thought. "Is the Persian threat troubling you, or is it something about me?" Melaina asked.

Hipparete was quiet, unanswering. Melaina watched the dark sympathetic eyes set in the woman's small oval face framed by curly black hair. Her son had taken his looks from her, so different from Melaina's own light-complexioned, blond-haired mother, easy and quiet, almost simple, without the nervous intelligent eyes. Melaina felt an unexpected comfort in Hipparete's presence.

Finally, Hipparete spoke. "I hope you'll be happy here in Kallias' home. It was mine until Hipponicus died, and I've stayed on to govern it until Kallias married. Many times, when the daughter-in-law takes over, she puts her husband's mother out in the street. My dowry is not large, and I hope you'll find use for me. I'm good with slave girls, a little weak at weaving, to be honest about it, but quite good with the ovens."

Until speaking with Kallias last night, Melaina had not dreamed of having such power over the household, and now this. Kallias' mother feared her. "Put your mind at rest," Melaina said. "As long as I'm mistress, you'll have a place in my home." Melaina took her mother-in-law's cold hands in both of her own, warmed them, saw tears in her eyes. "And as for the baking, I hate the heat. Weaving is my one talent. A perfect match, we'll be."

★

Late that afternoon, Kallias returned, and Melaina was anxiously awaiting him. "Any word of my mother?"

"She's been behind Persian lines searching for you. When the Hellene army heard, it created a sensation, and she's been quite a storehouse of reconnaissance. She's not pleased I've wedded you without her."

"No doubt. But how happy you've made me with word of her. This one bit of news gives me renewed life."

"Your mother retrieved six Eleusinian women from Mardonius. The mother of Agido was among them."

"And Anaktoria?"

"Not that I heard."

"At least Agido is not an orphan. But none of my jubilance rubs off on you. Trouble clouds your eyes."

"It's not you weighting my mind but the fate of Hellas. While Mardonius has retreated to Boeotia, the danger is not over. A great land battle looms. We've word of an oracle from Delphi that Hellenes will win if we fight before a temple of Eleusinian Demeter. Such a temple has been found on the feet of Kithaeron, and your mother has gone to resurrect the abandoned sanctuary. But another battle may take place in the Aegean. How it could be fought before a temple of Demeter is beyond me. I must join the fleet to inform them of this impossible imperative. I've three triremes outfitted for battle and tomorrow must sail for Delos, where the fleet harbors."

Melaina took this news much harder than she'd have expected. She didn't want her husband off at war. She dizzied, staggered, and dropped to one knee. She felt a small spasm in her throat, a heightened sense of awareness.

"Your eyes," Kallias said, "that heavy, lost look. Trouble with the child?"

Melaina rose to her feet and threw her arms about his neck. "My lord! Don't be angry. If you've compassion in your heart, find some for me now."

"What have you done?"

"It's not what I've done, but what I'll do."

"Pray quit speaking riddles. Is it a prophetic trance?"

"No! I have the sacred sickness."

His eyes still questioned. "Your cheeks quiver."

Lady Hipparete entered the room.

Melaina ran to her. "I haven't much time," she said. "You know the falling sickness?"

"Yes," she replied, "I've seen it in a neighbor's slave."

Kallias spoke to his mother. "Is she ill?"

"See this stays between my teeth." Melaina bit down hard on a leather strap.

CHAPTER 7: THE VISION

Consciousness came slowly to Melaina, a gathering of great clouds of confusion. She heard shouting, the scurrying of feet, saw shapes flitting about, shades. Have I gone to the Underworld? she wondered. Although the phantoms slowly became people, she recognized no one. She felt a great urgency to speak but couldn't. She slept.

Finally, Melaina opened her eyes but felt them oscillate uncontrollably. She hated Kallias seeing her like this so soon after being married. Even when she did manage to control her eyes, she could see from only one, so she kept the other closed.

Trying to collect her thoughts, she looked up at Kallias through her one good eye. "My mother described it," she said, "as similar to the sight of an ox whose throat has been cut: arms cramped, the head drawn back, and legs kicking in all directions."

"Much worse," Kallias said, standing back from her. "Your cheeks trembled, and your whole head swelled red. We had difficulty keeping the strap in your mouth. Your tongue protruded as might a mad person's. I was afraid you'd bite it off. Even after you came to your senses, you denied knowing me."

Hipparete took Melaina by the hand. "It lasted only a short while. Some say only the great have this affliction. The twelve labors caused it in Herakles." She looked at Kallias, "Don't lose your feeling for your young mistress. She'll bring you great glory."

But Kallias turned on Melaina. "Why did I not hear of this before the wedding? Look at you! One eye still squints."

"If you only knew my sleeplessness with this same thought, my lament not knowing if I still had it. I've been to Epidaurus for treatment and cured, so the priest said, only now to have the affliction return."

Kallias threw his arms into the air. "Great Zeus, what have you done to me? Oh, Mother! Forever I'll regret that day on the plane of Marathon when I asked and Kynegeiros gave his only daughter to me. Since then, I've been followed by jealousy of my wealth, laughed at because my wife comes to me already pregnant, and I now reap this new shame. This intolerable affliction."

Melaina said, "Though the seizures are a fright to look upon, Lord Kallias, they are a divine moment. I live a lifetime in an instant amidst a sacred warmth higher than love, fuse with the divine as if set afire. All doubt and troubles disappear."

"These feelings are a warning of the coming madness?"

"Warnings come for bad things. 'Tis a gift and sometimes contains a prophecy."

"I'll not tolerate it. A hopeless sickness is better off in Hades."

Melaina dropped to one knee before him. "I implore you, Lord. Don't abandon my child and me because of these troubles. You chose me, not I you. Horror was my first thought when learning you were to be my husband. But in these short days, I've developed a fondness for you. Live with this new knowledge a while before condemning me. Perhaps I'll be an asset in the end."

"She's spoken well, Kallias," said Hipparete. "Hate this odious disease, but not the afflicted. Take pity, my son, and reap great sympathy for it!"

"Remember you promise to my father," Melaina said.

Unannounced, Kallias' eunuch entered the room, a male slave hot on his tracks. "Trouble, Kallias," said the eunuch.

"What? In the name of Hades!" shouted Kallias, turning on the slave as if to strike him. "Now the whole of Athens is to know my evil fortune." He then turned on the eunuch. "Well you've already let the bastard in, and here with women present." He turned back to the slave. "Speak, you son of swine! If it's that important, say it here, in front of the women."

"Lord Kallias, two triremes are fully manned, oarsmen, hoplites, and archers, but the third is five short a full complement of deck hands. They quibble over the wage."

"They're fully rationed?" Kallias visibly calmed.

"Indeed. Though short an anchor on one and a sail on another."

"Stand at the gate. I'll join you shortly. These boat rowers will bankrupt me yet."

Kallias turned back to Melaina, but his mother stopped him from speaking.

"Let this matter rest, dear Kallias. See to your ships. Let your distemper cool."

"My distemper!" Kallias threw up his hands. "She's not been in my home a day and already has my own mother speaking against me. I will go to the docks. But rest assured, I'll settle this when I return." He strode from the chamber.

Lady Hipparete quickly took Melaina by the hands, saying, "I'll talk sense to him. We can't allow this grievous mistake."

Melaina said, "I hadn't remembered it until now, but the instant before the seizure consumed me, that splitting pain, I had another vision. It'll take a while to learn its meaning. Forgive me, Lady Hipparete. I must retire to a quiet place and think."

★

Melaina went into seclusion beneath a shaggy oak in the meadow of Kallias' garden. This beautiful setting is now mine too, she thought. She listened to the rustle of leaves while roaming crag and cliff of memory to retrieve an impression that occurred the instant before the pain came. Therein was an image, a frightening one, of herself large as a Cyclops, bounding across the waters of some bottomless sea into dark oblivion. She'd found it, thought it out. Now she needed Kallias desperately.

But as the afternoon wore on, she couldn't shake Kallias' words. "I'll not tolerate it," he'd said, meaning her, her illness. She contemplated what Keladeine at the Isthmus had told her, that at times our lives parallel the ancient myths and wreak great havoc. Melaina remembered that Iphigeneia's father had brought her to

Aulis under the pretext of marrying her off to Achilles, only to learn that she was instead to be sacrificed to Artemis. After her initial protests, Iphigeneia had gone to the slaughter stone willingly, giving her life for Greece. Melaina thought, I'll not be sacrificed, but I've certainly suffered a marriage tragedy.

Late evening, a rattle at the gates brought Kallias' voice calling the eunuch, "Pai! Pai!"

Roused from her thoughts, Melaina ran to him.

Kallias said, "Good that yours is the first face I see. I've made a decision."

"Never mind that, dear Kallias, though already I see the negative thought chiseled in your face. The fate of Hellas must be weighed first."

"Contemplating the affairs of state is not the lot of women."

"But the gods sometimes reveal their designs to women. It's the Pythia that sits astride the tripod at Delphi, not a priest. If you'll not allow this truth, then tell the Pythia to dismount, silence Apollo's voice."

Kallias lowered his eyes, studied the ground. "Point well taken. I'll grant a short audience on this."

"Just before the seizure you witnessed, I had a vision, as I always do. I was stone-stepping in a sea, striding from island to island."

"Childhood memories. Game playing only."

"A game's likeness surely, but with a deeper meaning. One island was Delos, the other Samos. I crossed them in two steps, as would a goddess, and saw smoke billowing from Samos. Then I came to a mainland where a great battle took place."

Kallias' shoulders slumped. He turned away from her and talked to the walls. "Father Hermes, who is this woman you've sent? Ever she plagues me. Twice I've been burdened with saving her from Persians, and now comes the pestilence of being married to an ever-chattering Pandora who thinks she's a goddess."

"That's not so, Kallias!" Melaina had tried to check her voice, but still it scolded. "Simply a vision, never had I a thought of being divine. Word of a battle between Hellenes and Persians to liberate Ionia, though it comes from a woman, cannot be ignored. I'd remind you that in ancient times all prophets were women."

This last remark stopped Kallias cold, and a worried look crossed his bearded face. "I'd hoped you'd speak deranged, but how am I to dismiss words that make sense, even if they come from a mad woman?"

"Sorry, Lord. I've no desire for inducing distress."

"You know of Ionia's request for liberation? This spring, an embassy from Chios came first to Sparta, then Aegina, where the fleet mustered. The ambassadors requested assistance for their revolt against Xerxes, saying the unexpected, that the Persian fleet was still in the Aegean."

"I know nothing of these things, Lord."

"Then your vision is all the more puzzling. We'd thought the Persian fleet would return home, and planned only for a land war. Now we're ever on guard against attack by sea. If we don't clear the Aegean of the Persian fleet, Hellas will forever live in fear. Yet our fleet can't be coaxed further than Delos, trepidation standing sentry over the dark water between."

"Listen, Lord Kallias. I see our fate clearly now and know what must be done. Don't be angry if I speak forcefully, but you must understand. Several months ago while on the way to Epidaurus I had a seizure, same as that you witnessed, wherein I saw two great land-battles, one hereabouts with Mardonius and another on a foreign shore. I know now the first will be at Plataea, surely that of which you spoke earlier, where my mother has gone. So far, I'd not been able to understand the second, but now, in light of my vision, I realize it will take place in Ionia, on the coast of Asia."

"Oh, if I could be sure this isn't just baseless speculation from a pregnant girl overestimating the trivialities of her own thoughts. By the gods, and it comes before a seizure."

"I'll remain silent henceforth, Lord Kallias. I only ask that you tell the generals of my vision. Much is at stake, and the gods have spoken."

Kallias thought for a moment, then answered though his voice had lost confidence. "If Eurybiades and Themistocles still commanded the fleet, perhaps. But now the Spartan king Leotychides has supreme command with Xanthippus leading the Athenians. They haven't Themistocles' courage and will resist budging from Apollo's sacred isle."

"I know this General Xanthippus," Melaina said. "He's expressed respect for me." She was silent a moment, then her conviction again flared. "Oh, they must fight, Lord Kallias! The gods will it. They demand it. Change their minds. Affirm divine will!"

Kallias' voice became conciliatory. "Long have I also thought Ionia's alliance crucial to Hellas' security but could never find sympathetic ears. I remember your performance last year when we needed a sign for the generals to keep the fleet on Salamis, and again the night before the sea battle. You've become a symbol of divine intervention to many. If these visions are truly sent by the gods, I must take you to the generals."

"Surely, your voice is the one to sway them. Besides my mind is still cloudy from the seizure."

"You'd have a day or so of traveling to recover. The voice of the visionary would be more influential."

"I'd not speak to them here in Athens?"

"No." Kallias thought a moment. "At Delos. My three ships leave late tonight. I have but to give word for you to board." He walked away slowly, stopped and turned back. "Are you up to such a voyage? Would the unborn permit it?"

"Such a sailing is indeed frightening, Lord, for my sake as well as the child's. But I admit that, since surviving the chariot racing to flee the Persians, a sea voyage would seem trivial." She also longed to once again be aboard a trireme.

"The generals have dallied about on Delos all summer, through the good-sailing months, lacking the courage to engage the enemy. They must hear your prophecy."

★

Late that night as they left for the docks, Kallias' mother threw her arms about her son and clung to him, weeping, knowing he would soon see battle. When Kallias broke away, Hipparete fell upon Melaina, squeezing her tightly and refusing to release the fond bonds of her arms. Finally, Kallias and Melaina stepped out into the dark, stars sparkling overhead. Melaina saw Aquila, constellation of the Eagle, the bird sacred to Zeus that he sent to eat out Prometheus' liver. She tightly clutched the Broach of Arrogance given her by Palaemon that now held together her cloak. She saw agony chiseled across Kallias' dark brow and wondered if he was reconsidering taking her. What if she had a seizure in front of the generals?

The docks were not as empty as she anticipated. Kallias' triremes were being outfitted for war and a thirty-oared galley loaded with supplies, but several other triremes, in for repairs, were to set sail with them. She heard the shouts of hoplite commanders, boatswains, and the echoing thud of dowel pins being hammered into place, the trills and whistles of flutegirls. She smelled the sharp odor of fresh pitch and saw its brown smoke rising from cauldrons sitting over glowing coals.

Before they boarded, Kallias called the crew and soldiers together and offered a prayer. "Hear, O King Hermes, father of my fathers, protector of all those on dark journeys, guide these ships along with my comrades safe and sound thither to Delos, thy brother's sacred isle, and back again to this great city. Then will we honor you once more, singeing fat-wrapped thighbones on your altar. Accept our sacrifice and protect us on this voyage, making the breeze soft upon our sails."

As he spoke, Kallias scattered barley meal, slew a sacred goat, and placed its entrails on the fire. "Prepare for departure!" he shouted.

A buzz of voices ran through the company of hoplites, armor clanging their excitement. "Listen!" Kallias said. "They remember you. The maiden at Salamis, who sent them into battle so well, is to go with them to Delos. What power you hold over people."

A priest of Apollo boarded with them and went astern, adorned it with a garland, and prayed. Then the hawsers were lifted from the landing lugs, and the ship drifted out of the slip. The boatswain poured blood-red wine into the sea, and the keel sank deep into the black water.

CHAPTER 8: THE COUNCIL OF GENERALS

The trireme rocked down the dark coast of Attica as the full moon rose. Melaina stood at the poop deck beside Kallias, watching the sleek triremes alongside theirs as they sliced through the sea. Although Melaina had told Kallias she could make the voyage and had believed it herself at the time, she now couldn't get the baby off her mind. She was in her ninth month and felt larger than she should, the child riding lower than normal.

Kallias was quiet beside her, pensive beyond his nature. Melaina felt lonely standing beside him and longed for her mother. But she remembered their wedding night in bed together, the warmth she'd felt lying next to him.

Shortly, they came to Cape Zoster where, back in primordial time, divine Leto had almost given birth to Artemis and Apollo. Leto, seduced and abandoned by Zeus, managed to drop her girdle on the coast there, but Hera, in all her jealous wrath, prevented Leto from delivering. Leto traveled further into the Aegean, the direction in which Melaina and the triremes headed now. As the dark land mass drifted behind them, Melaina saw a line of torches on the narrow sand spit, standing like a girdle across the Cape's waist, the land cinched to nothing where great reefs of dark cliff had tumbled to lie partially submerged in surf. The binding of Melaina's own abdomen felt too tight. She loosened Kleito's linen bandage, so the straps wouldn't dig into her shoulders.

On they sailed, the sky in the east turning pink, and at the windswept southern tip of Attica, Cape Sounion, Melaina saw the glowing temple of Poseidon, the stark marble columns towering over the cliffs of the headland, bathed in glorious sunrise. She knew that the silver mine at Laurium was not far inland. The slave children, the worms, she'd seen at Eleusis, worked the mine, and it had provided financing for the Athenian fleet. All that suffering, she thought, the suffering of children.

From the tip of Sounion, Kallias' little convoy slipped between the islands of uninspiring Kythnos, as well as mountainous, fertile-valleyed Kea. Past these islands, the triremes plunged into the heart of the Cyclades, the Aegean turning deep blue with the afternoon sun burning down upon the fleet.

Dark-maned Poseidon, divine ruler of the sea, had formed the islands himself, smiting mountains on the mainland with his three-forked sword fashioned by the Telchines. He then lifted them from their foundations as with a cleaver, rolled them into the sea, and rooted them in deep waters, all except Delos, which he left floating.

By mid-afternoon, the triremes sailed above the arid northern tip of rocky Syros, and passed south of Tynos' purple peaks just before sundown while the flat island of Reneia loomed to the right. Mykonos was beyond Reneia with Delos, their destination, between the two, close set by Reneia's eastern coast.

Ancient myths told of winds tossing Delos about on waves, but when Leto set foot on it, four lofty pillars rose from Earth's roots to hold the rock on their capitals. Leto gave birth to her divine offspring as she clung to a palm tree, knees resting on soft meadow grass that rose to form the base of Mt. Kynthos. Artemis was born first, then assisted her mother with the delivery of Apollo. Thereafter, the gods hailed the isle as the far-seen star of dark-blue sea. The twenty-one islands of the Cyclades were as a dancing chorus circling Delos, the crown of Apollo.

As the triremes rounded the northern tip of Reneia, Melaina saw warships dotting the sea beyond, patrols far out among the islands. But before her lay the small sacred isle, divine Delos, hordes of Greek soldiers roaming its shores, and battleships lining its coast. They entered the strait between the two islands, the beaches crowded with triremes, galleys, and fishing boats. Some had grounded on sand. Others docked alongside the mole of massive granite blocks forming the ancient harbor's breakwater.

Melaina had known that rocky Delos was small, but never expected this tiny, wind-swept, wave-beaten haunt for gulls. She could see past its southern tip not far in the distance, and its width was hardly more than a good walk. Kynthos, in her imagination a gigantic snow-capped peak, was but a hill, a rugged brown mass rising twixt two mounds. Kynthos was Artemis' sacred mountain from which the priestess Kynthia at Brauron had taken her name. Melaina saw the gleaming columns and walls of the sanctuary in the middle of a low-lying plane close to the harbor, the sun glowing on its marble columns.

Kallias finally stirred from his trance. "No mariners pass Delos, not even when in great haste, without going ashore and dancing for Apollo," he said. "Even before the Trojan War, this island was sacred."

They sailed into harbor, furled the sail, and oared the ship stern-first into dock. A priest of Apollo met Kallias and Melaina, stood in her path.

"No pregnant women," he said.

"She's a priestess," said Kallias.

The priest scanned her top to bottom. "She's too far along. I can't allow it."

"She's come with prophecies for the fleet."

"During birth, a human soul traverses the gulf separating our world from that of the gods. Screams and anguish of human suffering contaminate our communication with Apollo."

"Lord Kallias," Melaina said, taking hold of his arm, "perhaps I can ease his mind. May I speak?"

"If you can stay this man's antagonism. Please."

"I've witnessed this same prohibition at Epidaurus," she said. "I love Apollo and would never defile sacred Delos. I'll leave with the first labor pain."

"She'll not be here long. A couple of days only," added Kallias.

The priest hesitated. "As yet, we don't have an official order against it. Still, she should sleep aboard the boat."

"I'm a priest myself, Dadouchos of the Mysteries. I'd tolerate that for a slave, but not a priestess."

The priest turned to Melaina. "A merchant ship leaves for Athens tomorrow morning."

"She'll return when the generals say so," said Kallias. "Not before." He took Melaina's arm, and the two walked past the priest.

"First sign of labor," he shouted after them, pointing west. "All women give birth on Reneia."

They entered the sanctuary through the propylaea and entered a fan-shaped courtyard bordered by temples and filled with hordes of milling warriors. From across the way, a men's choir sang and danced, accompanied by an aulete, his music swept about by wind gusts. To Melaina's right stood a gigantic statue of Apollo, the god depicted nude, left foot forward, arms free and bent at the elbows. His head rose above the two-story buildings. When they reached the middle of the courtyard, Melaina turned back to see the great marble Apollo dwarfing the entire complex, outlined by Kynthos' dark craggy peak in the distance.

Kallias wasted no time presenting Melaina to the generals. As he escorted her to a large building at the end of the courtyard, darkness seemed to descend upon Delos like an oppressive daemon. Melaina felt another surge of loneliness. Here she was in the middle of the Aegean, on a tiny island a large wave could sink, walking beside a man who didn't want her although they were married, and about to enter a building off-limits to women. Her visions seemed trivial. How could she advise generals in war strategy? She wrapped her arms about her abdomen, clung to her baby.

Melaina and Kallias entered a chamber filled with men and stood amid a din of voices and the stifling stench of sweaty seamen. Melaina wished that Kallias had left the door open. Inside, she saw a gleaming hall, walls formed by pilasters that penetrated openings in the ceiling. The north side was a vaulted apse, the south a small temple with two polished columns in antis housing a small statue. Men sat in marble benches against the long walls. The beauty of the place lifted Melaina's spirits. She could barely comprehend the fact that the echoing hall was decorated in luminous gold, silver, and ivory, and couldn't imagine even Zeus' court on Olympus being more beautiful than this. Though lit by torches, all was aglitter as with moon-luster, or even more, fiery light from Helios.

Melaina was surprised that no one served food. There was no carved roast beast, no gold cups brimming with wine or baskets bulging with steaming loaves, no sweet entrails. Nor were any servants present, no maids or houseboys scurrying about. She realized how destitute Greece had become, how difficult it must be to feed an entire fleet.

Gradually, the din abated as all eyes turned toward them. Melaina heard the squeak of benches and rustle of feet against the stone floor, the flap of a palm against a tabletop. The commanding generals sat enthroned at the far end of the chamber, a great marble table before them. Melaina avoided their eyes and pulled her veil about her face. Dear Demeter, why have I come here? she wondered.

A general stopped his oratory. "I see that Kallias, son of Hipponicus, has joined us. It is indeed strange to see the rich Athenian bring a woman to a war council. But let's wait until we finish the business at hand before we allow him to justify this act."

Kallias told Melaina, "He's the Spartan, Leotychides, fleet commander."

Melaina peeked around the room from behind her veil, surprised to recognize several faces, although she could name but a few. She felt unexpectedly at home here among these men of war, strangely more so than she'd felt anywhere recently.

Leotychides sat and another man rose, Xanthippus, the Athenian she'd seen at Kleito's on the way back from Brauron and again at the Isthmus. She remembered his self-assured demeanor and soft-spoken ways, but he now had a glossy cast to his eyes, and his swift manner of speaking was labored. She remembered

Kallias saying Xanthippus now commanded the Athenian fleet.

"For the past week," said Xanthippus, "my squadron has run reconnaissance, venturing far into enemy waters, but steering clear of the islands aligned with Persia. What we have to report is not good. Piracy has escalated, cutting off supply ships to some of the islands and creating dismal conditions. Starvation plagues many. The Persian fleet wintered at Kyme, but now musters at the great naval base on Samos. We must prepare to meet their threat."

Leotychides came to his feet and silenced Xanthippus. "I have to keep reminding our Athenian friends that our presence here on Delos is meant only to ensure that our shores are free of harassment. Our troops on the mainland will fight the war. We'll stay put unless Persian ships sail west." He turned to Kallias. "Why wait longer? We must hear from Kallias. It has been days since we heard news of the army. Kallias, tell us of Mardonius and the occupation of Attica."

Kallias walked forward to the table, briefly turning to look back toward Melaina. She saw his dark features beneath his curly hair. "General Leotychides, fellow Athenians and members of other Hellene states. Not many days ago, Mardonius removed his army from Attica and set up camp in Boeotia, but before retreating, he advanced west as far as Megara and burned Eleusis, including the Telesterion where the sacred Mysteries have been held for the last thousand years. He also burned everything left standing in Athens."

Melaina saw the tired faces grow dark, heard their mumbling. Kallias paused. When the voices subsided, he continued.

"Shortly after Mardonius' retreat, the Hellene army gathered at the ruins of Eleusis and took an oath to defend Hellas to the last. They then crossed over the spurs of Kithaeron and took up positions on the southern bank of the Asopus at Plataea and opposite Mardonius' forces, where they now wait until those who practice seercraft say the time is right to attack."

A man interrupted Kallias, a great dark man with matted hair and beard, soiled tunic. He looked as though he could account for the entire stench of the room. Melaina recognized him as Kimon, one of the men who'd accompanied them on the return from Brauron. She'd also seen him at the Isthmus, where he'd expressed affection for her until Kallias shoved him aside. Both times he'd been flushed with wine, but now his face was red with rage.

"Let's sail the fleet back to Athens!" Kimon shouted. "Give us a chance to fight. I should have stayed on Salamis. Now I'm stuck out here in this godforsaken wasteland of an island daw-dling while Hellas burns and Mardonius thumbs his nose at us from Boeotia. All the cowards in Hellas have escaped here to De-los. Will we never fight?" He fell back in his seat like a walrus and sat there sulking. "I long for a glorious death!" he shouted. "You goat-phallused bastards want to rot in your beds on top of your women."

Kimon's voice left an echo in the large hall, and Kallias hesi-tated before continuing. "Could be you'll get your chance yet, Ki-mon," he said. "A while ago, word came of an oracle from Delphi foretelling that Hellas would be victorious at Plataea if the battle were fought on Athenian soil and before a temple of Demeter. At first, we thought all was lost, since we interpreted the oracle to mean that we must fight in the Thriasian plain. But the priestess at Eleusis knew of an abandoned temple of Demeter near Plataea, and there the troops have set up headquarters. Since the land was Plataean and not Athenian, Plataea removed her boundary stones. Such is the situation as we speak, seers sacrificing to determine the gods' will. But without the knowledge of the priestess of Demeter, they'd be floundering to fight Mardonius in a way that pleased the gods."

Kimon shouted again from his chair. "This doesn't help us waterlogged out here. I see no role for us in this." He turned again to Leotychides, "Send us back to the mainland where we can fight and die with honor in defense of our homes."

Leotychides didn't respond and Kallias continued. "I have with me the priestess of Kore, daughter of the priestess of De-meter. I'm sure all of you remember that, on the night before the battle of Salamis, her prayer sent us all so well into battle. This young woman has had visions of coming battles, one involving the fleet. She speaks of a favorable outcome, provided we observe the will of the gods. That's why I brought her to you this evening, although the presence of a woman before a war council is unprecedented. If she's right, we must act with haste. I'll not tell you of her prophecies myself but let her speak, if you chose to hear her."

A tall, middle-aged man jumped to his feet, face contorted with incredulity. "This is an outrage! I've divined for the fleet these past few months and see no reason to second-guess Phoebus. Has my reading of divine will been found faulty? The gods wish us to stay put."

Instantly, Melaina liked something about the man, although his argument ran against her. She detected an uncertainty in his manner, something sympathetic, an insecurity fueling his hot words. This man could easily be made an ally, she thought. Melaina whispered in Kallias' ear, and he stood once more.

"Deiphonus, no doubt you've read the omens rightly, but Apollo has little at stake in this as his temples at Delphi and here on Delos have been spared by the Persians. Other forces at work in the cosmos, those with a direct stake in the outcome, will determine our fate."

Xanthippus rose. "Deiphonus, seers are supposed to be versed in everything, yet you've not distinguished yourself since joining the fleet. Your oracles are long on excuses and short on action. Shut up and let the girl speak."

Deiphonus wasn't perturbed. "Your problem is not with me but Apollo's obliqueness. Tell us more of the woman's visions, if you are to hear them. They come from dreams or lunatic ravings?"

Kallias seemed to know not what to say. He looked back at Melaina, then turned to Deiphonus. "She has the falling sickness," he said, but seemed startled with his own words as shouts of dismay rocked the walls.

What's he done, thought Melaina, totally discredited me?

They'll stone me if he doesn't watch out.

Kallias continued, "Many of the greats had what's known as the diviner's disease: Herakles, Ajax, invincible Bellerophon who tamed the winged horse Pegasus. She's had it since conceiving a divine child."

This produced another uproar. "Conceived a monster, more likely. Get her out of here!" shouted Deiphonus.

"More reason to hear her!" shouted Kimon. "What harm would it be to listen? Surely we have the will to reject a woman's prophecies if they prove idle." He walked up behind Xanthippus, looked down at him as he sat with fear on his face. "And you, Xanthippus. You work you heart out to jail a honorable man, let him die in prison, but speak weak words in support of this glorious woman. Rise up before this council. You lead the Athenians here. Demand a hearing for her." Kimon waked back to his seat.

"Never should we hear her," shouted Deiphonus. "Epilepsy is but sickness of the soul and replete with false prophecies."

Melaina's heart plummeted. Surely a great seer such as this man would know her worth to the fleet. She was sorry she'd come. What a false sense of wellbeing she'd had thinking herself in the company of friends.

"She's Melaina, daughter of Kynegeiros!" shouted Kallias. "The dead will punish you for rebuking her."

Fnally, Xanthippus rose again. Kimon's attack on him seemed to fuel his words. "I say again, hear her! Memory of the great Athenian warrior demands it."

The general uproar supported him although Melaina thought it due more to curiosity than desire for guidance.

Xanthippus was still on his feet. "It's long been known that pregnant women glimpse the future. A priestess of the Mysteries cannot be ignored. And one of such lineage! I fought alongside Kynegeiros. No one here has his courage."

Kimon rose again, looking tired and disgusted with the whole affair, spoke directly into Deiphonus' face. "You speak as an idiot, undeserving as a child. I, for one, would listen to this daughter of

Kynegeiros regardless of her topic. Shut up! Let her speak."

Leotychides himself rose, held up his hand. "Silence!" he told them, then turned to Melaina. "Step forward, young priestess. We'll hear of these visions that so moved Kallias. Start with their nature. What god gives these prophecies? Such questions are of great interest."

Melaina rose and walked forward, carefully avoiding the eyes of the men focused on her. She stopped before the table and was provided a chair. Men from the back of the room squeezed forward. She took a deep breath but so crowded with child was her abdomen that she still felt breathless. She lifted her veil in a fold across her brow. She was surprised at how weak her voice sounded.

"I realize it's unfitting for a woman to practice other than silence and discretion, yet I come to speak not of my own will but that of the gods. I'll do the best I can in spite of my sex, not being a practiced soothsayer or orator. The frenzy that sometimes captures me is horrible to gaze upon, as Lord Kallias can attest. Still, before each gruesome seizure, I have such clarity of mind, such sense of peace, that one can only describe it as union with the gods. But then comes splitting pain and raging terror no mortal should experience, followed by deep darkness and loss of the senses. Whether these visitations are possession by Apollo, as the priest at Epidaurus told me; the god of frenzy, Dionysus himself, who also has prophetic power; or divine Demeter and Kore, I know not. Perhaps the child growing inside me holds the key."

Melaina heard the men shuffling about and could see that they were tired and losing interest. She had to get to the meat of her story quickly.

"As to the visions, one occurred outside Epidaurus, the other in Kallias' home. The first was of a split path, not mortal roads but Sacred Ways defined by the Fates. Both led to great suffering during battle followed by even greater glory in victory. In the second vision, I was lofted high into the air as if carried upon the shoulders of some awesome goddess. She strode among the Aegean islands, first to divine Delos, then Samos, sacred to Hera, where smoke trailed skyward from some great conflagration, then on to mainland Asia where a great groan issued forth."

She stopped for a moment to catch her breath. The hall was deathly still.

"I've studied this last vision for meaning and can only say that surely some great atrocity is to take place at Samos. The meaning of the agony in Asia can only signify a battle. But regardless of my interpretation, I can say for certain that Zeus wills you forth to battle against the Persians. You can meet nothing there better or worse than your fate."

The chamber remained quiet following her words. Finally, Xanthippus rose. "Mistress Melaina, I marvel at the sight of you. Your manner of speech, though maidenly, couldn't be more like your father's. That any daughter of his could speak so well is no surprise. You've come among us with your wisdom, goddess-like, yet humble as befits your gender. I, for one, would heed this advice, take your prophecy as truth, and proceed on the attack. But I've not the deciding vote. We must haggle amongst ourselves to learn whether we have the courage to accept the challenge you put before us. One would hope for swift action, but our short history here on Delos wouldn't foretell it. Retire to your accommodations here on the island. We'll trouble you no more."

Kallias took her by the hand and led her from the building, through the courtyard, and to a temple where the priestesses lived. Kallias was lost in thought, and Melaina wondered at the impact she had on the generals.

"What'll they do, Lord Kallias?" she asked. "I'd expected them to decide one way or the other. I've failed you, and them also, by being unconvincing."

"Oh, but you were convincing. You must understand. Generals are timid creatures, overwrought with political motives. We've done our best. Let matters fester."

As they entered the temple of Artemis, Melaina caught sight of a tall girl in a short bare-armed chiton. The girl looked familiar, but Melaina thought it impossible that she'd know someone on the island. Still, the face was unmistakable, and the girl stood tall as a man, head and shoulders above the other women. She had a wolf at her side.

"Keladeine!" shouted Melaina.

It was the young priestess from the Isthmus of Corinth.

CHAPTER 9: A VIEW OF THE FATES

Keladeine looked back, and then turned away as if she'd only imagined someone calling her name.

Melaina shouted after her, "Keladeine, don't you recognize me?"

Keladeine wheeled about and raced toward Melaina, threw her arms around her. "Melaina, how could I? You've changed so."

Lykos bristled at Kallias, uttered a low growl with teeth showing. Kallias stepped back. "Stay the beast!" he said.

"Lykos!" said Keladeine. "Heel, Lykos!"

"Lord Kallias, forgive me," Melaina said. "I've met a friend."

"Then you're in good hands," he said, looking relieved the wolf was no longer eyeing him. "You'll not see me for a while, but I'll contact you when I decide you should return to the mainland." With that, he left the temple.

Keladeine took Melaina to a chamber where handmaids fixed a bed beside hers, covering it with embroidered quilts and thick firs. Then the two girls sat facing each other and clasped hands.

Melaina spoke. "Tell what's happened to you first, Keladeine, why you're on Delos. What brings you so far into the Aegean?"

Keladeine was more radiant than Melaina remembered, still dressed in her short, sleeveless chiton, skin golden from Helios. "Oh, how I wish to get off Delos!" Keladeine said. "I've been stuck here two months by the Persian threat. The warriors won't leave me alone, always singing the praises of Aphrodite and trying to get their hands on me. They never understand the path of a virgin. I've been alone and wretched, without a friend."

"But why are you here, Keladeine. It's strange to see you so far from the Isthmus."

"Apollo has ordered me to Ephesus. Word came from Delphi that a priestess must be sent because of a transformation about to occur in Ionia. My dream of living at Ephesus has come true, but I can't fulfill it. And this general, Kimon, he's ever after me like a viper."

"Yes, I know him," Melaina said, "quite an appealing fellow."

"That's the bad part, my own disease. I crave him with a sort of distemper, ranting and raving I am like a lunatic, but won't let him know. I've got to get off this island before I end up in your condition." Keladeine squeezed Melaina's small hands with her large ones until they hurt. "Tell me what's happened. Whose child is this? How could you go against your vow to Artemis." Keladeine's face showed more than concern. It projected irritation.

Melaina felt humiliated. Not since learning she was pregnant at Epidaurus did she feel such guilt. No one but Keladeine could realize the dread consequence of her pregnancy. She tried to talk but could only cry, tears spilling down her cheeks. "I don't know how to begin. First, you must know that I have the falling sickness, epilepsy."

Keladeine became quiet, and Melaina told of falling at the battle of Salamis. How she'd known she had epilepsy even at the Isthmus, but thought she'd been cured and hadn't mentioned it. She told of Sophocles, how she'd developed great affection for him and become jealous, that she'd made a mistake one night and left herself open to the influence of Aphrodite. She told of the strange coupling, how it had all seemed a dream and that she knew not who'd visited her bed. She told of the trip to Epidaurus to seek a cure for the epilepsy, learning of her pregnancy while there, and of Kallias saving her during the burning of Eleusis, marrying and shunning her after learning of her illness, all within a single day.

"Is your baby the divine child talked about all over Hellas?"

"I've wanted to think that it's Sophocles' child, but memory of that night, while unclear, refutes it. Oh Keladeine! How can one suppose herself to be carrying a divine child?"

Melaina fell silent, and Keladeine said, "When I met you at the Isthmus, I realized that your life was but clay on the potter's wheel of the gods, some deity spinning and shaping it to divine will. Remember? I told you this then. Even being with you takes courage for any who have the ability to sense divine presence. We're all in your service, as evidenced by my sweet sister giving her life to rescue you. Even my being here on Delos may be but support for you in time of need. Tell me, what brought you here? The island buzzes with news of a priestess come this very evening on a mission from the gods. Could that be you also?"

"It's but my own foolishness, Keladeine. Before each seizure I have visions, some of great battles. I'm here to tell the generals, so they can decide if my visions be omens of future events or baseless hallucinations. Kallias didn't believe so but brought me anyway, unwilling to decide against me himself. I went before the generals this evening after arriving."

"All you tell fits a divine pattern, but one thing concerns me greatly. Artemis deals harshly with those who stray. Have you prayed to her about this?"

"O Keladeine! If you knew the anguish this very thought has caused me. After learning I was pregnant, I went to Artemis at Epidaurus and tried to propitiate her, but felt the goddess remote, not listening. The priest at Epidaurus thought Apollo must be the father of my child. Such he read from the dream I had in the Abaton. He said that Artemis rebuffed me by appearing with Apollo as a hind instead of in human form."

"If this is true, you've come between divine brother and sister, not an enviable position. But I don't believe it. At Iphigeneia's sacrifice, Artemis substituted a hind in her place. Could be she was simply showing you the same principle of mercy."

"I fear not only the wrath of Artemis but also Hera. On the way to Epidaurus, I stopped at her temple to pray, but felt great hostility from her."

"Perhaps Hera will soften her anger now that you've married.

Could be the gods are taking turns with you, each working their will on your life. Artemis is a complex deity. In Asia, she's known as the great mother goddess. Her worship there is even more ancient than in Hellas. That's the reason I'm going, to merge Hellene and Asian views of her. Perhaps out in the middle of the Aegean, as we are here on Delos, her influence over you is mixed, ambivalent."

"But lately I've felt close to Athena. Ever I come closer in temper to that of the fleet. Sailing in a trireme is such a joy."

"We must get you up the mountain to the temple of Athena tomorrow morning. If Athena is influencing your fate, we must pay homage to her. That you've married an Athenian certainly makes that likely. Athena has taken you into her charge for the sake of Athens."

As the two young women talked, sounds from outside, of dancing feet and singing choruses from all over Greece, lofted into the chamber. The island seemed in continuous festival. A group of girls, who called themselves Deliades, entered the chamber and formed a circle around Melaina and Keladeine. They were the friendliest creatures Melaina had ever met, dancing about like children begging attention, laughing and poking at her until she thought them a nuisance. They were unusually interested in her pronunciation of words, the way she used her mouth while talking, and her hand gestures. They would set her in motion across the room just to watch her walk.

Later that evening, Melaina and Keladeine left their chamber to see the festivities. They entered the courtyard and passed a modest temple of Artemis beside the Keraton, Palace of Horns. Choruses came from within it dancing the Crane: an invocation of birds, swamp walking, and maneuvering the Labyrinth. Melaina and Keladeine stood and watched. First came long-robed Ionians, refugees fleeing Persian dominion, performing dances of great solemnity and dignity. Keladeine joined the thin-veiled women cloaked in flowing garments. She danced like a delightful dove, tilting her head first this way, then that, her feet placed in precise measure to the beat, a gentle lifting of the arm, a pose. The aulete's tune was slave to her song.

The Deliades also returned to the festivities. Many people of different origins came to Delos. These the Deliades mimicked, imitating dialects and chatterings of all men. Then Melaina learned why they'd been so interested in her back in her chamber. One of the Deliades stepped forward, her chiton stuffed with a pillow, puffed her cheeks and stiff-legged about the courtyard to the aulete's beat. She twirled about each stiff leg and lumbered from side to side.

Melaina fell against a wall overcome with hilarity at her own likeness. "They use laughter as a lethal weapon. Tell them stop it, Keladeine, or they'll have me delivering the child."

The Deliades praised Apollo with a hymn by ancient Olen, like that Melaina had heard in the thymele at Epidaurus, one to Leto and arrow-pouring Artemis. Melaina sang too, voice lifting, lofting. She sang with a gleeful force she'd never before achieved. It came from pure ecstasy. With Melaina in the center, the chorus circled, then twirled so fast that their hair stood out straight from their shoulders. Melaina loved the flickering torchlight, the smell of trailing smoke winding a path among the dancers. The lyre player stepped onto the dance floor and smote the ground with flashing feet. A throng stood around the courtyard clapping.

Melaina felt the mildest confusion and was momentarily deprived of her senses. She experienced a throat spasm, cheek twitching, and suffered a minor facial convulsion. She heard a call go up from the chorus for the deity to join them, and they all began an ethereal dance, mimicking the movement of heavenly bodies. Frenzy overtook the crowd, hysterical, wild dancing. Melaina felt a rush at the flurry of pounding feet, the deafening screech of the pipes, and her vision shifted. She saw dancing stars spiral above, a gigantic vortex of cosmic motion, and felt the Cyclades spinning about Delos.

A swirl appeared in the middle of the dance floor, and grand Apollo himself swooped down from the firmament to high-step a tune among them. All mortals spun about him, his satellites, as the cosmos circled above. The great Spindle of Necessity, she saw, and round it whirled the planets, moon, and sun, each assigned a humming Siren. The three white-robed Fates, divine spinners of lives, chanted while twirling the axle of mortality. Each sang in turn of the past, present, and future. It was as if Melaina viewed the creation of the Universe, the machinery of the gods weaving human reality from primordial chaos.

Melaina didn't cry out or fall. She had no splitting pain, but recognized her affliction, the vertigo and stupor, followed by a period of incoherence and the slow return of understanding. She had thoughts of violence and felt malice toward everyone.

I'm having a partial seizure, she thought, one seemingly without end. She saw other divine Olympians: Artemis, Athena, Zeus, and Hera. The frowning warlord Ares stood alongside the sea-god Poseidon. Divine Demeter, without her daughter, sat on a golden throne. Aphrodite danced nude.

When Melaina fully roused, she realized Keladeine had hold of her hand and was talking to her calmly, her voice coming from far in the distance. "Come back to me, Melaina," she was saying, "I'm here when you return."

Melaina watched as Athena leaned forward and touched Zeus, her father, on the shoulder, whispered in his ear. Melaina saw Zeus nod.

"Zeus has just decided our fate," Melaina said aloud. "Woe be unto Persia."

CHAPTER 10: THE BROACH OF ARROGANCE

Melaina woke late to find Keladeine missing. Instantly, she felt abandoned and longed for Kallias. She left the temple and walked the courtyard grounds alone, but couldn't find Kallias or the young priestess. The weather had turned cold and a group of men recognized her and offered help, but she refused, sinking into depression. She worried about the child, felt it shift inside her, and wondered how she could have talked Kallias into bringing her to desolate Delos.

Finally, she found Keladeine with a strange-looking man, the two shooting arrows into an old tree stump out by a shallow marsh. Keladeine had a quiver stuffed with handmade arrows strapped to her back. Melaina thought her companion looked unmanly, his dress effeminate. Keladeine called him "Colaxais" as he showed her how to sight along the arrow and gauge the elevation of its tip to allow for fall during flight. Lykos and an even larger black dog stood to the side, obediently staying their ground.

Upon seeing Melaina, Keladeine dismissed her teacher, speaking to him in a foreign tongue.

"What an odd fellow. Who is he?" asked Melaina.

"A noble-blooded Scythian of great wealth. He makes his home on the banks of the quiet-flowing but mighty Don River."

"What! A Scythian? Scythians are uncivilized, and have uncouth eating habits."

"Ah, he's not so bad, once you get to know him. Besides, they're not always after pleasures of the flesh."

"I've heard they don't allow the elderly to die of old age, but include them in a sacrifice with their cattle, their human flesh boiled and eaten along with beef."

"Don't believe everything you hear, Melaina. And they are handy. Second to none with the bow. And the gods enjoy their presence. A Scythian's nature attracts them."

The two girls walked to the rush-overgrown marsh marking the shallow, sacred lake, 'the Wheel' as the Delians called it. A small stream flowing from Mt. Kynthos kept the lake brimming with fresh water. On an oasis in the center, a tall date palm grew. Melaina stared across the water at it. She was still dizzy, reeling from her vision the night before.

"Yes," said Keladeine, "Leto spread her arms around that tree while giving birth to Artemis and Apollo."

"Wow!" said Melaina. "What a sacred site." She watched as tuneful, muse-inspired swans swum, lacing the eddying mere where bulrushes hid the far shore and the sun's heat drew mist skyward. Along the western flank, between lake and sea, stood a row of roaring lions, statuesque guardians of the lake.

Melaina spoke with Keladeine of last night's vision, explaining that she'd seen the gods and knew their will concerning the forthcoming battle in Ionia. She didn't know how to speak to the generals about it, yet knew she must. Melaina hadn't seen Kallias since the night before and missed him considerably. She'd come to appreciate a man's presence.

She and Keladeine left the lake and walked up Mt. Kynthos to the temple of Athena. Melaina stopped every few steps to catch her breath. "Gone are the days when I could bound about like a young rabbit. The child takes my strength." But she didn't have to walk the full distance. A small donkey-drawn cart carrying supplies for the temple allowed them aboard.

They said prayers at both Athena's temple and at that of Zeus the father. Keladeine officiated, speaking the words for Melaina. They stepped back outside. From the top of Kynthos they viewed the entire world. The hilltop was formed of broken boulders and curious skull-like formations. Delos itself was a thin sliver of rock, beneath a stark-blue sky, surrounded by sea. Keladeine pointed

out the islands of the Cyclades visible from the lofty peak: close-
by Reneia and Mykonos, of course, but also Paros and Naxos,
twin shores to the south.

Melaina noticed three ships sail around the southern tip
of Mykonos and Greek warships immediately intercept them.
"Look!" she said.

"Something's happened," said Keladeine. "We must hurry
down."

They again sought the cart and descended the hill. As they
reached the village, Lykos saw Kallias first and would have attacked
except for obedience to Keladeine. "Off, Lykos!" she scolded.

"Lord Kallias," Melaina said, "we've seen three ships accosted
off the tip of Mykonos. Do you think they're Persian?"

"No. We've just received the news ourselves. They're Hellenes
from Ionia and requesting council. The generals bid me summon
you also. Seems I've become your herald. Descendant of the divine herald, as I am, is it any wonder?"

Keladeine returned to the temple of Artemis, and Melaina
entered the council chamber with Kallias amid great confusion,
everyone excited and shouting at once. "Show them in as soon as
they arrive," said Leotychides. "Word from the Aegean's far shore
is food for the ears."

The three Samians entered, dressed in full war garb with
swords hanging from their belts. The eldest, gray-haired and
hump-shouldered, stood in the center of the chamber and spoke,
his excited voice echoing in the hall. "We've been sent by all
Samians without the knowledge of Xerxes or Theomestor whom
the king left as tyrant over our island," he said. "The Persian fleet
musters on Samos as we speak, but not for battle. After their defeat
at Salamis, low morale affords them little more than the strength
to stand watchdog over Ionia. The time is ripe. Liberate us!"

Leotychides spoke. "Your request adds to that we heard yesterday saying the gods also wish us to force the issue in Ionia. But
we Spartans serve only our own security. Meddling in the affairs
of others is ever a great plague on humanity. Your words are com-

forting, but demonstrate even less reason to press the attack." With that Leotychides took his seat.

The hump-shoulder Samian leader looked perplexed and waved his arms but was speechless. Finally, he found his voice. "At the mere sight of Hellene sails on the horizon, not only Samos but all Ionia will revolt against Xerxes. The Persians can offer little resistance. You'll reap a great harvest. Although it serves our good, it also serves yours. Xerxes will use Ionia to harass the rest of Hellas far into the future if you permit this continued occupation."

Leotychides rose again. "We haven't the means to attack the lion in its lair. Our ships are badly supplied and ill-prepared for a long siege. When Agamemnon invaded Asia, Hellenes pounded Trojan walls ten long years before they fell."

"Not so this time," said the Samian. "Persian ships are unhandy and no match for yours. Surely you learned that at Salamis. That Hellenes would attempt an assault on Ionia has never entered Persian thought."

"Persians don't think of it, because it's foolish," countered Leotychides.

Xanthippus rose. Melaina could see that the Athenian, though second in command, carried more weight with the men than did Leotychides. "Endless excuses," he said. "Did all brave Spartans die with Leonidas at Thermopylae? We Athenians are by our very nature disposed toward action. Let us not pass up this opportunity. The Ionian is right. All Hellas is at risk so long as Persia holds sway over Ionia."

Leotychides countered. "Athenians are ever eager to voice an insult, yet even Delphi's oracle speaks against action. Did not Apollo dictate that all battles must be fought on Athenian soil? Kallias said as much yesterday."

Kimon had remained quiet, but now jumped to his feet, his voice booming the hall. "You vomit stupidity! We can rot on Delos no longer." He turned to Melaina. "Even our women prod us forward. You filthy cowards! You're fit only for the dung heap."

Leotychides seemed to falter, then said, "We'll have to talk to the Ephors at Sparta before making a decision. I can't risk troops without authority."

The leader of the Samians spoke again. "Never would I have imagined such faintheartedness. Tigranes is the only warrior of any talent among them. Beware the man who has to face him in single combat. But he is only one man. In the name of honor that all Hellas holds sacred!" he shouted. "Save us from slavery. We are men of the same blood as you. Expel the foreigner from our soil."

Leotychides seemed a coward to Melaina. She could see it all slipping away. The generals would indeed stay on Delos and the Aegean remain forever a haunt and refuge for Persian warships. A wave of grief fell upon her, and her hand touched upon the golden Broach of Arrogance. The symbols on it were chiseled into her mind's eye such that she could see them without the broach before her. Now they burned bright as never before, flames licking the edges of the stylus strokes, the script on fire. The ancient tongue spoke to her, *The command of Zeus is ever upon you, his struggle is yours.* Great anger emanated from each letter.

Melaina jerked the broach from her cloak, stood, and walked among the generals, holding it up for all to see. "Here!" she shouted, her eyes flashing across theirs in flagrant disregard of feminine custom, recording their astonishment. "This golden broach given to me by the blacksmith at Eleusis was formed using the Telchines' ancient art. The eagle, whose shape it has, is that which gnawed Prometheus' liver, a bane for the god's arrogance when he stole fire and gave it to mortals. This broach warns against that arrogance all mortals inherited with the fire. Xerxes, yea all Persia, is the embodiment of arrogance. He claims to be King of Kings, yet is no more than any Hellene citizen."

Melaina saw Kallias shift uncomfortably in his chair and shake his head, while Leotychides fidgeted and looked about him, not knowing if he should stoop to argue with a woman. He finally spoke, "But consider this, daughter of illustrious Kynegeiros. Realize Delphi's imperative that the struggle for Hellas be fought before a temple of Demeter and on Athenian soil. Kallias tells us this. Yet none of Ionia, Aegean islands or Asia, belongs to Athens."

Melaina turned her eyes directly on him, her brow wrinkled in anger. "No matter that none of it is lawful Athenian soil. The Gods speak of their view of the land, not the idle opinion of mortals. In ancient times, the sons of King Kodrus of Athens by divine decree sailed to Asia and founded Ionia. It will always be Athenian in the heart of Athena and Zeus the father. This wrangling is simply an excuse to escape divine will. In my vision on the way to Epidaurus, the Fates hadn't yet sewn the cloth of our fate. But last night while watching the dancing in the courtyard, I had another vision, and watched as Athena asked, and Zeus chose sides. Divine will now stands with Hellas. Zeus has already decreed Ionia unshackled. You have but to deal the divine blow."

Leotychides' face went blank. Melaina knew she had him in a tight spot. Not only was a woman telling a man to show courage, but she also, by pronouncing the gods' decree, had removed all their excuses.

Since he sat in shameful silence, she spoke again. "The three divine crones, daughters of Nyx, weave the future as we speak. As long as Xerxes has a single Hellene city within his grasp, he'll covet the rest. Xerxes will be defeated. The only question is whether you have the courage to be part of it. Let me tell you this…."

Melaina felt herself jerked backward. Kallias had hold and pulled her, not only from in front of the generals, but also from the chamber and into the fading afternoon sunlight. Once outside he told her, "I've saved you from the very arrogance you speak against. It's not a woman's place to scold generals."

"How else could I cure their blindness?" But even as she spoke in her own defense, guilt overcame her. In her zeal she'd overstepped her bounds, as she was so apt to lately. How could she have progressed so quickly from fear of even speaking to the generals, to ordering them into battle?

"I'll return to see that their wrath goes not too strong against you," said Kallias. "Perhaps they'll impose a mild punishment. You're young and intend good." He walked away.

CHAPTER 11: READING ENTRAILS

Kallias was gone but a short time and returned forthwith, the fleet seer trailing after him. "Ever your impact on people amazes me," Kallias said. "For when I reentered, the generals were discussing not which chastisement best suited your crime, but how to further explore the will of Zeus. Here with me stands Deiphonus, soothsayer extraordinaire, sent by Leotychides. He's to divine the god's will with you assisting. From now on, limit your outspokenness so as not to overly concern me."

"Which way flows the tide of opinion?" she asked.

"Amazingly, the generals lean toward going. After suffering your assault on him, Leotychides weakens from his steadfast opposition. The sacrificial omens will swing the balance. You two are to set up the sacrifice for the generals' observance."

He left her in the hands of belligerent Deiphonus.

The two walked silently in lengthening shadows to the temple of Apollo, past the colossal cult statue, the monumental gilded image of the god holding a likeness of the three Graces in his right hand and a bow in his left. Inside was the fireplace covered in ash, glowing charcoal, bones, and the slaughter stone stained by blood, oil, and wine. Vessels of all kinds stood about along with roasting spits, axes, and cauldrons on tripods for boiling sacrificial meat. She knew Deiphonus didn't want to share the sacrifice, but looked strangely afraid. He fidgeted with his himation, kept throwing the end over his shoulder.

Of all the men in the meeting they'd just left, he'd seemed the only clean one. His chiton, warn next to the skin, appeared new or at least recently washed. His himation was so clean and white that it glowed in the pale torchlight of the temple. His himation was girded about the waist by a band of the finest silk, almost like a woman, she thought. Everything about him shouted pretense. The scent emanating from him was saffron.

"Don't worry," she said, "I've learned my lesson. I realize a fleet seer of your reputation could teach me much. I'll but observe the intricacies of your art, and try to learn from a master."

Deiphonus looked frightened and turned away, stroked his beard nervously. He said, "To learn to work together we'll need a practice victim." He disappeared.

While he was gone, Melaina rekindled the fire, but he reappeared quickly with a goat from the holding pen, a bit of confidence returning to his troubled face. He sprinkled the goat with meal and wine, waited for it to shiver assent. This he did with great flourish. Melaina uttered the woman's cry as he slit the animal's throat, then elevated the back legs to encourage the blood flow. Just when she expected him to open up the animal, he paused. She saw his hands tremble. He's afraid, she thought, but of what? When he slit the animal down the middle and broke it open, he paused again.

"Are you going to read the entrails, or not?" she asked.

He sat to the task, but started unfolding the large intestine, laid it out on the ground. Then he grabbed the heart with the left hand while he cut it loose from the arteries with his right.

"What are you doing?" she asked, unable to contain her curiosity. She suppressed a laugh. "Start with the lungs, heart, then liberate the gallbladder and liver."

"I've never done this in front of a priestess," he answered.

She wondered how a grown man, a fleet diviner, could be afraid of a girl only fifteen, when she realized, with a jolt, that the man was a fraud. "You have a problem?" she asked.

"I know that with the knowledge you've shown just this far, you'll see through me, so I must tell you the truth. I have no reputation. Many chide me over my lack of skill." He still wouldn't look at her. "I've but taken the name of a great diviner's son and have little knowledge of seercraft. If the generals find out, they'll have my head."

Melaina thought to herself, So that's what's behind his façade. Instantly, she made a decision. "No one need know," she said, then thought, How fragile and transparent are the hearts of men! "I learned from an aged blind man at Epidaurus, a descendent of ancient Teiresias. We'll work together to bring forth a prophecy so pure, it'll sway the hearts of even the most ardent disbelievers."

She took the knife from him and severed a large vessel coming from the head. "Note," she said, "on its path to the liver, one-half the vessel runs beside the kidney and loin to the thigh, then continues to the foot. It's called the 'hollow vein.' The other half courses the diaphragm, lying close to the lung, then branches to the heart and arm."

Deiphonus stared into the bloody victim, observing Melaina's hands as they quickly severed the connecting veins and raised a dark mass from within the bloody chamber. The hot, sticky fluids warmed her cold hands. "This is the liver with gall bladder attached."

"What part indicates divine preference?" he asked. "I know the liver, spleen, heart. Even their function in nourishing the body is no great secret. But I find no god residing there."

"Oh, but you must think in terms of the wits, the way thoughts come to us." Melaina took a deep breath, realizing she'd better start at the beginning. "The brain contains the higher principal, the divine element of the soul," she said, "and the body the lower. The neck is the isthmus connecting but restraining passage. The higher principal contains reason, reflection, and understanding. The lower houses terrible but necessary feelings: pleasure, pain, confidence, and fear, the appetites. It's irrational, falling easily under the spell of phantoms. The heart, filled with courage, passion, and love for contention, is set at the guardpost before the gate to the divine citadel, demanding temperance and enforcing the rule that only the best shall pass upward."

"True enough," he said. "But this tells nothing of divine will."

"Patience," she said, "I'm coming to that. We feel the gods, experience their presence inside ourselves. They influence us mortals through our entrails and demarcate animal entrails in the same way."

Melaina laid the dripping mass in his hands and stroked the surface to indicate the condition of the various parts as she spoke. "Diviners use the nobler entrails, in particular the liver, which resides next to the irrational part of the soul with its weakness for hallucination. The liver transmits thoughts to the soul under the influence of the gods, receiving and reflecting images as a mirror. It's there, into the liver, that the gods throw their ideas and feelings."

"But how to read it?" Deiphonus' voice was high-pitched, full of panic. "What discernible signs could possibly manifest there?"

"When the gods wish to express dissatisfaction, they cause the liver to become bitter and threatening, thus giving off bilious color while becoming wrinkled and round. The lobes bend and shrivel. Conversely to express pleasure, the gods use the liver's natural sweetness to provide gentle thoughts, allaying bile and bitterness to render smoothness, perfection, and thus furnish happiness and joy. All this occurs within the livers of humans and animals alike and is the reason seers divine using sacrificial victims. To read divine will in the entrails, one simply unfolds the liver as a writing tablet, opening and inspecting it."

"Beyond strange, but simple enough," he said, his voice returning to its normal state of feigned confidence. "The lower portion of the soul, though irrational, sees the future?"

"Necessarily so. As proof that divination comes from our innate foolishness, not wisdom, realize that I don't attain prophetic truth and inspiration when I have my wits about me but when I'm demented. Only later, when I have recovered my reason, can I judge the meaning in my apparitions and interpret whether they are favorable or contrary."

Deiphonus' eyes were large, and his voice filled with wonder. "How did mortals learn such things?"

"Prometheus, Forethought himself, taught mortals divining

when he stole fire. As punishment Zeus sent his winged hound, the eagle, to banquet on Prometheus' liver. Since Prometheus taught us to read the liver, Zeus tortured Prometheus' own."

"Yes, I've wondered about that. But hurry. Let's set up the sacrifice. The generals will arrive shortly."

Into the garden the generals came, the temple overflowing with warriors and seamen to witness the sacrifice. Melaina had slaves cut them all tender myrtle sprays to bind their brows. She and Deiphonus then purified their hands in the sacred mountain stream, while one servant brought baskets and another a bowl for slaughter blood. They kindled the fire and set cauldrons around the hearth, the clang of metal ringing.

"Bring a lamb," she said.

"Will any do?" whispered Deiphonus.

"Select haphazardly, as in casting lots, so divine guidance that pervades the universe will direct the choice."

While he was gone, Keladeine appeared, Lykos at her side. Melaina whispered a few words to her, and Keladeine spoke sternly to the wolf. Melaina then patted him on the nose. Keladeine stood back with the other observers, Kallias at her side. Melaina regarded him briefly, then turned back to the sacrificial fire just as Deiphonus returned carrying the lamb under his arm.

Melaina turned to Leotychides, and asked him to agree to a twofold question. She offered, "Is it better and more proper for us to wage war on Persia in Ionia than to remain at Delos?"

"Yes, that is the question," Leotychides assured.

Melaina cast barley meal upon the altar and spoke. "Apollo of rocky Delos, vouchsafe victory for Hellene forces and ruin for our foes."

From the basket, Deiphonus took the straight blade, sheared a lock of lamb's wool and cast it upon the flame. Then he slit the lamb's throat.

With the filleting of the animal, Deiphonus showed considerable skill, slitting it down the middle with the sharp blade, and breaking it open. Melaina took the knife from him and bent to the work of severing the large vessel from the head to liberate the liver. She stared at it intently. But the liver was less a lobe. Melaina knew only a healthy sheep could be used and studied the visceral side of the liver, which also contained a deformed gallbladder.

Deiphonus gasped. "Evil portents, foreshadow of disaster!"

A murmur of concern passed among the generals.

"Hardly!" Melaina scowled. "The lamb is diseased, the omens spurious." She turned on him. "You've brought us a bad victim. I'll have to select one myself."

Deiphonus threw the carcass to the stray dogs standing about, and he and Melaina left the temple together, walked to the sacred holding pen. Several lambs approached the two seers, and Deiphonus was ready to take the largest, but Melaina spotted one in a far corner. "That!" she said. "The word of Apollo is elusive. We'll take one reflecting his nature."

Back in the temple, Deiphonus drew back the lamb's head with great flourish, cutting through sinews of the neck, and splashing red the stone altar. After the filleting, he offered the gods thighbones wrapped in glistening fat.

Melaina said, "Listen. Hear the fire crackle? That's Hephaestus laughing. A favorable sign." Then she grasped the noble entrails and inspected them, Deiphonus looking over her shoulder.

"The liver is sectioned as a picture of the world read from the night sky, a model of the heavens," she said quietly to Deiphonus. "Read from the top, going around to the right. I read a favorable sign from Hera," she said, "obviously concerned for her temple on Samos, her birthplace."

"Yes," said Deiphonus, then raised his voice so all could hear, "a favorable sign from divine Hera, her temple on your island in jeopardy," he said to the Samians.

This brought murmurs from the crowd, "Ah, yes," they said, but still Melaina saw confusion etched in their faces. If I don't get on with this, she thought, they'll lose confidence in me.

Melaina knew that the regions of the liver important for interpreting Demeter's influence also carried significance for Kore.

She stopped, her courage shaken, then regained her composure. "This is from the divine daughter and pertains to me alone," she said.

Melaina's silence had caused some in the crowd to believe she'd lost her confidence. Kimon said, "She hasn't the courage to speak the will of Zeus. Shout your thought in the midst of us, Melaina. Does cowardice master you?"

Leotychides chimed in. "She's lost her way in the reading," he shouted. "If you utter a vain prophecy, lead the fleet to disaster, think how to escape my hands alive."

Melaina's face flushed and for the first time she panicked. Deiphonus was not the only fraud here. Never before had she read entrails on her own. Yet she knew she could do it. Had they already lost faith in her?

Kallias then stepped in front of the general, his face red with anger. "Hold your tongue when addressing this priestess for she is my wife. I'll send you to the Undergloom if you threaten her again."

Another murmur of surprise passed through the crowd, and they seemed to look upon her with new respect. This was the first time Kallias had mentioned their marriage in public. Melaina was struck dumb by the statement and felt immeasurable gratitude for this magnification of her stature. Now she was not only a priestess but also the wife of the richest aristocrat in Athens, a field commander's wife. She could do this.

Melaina addressed Leotychides' fear. "I falter not from lack of knowledge, sir, but overabundance. Never have I seen such beautiful entrails. The liver glistens with more brilliance than the heavens. The fate of all present here is written therein, just as in the stars. Any of you, step forward. I'll read your fate in the coming days."

The two generals who had spoken against her shuffled about uneasily, each standing first on one foot, then the other.

"I see the end of all your lives," she said, "you have but to ask to know if it comes tomorrow or in a hundred years."

But not one had the courage to look his own fate in the face. Kallias shamed them. "Ever you find fault with soothsayers, but tremble before her seercraft."

Since they all remained silent, she proceeded with the reading. Deiphonus crowded in behind her. The two spoke quietly, then Melaina addressed the generals.

"Deiphonus allows me to relay the final word of Apollo as he prophesies the will of Zeus. The condition of the entrails is perfect. Never has either of us seen such glistening liver fat. Zeus has spoken again, his word unchanged from past prophecy." She raised her hand in the air, made a fist. "Ionia is ours! Death to Persia!"

But her enthusiasm was slow to move the crowd. Leotychides spoke for the group. "This is the final word then? A favorable reading from the entrails?" But Melaina could tell he was still unstirred.

"One more word will I speak," she said. "The vision came to me as I read the entrails. The Persians have burned Samos. Red flames lick timbers on the holy island as we speak."

The Samians shouted in dismay. "Ever more urgent is our need," said their aged leader. "Proceed quickly."

Melaina continued, "If you had doubt that those on Samos would revolt against the Persians, this should settle the issue."

Seeing that the omens were favorable, Leotychides asked the Samians for their names, "Perhaps they will contain another good omen," he said.

Lampon was one, another Athenagoras. The Samian who'd done all the talking stepped forward, the old humped man. "Hegesistratus," he said, Leader of the Host.

Melaina thought this a curious name and wondered if she hadn't heard it before.

Quickly, Kallias came alive, drew his sword and advanced on the man. "I'll hack your head from your shoulders," he said.

Melaina wondered if Kallias had gone mad.

"Show your leg!" demanded Kallias. "I'll see the right foot, or take your head."

The Samian pushed back, wanting no part of his body vulnerable.

Then Melaina's own confusion over the name resolved, and she realized Kallias' worry. She stepped between them. "Lord Kallias! I know your mind and can assure you he's not who you suspect."

Kallias turned to her incredulous. "You know him?"

"No, but I've met a man by that name, Hegesistratus the clubfoot who divines for Mardonius." She turned to the Samian. "Sir, offer up the limb. I'll see to it that he, my husband, not cleave it from the trunk."

The man cautiously stepped aside, raised his tunic.

"Yes," said Kallias, "the woman is right. No carved timber you walk upon. Forgive my outburst. I thought we had an enemy amongst us." He turned to Melaina. "Who in Hellas or Persia, or in all the world for that matter, don't you know? Women are supposed to come to marriage as a clean slate, a piece of papyrus for their husbands to write upon. You come to me a book of screeches and ravings, full of enough lunatic learning to baffle an aged philosopher, and not yet past your fifteenth year."

The tension broke, and Leotychides spoke to Hegesistratus. "The meaning of your name is indeed a good omen. I'll cast my vote also for liberating Ionia. But before such an undertaking, let us take an oath of offensive and defensive alliance. This young priestess here would seem an excellent choice to give it. Let her be the one to pour wine and administer the words." He then looked expectantly at Melaina.

Melaina was astounded with the distinction given her. But the thrill quickly turned to foreboding as she looked at Kallias and remembered his vacillation concerning their marriage. Even with his recent admonition, the fact that he'd faltered for a while still stung her. Can a man keep an oath? she wondered. "Greatly do you honor me, sir," she said to Leotychides. "What holds Hellas together is the oath. Still, without wishing to seem ungrateful,

I'll not do it with wine."

"She's temperamental," said Kallias, "and unreasonable at times. Perhaps someone else would be a better choice."

Melaina ignored him and continued addressing Leotychides. "I'll use water from the river Styx carried in a golden goblet, as do the gods."

"Impossible!" shouted Kallias, and the murmur from the rest told that they shared his alarm.

Anticipating such an outburst, Melaina maintained her composure. "The islet west of Delos is sacred to both Hekate and Iris. A sacred spring flows there with water forbidden for use other than oaths. It comes from Styx in the Underworld, and Iris herself draws water there for the gods' oaths. I'll use it unless your oath is insincere."

Leotychides questioned her. "Why such extremes for oath taking? I've heard nothing like it."

"Kallias has taught me well of men's fickle hearts," she said. "I'll not give an oath that can be taken lightly."

"What of this, Kallias?" asked Xanthippus.

Kallias, face beaming brilliant red, turned his back to them.

Then, all stood still, each hoping the other would know how to satisfy her. Finally, Kallias turned back, spoke. "I'll take her to the island. She can draw the water herself."

"Hurry," said Hegesistratus, "Helios' light fades."

From Apollo's temple, the priest retrieved a large golden goblet that Melaina carried in both hands on the walk to the dock. Quickly, she and Kallias entered a small fishing boat. Kallias, at the oars, facing the stern where Melaina sat, negotiated the narrow channel as the pink glow of sunset faded from the western sky.

On the far side, they exited the boat, and Kallias helped her up the shallow incline and past a small abandoned building, a temple of the divine oathgiver Iris, Hera's winged messenger, the angel. They came to a grove of oak trees, all stunted by rocky soil. Within the shaded grove, they found a cliff and through a cleft in it heard, but could not see, running water. Melaina removed her chiton and unwrapped the bandage supporting her bulging abdomen, then folded and laid both on the ground. She stood naked before Kallias, holding the golden goblet.

"I'm afraid of the dark," she said. "Talk to me while I enter."

"So you do still have some of the little girl left in you," said Kallias, then kept up a stream of words, nonsense really, as her bare feet stepped into the cold water. She squeezed between rocks into the cleft, wetness splashing her, then held out the goblet until she felt it overflow. She backed out of the cleft to Kallias.

"Quickly, Lord," she said. "Dry me. This water has death in it."

"Is it really from the Styx?"

"So it's been told by priests since primordial times. To drink it brings death, to get it on the skin causes those closest you to grow remote."

He dabbed the cold water from her with the bandage, then stood looking at her. "Though eight months pregnant, you're by far the most beautiful woman I've ever seen, Melaina. I've come to love you in spite of this terrible falling affliction." His voice was smooth there in the pale moonlight, touched with sadness. He took her into his arms.

Melaina felt an exquisite internal warmth and a quiet compassion for him, though she'd not call it love. But she did kiss him, kissed him as if she loved him. Then she donned her chiton and they returned to the boat by torchlight.

She warned him, "Careful the waves not rock the boat and splash this Styx water on deck." She held the torch while he rowed.

Once again before the generals, Melaina said, "My final request."

The generals then looked askance of one another, nervousness besetting the group. Kallias stood aside, refusing to argue with her.

Melaina looked at them as if they were her group of girls back at Eleusis. "I'll need a lump of iron for each general, and a single hand-bellows. Following that I'll give the greatest and most awful oath possible."

From within the city grounds, slaves brought forth several heavy ingots and placed them and the wheezing bellows before her.

"Fire them!" she said. "They're of no use until white hot."

She stood before the fire squeezing the bellows as she'd seen Palaemon at Eleusis. Great flames grew but gradually died as the glowing coals became hotter and hotter.

"This water bears a curse," she said, holding up the goblet, "therefore drink none of it. It comes from far below Earth's wide paths, a cascade from the briny deep. If any god of snowy Olympus pours a libation of this water then swears falsely, he lies breathless a full year, wrapped in evil coma. When this trial subsides, another seizes him: nine years banishment from council and feast. Mortals suffer ten years exile plus whatever other evils the gods devise."

Deiphonus, along with a warrior he had sequestered, brought forward two ewes, one back, one white, and while Deiphonus slit their throats, spilling black blood into a bowl, Melaina called forth the gods. "Immortal Zeus, father of all mortals and immortals, wrathful and invincible god ruling from Olympus; bright-faced Helios, whose eternal eye sees all; and rabid, arrogant Furies who howl Necessity's dictates and wreak vengeance for false swearing; all you gods witness this solemn oath."

Then the generals, each in turn, retrieved their glowing iron ingot from the fire and, using the sacrificial victim's skin as a sling, cast the hot metal into the sea. "We swear never to break our mutual friendship until the masses of iron float up of their own freewill, still red hot."

With that, she poured upon the ground water from the golden goblet, the generals scurrying from its trailing path lest their feet become wet with the fearful liquid. Melaina prayed again. "Ethereal and blazing Zeus, and all you other vengeance-mindful gods; whosoever is first to do wrong against this oath, may his brain spill out on the ground as does this water, his wife be a captor of other men's desires, and his children reflect the face of his enemies."

Kallias flinched at the mention of children and wives, then looked daggers at Melaina. The generals plunged their right hands of fellowship into the warm, sacrificial blood, and Melaina spoke words binding each to the other, those from Samos pledging wholehearted support of the Greek cause during the coming battle. Henceforth and forever, the generals Leotychides and Xanthippus pledged both liberation of Ionia and protection against Persia.

The oath complete, the meeting broke up, generals to the docks, Melaina and Kallias to the temple of Artemis. They entered her chamber and closed the door.

Kallias said, "I'll leave you here and board one of my triremes for the trip to Samos. You'll return tomorrow morning to Athens or perhaps Eleusis, whichever you prefer. I only ask that you send word to my mother of your decision."

"Me, decide?" said Melaina. "How am I ever to understand you and your vacillating commitment to our marriage? In Athens, you sealed my fate saying you'd not suffer my illness. Then you acknowledge our marriage here before the generals. And now you act as though it's been me vacillating all along."

Kallias looked apologetic, yet remained quiet. Just as he seemed ready to speak, he was interrupted by a knock at the door.

Xanthippus entered smiling. "We want Priestess Melaina with the fleet," he said. "They would sail the triremes through the Gates of Hades for her if she willed it, I swear. We took a vote and gained unanimous consent."

Melaina slipped back behind Kallias, not wanting the general to see her face. Mention of sailing further east brought sudden fear to her.

Kallias told him they'd consider the matter and give a decision before the fleet sailed. "She's heavy with child," he said.

The general left, and Kallias turned to Melaina. "You can't withdraw your support now."

But her courage had left her entirely. "O Father Zeus! What a fearful thing to ask," Melaina said. "Let me think. Had I to say this moment, I'd return home. You promised my father you'd take care of me." As she spoke, tears filled her eyes. "The unborn babe, my lone feeble ally in anguish, just kicked me in the ribs. It too senses the peril. But to give the warriors an example of cowardice, when they desperately need a call to valor, would be unseemly. Allow a little of this night, Lord Kallias, for me to find my courage."

CHAPTER 12: A CALL TO COURAGE

Melaina settled down for a rest while Kallias gathered his armor in anticipation of an early start, but a fierce tempest arose, and he feared they'd be kept from sailing. Violent blasts stirred the sea, the rough surge setting ships pitching and rocking. Melaina rose again and stepped outside to watch the crews scurry to bring the beached crafts farther upon the sand to prevent them from being ripped apart by the raging waves. Priests worried the winds, and Melaina, with her robe wrapped tight about her to deflect the gusts, fell to wondering if somehow she'd further offended the gods.

Kallias and the generals seized the opportunity to sleep, but Melaina, with her insomnia, kept dreamless vigil over their slumbers. She thought of seeing her mother again, that she might comfort her over the Hierophant's death, and she longed for Eleusis even in its ashen state. Oh, how I long for the sight of home! I really am an exile, she thought. Will I ever see my home again?

After hours of listening to thunderstorms unleash their fury, Melaina also dozed and had visions of Iphigeneia with her father Agamemnon. She woke briefly, dozed again, and dreamed of herself at the slaughter stone on Delos as Iphigeneia had been at Aulis. She woke remembering the children who'd worked the silver mines at Laurium, the worms, how their labor bought the fleet of ships that saved Greece during the battle of Salamis, and now made the liberation of Ionia possible. Their toil must not be in vain, their suffering come to some good. My own child could end up there, she thought.

A noise startled Melaina. On the windowsill above sleeping

Kallias hovered a small, big-billed bird with a bushy crest, a halkyon with a fish in its beak. Some god had turned it aside while it flew aloft and settled it upon the pane. Melaina didn't know whether she was awake or dreaming. She'd thought the halkyon was a mythical bird with no earthly form, as legend told of its calming the waters to nest at sea.

"We are two of a kind, sweet twittering shuttle," Melaina said, "I may weave my own nest upon the sea before long."

The halkyon beat the fish upon the sill to kill it, as if knocking upon the door of Hades, swallowed, then uttered a laughter-like screech.

Melaina realized its clatter was fraught with omen, and that its shrill voice prophesied the ceasing of winds. Melaina spoke to it again. "O halkyon, sing your doleful song. I know you ever bemoan a homeland. I match your tearful cry, an unwinged songstress longing for Eleusis."

A thought came to Melaina, a twinge of guilt with it. On the far side of the Aegean, on some ancient Asian shore, a happenstance might occur in which she could avenge her father's death, as she'd promised him. She took a deep breath and made her decision. "My sweet Lord, see your grandchild through this."

She touched Kallias as he lay wrapped in soft sheepskin. "Kallias! Wake. You must climb rugged Kynthos and propitiate Artemis. We must dedicate me to this voyage, and the stormy blast shall cease."

He stirred, stared at her in alarm. "What daemon has hold of you this time?"

"The halkyon, kingfisher of the sea that knows the whims of waves, spoke as you slumbered. By the power of Artemis and no other will the sea be calmed, even as favorable gusts were given Agamemnon at Aulis when he sacrificed Iphigeneia."

Kallias wiped sleep from his eyes. "Ridiculous! I see no bird. The gods haven't demanded a human sacrifice in hundreds of years."

"Not sacrifice, Lord Kallias, dedication. I'll bend to the generals' request and sail with the fleet. I can't follow the path of the divine virgin, but she still has use of me. We'll offer a hind in my place."

Kallias took her hands in his, shook his head. "Last night, your tears provoked my pity. I now call back what I said. Don't risk this trip into the jaws of death. I can't bear to see you and the child in peril, two lives joined with mine as I've sworn before Zeus."

Melaina wondered again at this renewed commitment, but put a finger to his lips. "Listen, Lord Kallias. It's as if the winds here on Delos are those absent at Aulis that cost Iphigeneia her life."

"Still, this is a man's war."

"Look at it through mine eyes, and see the right of it. The first time I set foot on Salamis, during the earthquake, and during my prayer the night before the sea battle, all the strength of Hellas turned to me. And now, these ships, whither they sail, depend upon me."

"No. It's blind arrogance to think that all depends upon you."

Melaina faltered. She fell quiet a moment, but then took Kallias' hand, pulled it to her breast. "Dearest Kallias, how I wish you were right, but I know better. The battle must be fought before a temple of Demeter and Kore. Just as my mother must be at Plataea before a temple there, so must I be at one in Ionia. Put me where you will, in the bilge, on the prow, at the stern. Wherever I'm least likely to cause disruption."

"But this will be a sea battle. You were right earlier. I did promise your father that I'd keep you safe."

"He'd want his daughter to show courage. Besides, you'll need me even more if fighting at sea. I'll create a temple aboard ship. The wrath of Demeter over the burning of Eleusis howls inside me. Through the Mother and Maid, goddesses of divine deliverance, we have the power to rid the Aegean and all Ionian Hellas of barbarian suppression forevermore."

"This would be unfair to the unborn. Board the next boat back to Eleusis and the arms of your mother."

"And not to your mother and our home?" she said, once again noticing his vacillation. Still, her mind in this matter was set. "I mustn't cling to life too fondly, Lord Kallias. If the unnamed babe is indeed divine, let the deity who came to me in the dark protect it. I'll give my life, as centuries ago did Iphigeneia, for Hellas. I'll even risk the divine child's life. But take me aboard, and throw off the yoke of Persia."

Thus, she spoke convincingly, and Kallias rose from bed, leaving to wake his comrades.

"She's agreed to go," he said.

Word spread like fire along a dry hillside in autumn when all turns golden and lifeless, and a spark of flint may start a raging heat. So the warriors were heard in song throughout the island, their hearts inflamed. "The priestess accompanies us!" rang the cry.

"We'll need priestess Keladeine," Melaina told them.

Quickly, they drove a red female deer from the sacred herd to the mountain's lofty summit, ghostly shapes of nearby Mykonos and Reneia hovering off shore, exposed by the blinding flash of Zeus' lightning. The men heaped a stone altar, and all hunkered over at the crash of thunder, wreathing their brows with myrtle.

Priestess Keladeine came forward, invoking Artemis with many prayers as she poured libations on the blazing hearth, and with Kallias, beseeched the goddess turn aside the stormy blasts. At Keladeine's command, youths danced a measure in full armor, clashing swords against their shields to lose the ill-omened wail of wind in the din.

At the edge of firelight appeared beasts of wild wood, wolves and rabbits that had left their lairs and thickets to witness the dedication to their patron goddess. The generals feasted and sang praise to the goddess of Kynthos, Artemis most venerable.

As the fire raged, Kallias cried, "Look, Melaina, in the east! What constellation is that rising above Ionia's far shore?"

"Giant Orion," she answered shouting over the wind's blast, "Artemis' hunting companion and her one true love, chasing the

Pleiads' sevenfold track. A son of Poseidon, Orion could walk on waves. This is just one more sign that Artemis broods over this narrow isle and directs us ever toward Asia. Stack on the rest of the hind, Lord Kallias, lean rump pieces and sturdy shanks."

"Thigh bones and fat are all tradition demands."

"Artemis would have more than my fat and thighbones."

Melaina saw priestess Keladeine step back out of sight, Kimon standing alongside her, and the effeminate Scythian close by. She'd not noticed them before, but now the Scythian led two blind slaves on ropes. She started to ask about them, then thought better of it. Melaina remembered the reason Keladeine was here at Delos. "I have but one additional request. Keladeine must go with me."

"By whose will does her plight carry any importance?"

"Apollo at Delphi commanded her. She's been on Delos two long months awaiting a boat to Ionia. Yield to divine will, Lord Kallias. Artemis is the great mother goddess of Asia. Long she's suffered her temple at Ephesus in Persian hands. She needs Keladeine as priestess there."

Keladeine stepped forward from the dark. "I beg in the name of all you have at home, do not leave me here."

Kallias shook his head, but spoke to the generals, who eagerly consented.

"Then bring the dog too," Kallias said. "We'll see if he's any more than a nuisance." He took a long look at the Scythian. "Bring the barbarian also. We'll need all the help we can get." But he balked at the blind men. "The sightless will be of no use. See that they remain on Delos." He turned to the Scythian. "By the gods, man. What form of being is a Scythian that he'd blind another man and lead him about on a rope?"

Melaina held young Keladeine fast to her.

The sacrifice complete, the generals scattered the ashes, descended the hill, and the call went out urging all aboard.

"Hegesistratus!" cried Xanthippus, "stand lookout aboard the lead trireme, guide us to Samos. The other Samians can return in their own ships. In ancient times, Agamemnon missed Troy and made an aborted assault on the wrong city. Let that not happen to us."

Crews frapped their ships with papyrus cables to withstand the violent sea, undergirding hulls weakened during the battle of Salamis. The fleet drew anchor, loosened hawsers from the sacred rocks, and rowed out of Delian harbor, wind and sea still lashing the shore.

★

Melaina stood at the poop deck, watching the lights of ships. She felt moisture between her legs, a sudden sharp pain and gush of water. A wave of panic seized her, and she grabbed Keladeine's arm, realizing that her embryonic membrane had ruptured.

CHAPTER 13: VOYAGE TO A DISTANT SHORE

Melaina fought through the throbbing pain that gripped her abdomen while watching the constellation of lights from nearby warships that broke the darkness. The armada emerged from the shores about Delos and fell into formation. She held to Keladeine and refused to go below while the violent sea still churned. She wondered if she'd brought the fleet to doom in the pounding surf.

Kimon had come aboard with them, Aphrodite stalking Keladeine.

The ships' crews broke into song to bolster spirits, some only whispers on the wings of distant wind, but Melaina's own crew cried loud and strong. "O Paean! Paean, never leave us! Arrogance is the ruin of cities, but brave men stand as their loftiest bulwark. Gods are wrathful with a coward, so may I fly far from that reproach. Courage is ever a tower raised against the foe. Oh joy, Paean! Oh joy! Paean, never leave us!"

They shouted louder and louder, drowning the sounds of the sea-lashing wind and the creaking sailyard. She'd never been with men going off in defense of country and felt the yoke of comradeship, the call to glory. This was the antithesis of Artemis' euphoric freedom. Gray-eyed Athena, dreadful and mighty goddess, who stirs men to battle and delights in the clash of arms, she has shackled me, Melaina thought. Oh, dear goddess, strengthen my resolve against this contraction-caused pain.

The roaring bellows of Boreas still raged, and Melaina, refusing Keladeine's attempts to get her below deck, watched as gusts shook shrouds and billowed the fine-linen sail. The oarsmen turned their profitless oars aside ship like the wings of sea birds. As the ship entered open water, Melaina sensed the goddess adding flame to her heart and felt the stab of birth pains lift.

The helmsman astride his poop-deck seat fought the tiller, a frightfully wild thing in a tempest. Melaina lifted her purple veil, tying it around the man's waist, as had divine Ino to save Odysseus from a harvest of evil winds. Dowels and belly-timbers groaned, holding the ship together.

Melaina recognized the worry of the troops and prayed directly into the stormy blast. "O goddess Leukothea, mistress of deep-bosomed sea, Ino, who delights in waves but delivers mortals from wretched death in the deep's destructive ire, defend these well-benched ships from old Oceanus' stormy waves and bring upon Poseidon's raging sea a fair stillness. At the end of our voyage we'll work the wrath of the gods who dwell on snowy Olympus."

The crew had not long to wait. Soon, as the halkyon had prophesied, windless air smoothed the swirling waves and lulled the sea to rest. They dropped sail, trusted in the calm, and mightily at the oarlocks bent to rowing. Their broad blades tossed sea spray threshing, heaven's brightest star finally rising to announce the light of young dawn. Melaina slipped below as the oars bore the ships on, strong stokes slicing silent sea. Not even the storm-footed steeds of Poseidon could have overtaken them. Dawn rose without a breath.

From under the poop deck where she'd fashioned a resting-place on furs and old clothes, Keladeine ministered her medicines, having brought a bag of herbal remedies from the Isthmus. Melaina rested and gradually gained strength. She felt as safe in this young woman's care as with her mother's, and the baby became quiet inside her abdomen. No longer did it struggle to enter the world. Melaina slept.

When bright Helios' chariot reached its zenith, Melaina and Keladeine came on deck to watch the gleaming plains of Ikaria, golden-grassed isle, appear to port. Melaina had to raise her voice for Keladeine to hear above the rhythmic patter of oars, the au-lete's tune, and the grunts and groans of cursing seamen. As the broad blades broke the water's surface, Melaina saw rainbows in the spray, little phantoms of purple that were glittering symbols of Iris, the winged oathgiver and messenger of Hera.

As afternoon wore on, the aulete grew tired and clamored for relief, but no one else had the skills to keep a beat. Melaina felt so rested she stepped forward, her own aulos strapped about her neck, and matched his beat. The boatswain then motioned the aulete below for a rest, and Melaina took over to lighten the oarsmen's work. She sat at the mast amidships, her aulos playing a stout measure for the long-stroking oars, now a swift stroke, now a pause for the blade of pine. Leading the mighty formation, they swept forward as she'd seen Kallias' stallions surge under the whip. Apollo sent music-loving dolphins to gambol around the dusky prow as he'd done for Achilles on his way to Troy centuries be-fore. Bewitched by Melaina's aulos music, they leapt for joy while escorting the fleet to the far-off land.

"Ho!" went up a shout from the bow officer. He'd spotted a column of black smoke trailing skyward in the distance. Hegesis-tratus looked toward Melaina. She knew he was thinking of her vision of Samos burning. Had she been right?

A squall overtook them, lightning flashed among dark clouds, and the aulete returned from his rest to relieve Melaina. She and Keladeine went below to the treasured water tun and brought up a glistening cup for each oarsman.

The ship was long-seasoned and weather-stained, wrinkled, hull black with pitch and tiller handle overlaid with ancient ivory. The reconditioned ship was formed of silver-fir, the cutwater and cathead of manna-ash. At the center prow, Kallias had fitted a creaky beam of old oak from Dodona that now uttered a wordy groan with every roll and jostle. Was it a tree prophet? Melaina thought its voice sounded human. She'd had enough of augury and shuddered against reading the future there.

As darkness again encroached, the bo'sun lit the ship's three bronze lanterns astern for those following behind, and they cast a glow that glistened on the sweat-streaked cheeks of the oarsmen. Melaina, captured by the aulete's beat, hummed along as she had on her boat ride to Salamis, her clear-ringing voice lofting like wings of high-flying birds. Shortly, Keladeine sat beside Melaina, her lips adding a lily-like maiden voice, and the two hummed an alluring, wordless melody. Their voices were more melting than the zither's note.

The oarsmen delighted in their song, and each rowed steadily stronger. But a single word raced amongst them, and the oar-beat instantly slacked, their drive stolen. "Sirens!" someone said, flashing fear in every heart.

"They think we're the clear-voiced daughters of Achelous," said Keladeine.

"No wonder," said Melaina, "Kore sends Sirens from the Underworld to lure seamen to the land of skulls. They think we'll draw them to their deaths."

The girls were interrupted by a shout from the bow officer, "Ho, yonder!" The ship floundered instantly, oars held dripping in bright moonlight while all stared out at lantern lights in the distance. "Persians!" shouted Leotychides. "Even in the dark I know their shape. We've lost the element of surprise."

"Yes," said Kallias, "but they sail away."

The captain ordered oars in the water again, and the fleet slipped silently forward. Soon, a distant light signified land, the southern coast of Samos. The fleet then fell in behind the lead ship, and all navigated the shore northward.

Another shout rose up from the bow officer. To starboard were faint lights of ships' lanterns in the distance.

"The Persian ships are skirting the coast of Asia," said Kallias. "They've retreated as Hegesistratus foresaw."

A shout of dismay went up from Hegesistratus. "Flames! It's the temple of Hera."

Melaina stared off to port into the flickering light on shore.

As they got closer, flames scintillated, coals glowed. The column of smoke they'd seen earlier in the day had been the first omen. Melaina sensed all eyes turned upon her. Why couldn't I have been wrong, just this once? she wondered.

The Greek fleet sailed into the deep harbor unmolested, and, dropping the yardarm and stowing it inside the hollow mast crutch, turned outward and rowed violently to drive the ship sternwards to a mooring. Once inside the breakwater, all was quiet. On shore, Melaina saw shadowed shapes run about in the dark, then torches. Archers amassed at the poop deck and fitted arrows to taut strings in case Persian warriors should appear. Melaina heard the softened strains of wind-blown music and saw a band of soldiers moving, moon glittering bright on lance heads.

Hegesistratus stepped forward. "Ho!" he shouted, "is the island free of foreign menace?"

A large, cow-eyed woman stepped from the crowd. "No barbarians here. Nor in the city north."

"How about the tyrant Theomestor?"

"All Samians enlisted to fight were taken with the fleet, Theomestor also."

The fleet coasted into the slips, tied halyards, and lowered gangways. Leotychides called for assembly.

As Melaina stepped onto the dock, the woman, more beautiful than she'd first appeared, greeted her.

"I'm priestess of Hera," she said, "Chera, they call me." The widow.

"I'm from Eleusis," said Melaina.

"The sacred temple of the Mysteries?"

"Yes, my mother is priestess of Demeter."

The woman stopped, her tresses waving in the breeze and her large eyes opening even wider. She wore an excess of bracelets, and her snowy chiton swept wide with every step. Chera was a middle-aged woman, one of great dignity, with braided locks carefully arranged over her breast and shoulders. "I've met your mother," she said. "I was initiated years ago. We ourselves have a temple of Eleusinian Demeter close by, on the coast of Asia below Mt. Mykale. It's nothing compared to that at Eleusis, but still, we cherish it." Chera walked Melaina and Keladeine to the sacred precinct, her purple robe wafting aromas of exotic ointments. "Hera's sanctuary was at one time the largest in Hellas, but is now in ruins." She spoke to her handmaid. "Bear the fire before us. Scorch the air so we breathe heaven's breath free of Persian miasma."

"So is Eleusis," said Melaina, "burned to the ground."

Chera stopped again to stare in wonder. The slave woman went before them, carrying the blazing torch close to the ground and passing the hot flame from side to side along their path. She continued her expurgating ritual into the chamber, carefully singeing every corner.

"Sweep the flame wherever the tread of unclean feet has soiled," said Chera. After the woman had left the walls black with soot, she added, "Quench the torch. You've paid heaven, now bear it back to the hearth."

The group of generals and other commanders converged on the small building and packed inside. Leotychides spoke, first of their good fortune, then of Persia having abandoned all the Greek islands. "I question proceeding any further," he said. "Why tempt fate? We've liberated Samos. Let's return forthwith and savor our conquest."

Xanthippus, not yet having found a seat, turned on him. "Don't second-guess your decision at Delos. The task was assigned not here on earth but in Heaven. My friend, why cherish an incomplete victory? Fate beckons with no need of a helmsman to show the way."

But the commanders milled about, mumbling under their breaths, not wanting to risk the lives of their men so far from home. Some wanted to proceed to the Hellespont, capture Xerxes' cables used to cross into Europe, then return.

Kimon walked among the generals, speaking insultingly first in the face of one, then another. "Long we've heard Spartans brag of courage, yet all those here would seem cowards. Who amongst you has the legs to finish the task?"

Leotychides grew red in the face. "Kimon, I warned you about insults. I'll not tolerate them further!"

Melaina could no longer remain quiet. She rose to her feet and walked out among the generals, searching the eyes of each. She could see the weariness there, but knew the job was not finished. "Wherein lies reverence for the solemn oaths you've taken?" she asked. "Remember the Styx water? Yet, already your capricious hearts cry for release from your vows."

Kallias fixed her with a stern glance, and Melaina realized she shouldn't invite further shame. Yet her heart was firm. "Zeus demands action!" she shouted.

"Listen to the girl. What courage!" Kimon cried. "Have our men become women, our women men?"

"She won't have to face Tigranes," shouted one. "He's the best-looking man in the Persian ranks. Perhaps she covets a look at the general."

Laughter broke out, and Melaina realized that her woman's opinion carried no weight now. She'd heard much of this Tigranes in the two days past, but not of his good looks.

Kallias took Melaina by the arm, but Kimon's outrage boiled over onto her. Melaina turned on them again. "You dipped your right hand in blood and made a promise. Though the early path home seems less risky, think you not Zeus ever forgets a promise. Remember the returns of those who sieged Troy then lost the gods' favor. Corpses thronged the great sea highways and piled up on beaches from Asia to Attica." She stopped when Kallias' grip on her arm became painful.

Then Xanthippus glanced at Kimon. The verbal thrashing Kimon had given him on Delos still seemed to fuel his actions. "A single sea battle will do the job. Let us offload masts, yards, sails, and lines, and make for the coast of Asia."

Just then, a herald entered the chamber. "Attention!" he shouted. "We've received word from our scouts that the Persians have dismissed the Phoenician contingent of their fleet. We outnumber Persia two to one."

A great roar rose in favor of battle.

Leotychides turned to Melaina and Deiphonus, "Perform another augury. I'll not go into battle without favorable omens."

Melaina remembered the thunderstorms that had passed the fleet earlier in the day. "We'll augur lightning," she said, "read Zeus' will directly."

She and Deiphonus stepped out into the night and climbed a nearby hill. Melaina selected a stick of old wood and staked out a space on the ground for observations, as she'd seen Udaeüs at Epidaurus. At midnight with clear sky and calm winds, she took up her position. After praying and sacrificing to dedicate the ground, she bid Deiphonus sit praying to the gods for a sign while she scanned the heavens.

Melaina saw flashes followed by distant rumblings, but wondered how she'd ever decipher them. She recalled Udaeüs' teachings and concentrated on the color of each flash, the quality of sound.

Deiphonus questioned her about such augury. "Seems lightning arises because clouds bump together. How could that reveal divine will?"

"I say, clouds bump together to cause lightning, to send Zeus' council."

"How do you tell which contains a good omen, which bad?"

"High-thundering Zeus stands on starry Olympus, hurtling any one of three thunderbolts forged for him by a Cyclops. The first he launches on his own, as a warning. These are mostly seen in cloud tops and never touch the ground. The second, both terrifying and dangerous, but of good omen, strike the ground causing no damage. These he throws after deliberation with his twelve counselors. The third, destructive and final, he sends only with the Fates' permission. With this third, Zeus killed Asklepios after he'd raised the dead."

"Passing strange! Zeus throws the same ones over and over?"

"Yes, but above all, the favored section of heaven holds the key."

The generals gathered around but Melaina shooed them beyond her marked sacred ground. She faced north, stretched out her arms. "Look!" she shouted, "to the northeast. Flashes illuminate the clouds closest to heaven. These carry the warning I spoke of, but to the southeast, lightning strikes the ground along the coast where the Persians lie in ambush."

"What does it mean?" asked Leotychides.

"Did not Zeus send Agamemnon a lightning bolt on the right as a favorable sign to siege Troy?"

"Yea, so Homer tells us."

"What more do you need! Can Zeus be any clearer?"

Still, the generals milled about mumbling. What was she to do? She heard an owl's haunting hoots, saw it fly east into the darkness. Then remembered blind Teiresias' bird observatory at Thebes. "There!" she said, "an owl, a favorable omen from Athena, daughter of Metis most wise of all immortals. It cuts a course east toward Asia into the lightening."

Deiphonus asked, "Is there no difference in these signs, the lightning and the owl?"

"Much difference, Lord Deiphonus. The lightning was a requested sign, granted in response to your prayer. The owl is an offered sign, a call to fulfill divine will. Amazing! Since Athena, Zeus' war-loving daughter, is protector of Athens, we can but follow. I've never seen such favorable portents." Melaina turned on Leotychides. "You rebuff Zeus, fail to heed such omens, and we'll suffer divine wrath. If you want to make it home, your path leads only through Asia."

Many voices raised in favor of fighting. She'd spoken well.

Xanthippus glanced toward Kimon, pushed Leotychides aside. "Are we to spend an eternity groveling our fate? Back to the ships!" he cried. "Clear the decks of masts and sails. Bring up the boarding bridges. Weigh anchors. You heard it from the Maid. Death to the barbarians!"

CHAPTER 14: REVIEWING THE TROOPS

Melaina would have stayed on Samos but for the fleet's tenuous state of mind. She boarded over Kallias' objections, but with Xanthippus speaking her part. Then Kallias motioned Keladeine aboard also should Melaina again experience problems with her pregnancy.

They launched the ships, stored the white sails in the hold, let the rudder down astern, and fastened it securely. Now that they were finally going into battle, everyone voiced a complaint. Shouts of shortages went up, some grumbling about broken oars, others of missing ropes or anchors. Hoplites scurried to ready armor, gather axes and spears. Archers strung bows and sharpened arrow tips.

"This is not sound reasoning, taking a pregnant woman into battle!" cried Kallias.

"You made the decision when we left Delos," answered Xanthippus.

"Yes, but her water hadn't broken then." Kallias watched Keladeine and Lykos, ever fearful the wolf would nip him. He scowled in disgust at the Scythian.

Melaina didn't mention her own misgivings. She'd had light, periodic pains since landing on Samos, although she'd not even told Keladeine. Still, she chided Kallias. "How is it men by the thousands give their lives for Hellas, yet you bemoan a single woman who's caused you so much trouble?"

Kallias was slow to speak. "Perhaps, my feelings. You're certainly no longer the girl the camel frightened." As he spoke, dawn kindled on the eastern horizon, a blaze of yellow. "Death in battle may come to us all," he added. "If the time comes, you and I, we both will be at death's door together."

Melaina felt the cool breeze and shivered, then looked into the face of the wind as the ship drifted from the slip. Feeling herself cower inside, she pulled Keladeine close and wondered what dreadful fate they sailed toward, if the outcome would come swiftly or drag for days. She felt as if she stood before some dreadful abyss. The baby shifted, strained against her abdominal wall as if readying for some stroke of doom.

She and Keladeine stood at the rail of the poop, next to Deiphonus. Grave and beautiful they were, white-clad, golden-haired sisters. When would she ever return to Eleusis? She couldn't imagine it now in ashes and her grandfather no longer stalking its halls. Ever she missed her mother and prayed to the gods for her safety with the troops at Plataea. Melaina rubbed her tired eyes. She'd only caught a little sleep in the last two days, and even it had been disturbed by turbulent dreams.

The ship resounded with shouted orders, churning oars, and the rhythmic toot of the aulete. Hoplites shuffled about on deck, rattling swords, shields, and greaves. Oarsmen put up side-screen leathers, shallow tents extending along both sides of the ship to protect themselves from the rain of Persian arrows. Yesterday, they'd come into Samos in line-abreast formation, but now, coming to Asia's coastline, they assumed line-ahead, two long strings of ships extending into the channel behind.

Midday, the late-summer sun bore down as they skirted the southern coast of the peninsula jutting out toward Samos, brooding, forested, shadow-laden. Long they strained their eyes over the choppy sea, looking for mustered enemy ships in the bay, but none came to meet them. When they drew alongside the coast, a cry went up from the bow officer. "There!" he shouted, "fresh-cut timber." The Persians, knowing their vessels were unequal in battle, had beached them, thrown up a wooden palisade, and dug a ditch. They laid in wait.

Melaina saw a mountain looming inland and called to Hegesistratus. "What peak is that?" she shouted above the threshing oars.

"Mykale, mother of ferocious beasts, by all accounts."

Melaina remembered Chera's words. She'd said that a sanctuary of Eleusinian Demeter lay nearby on the coast of Asia.

"Kallias," Melaina said, pulling at his arm. "Legend tells of a sanctuary of Demeter in Asia founded by Philistus when he accompanied Neileus, son of Kodrus, who came here to found Miletus. Could that be it? This would fulfill the oracle's final requirement."

Kallias called out, "Leotychides, Melaina has spotted the temple of Demeter mentioned by Chera. Delphi said the war would be won only if fought before a temple of Eleusinian Demeter and on Athenian soil. Athenians founded that temple."

Melaina added, "Zeus wouldn't have brought us here if the temple wasn't nearby."

"They'll have summoned reinforcements from Sardis," said Leotychides. "If they hold up inside the palisade, we'll never win a siege. But I'll not tolerate another accusation of cowardice from Kimon. This is my last chance to avenge Leonidas' defeat at Thermopylae. We've been hoping for a land battle." He waved Xanthippus' ship in close and shouted across the short span of water. "We'll siege the palisade! You'll soon witness Spartan courage."

"But we've prepared for a sea battle!" Xanthippus shouted back. "Haven't the troops for a siege. Not only that, if the Phoenicians return, our ships will be sitting ducks. We'll have no way home."

Leotychides waved him off, and though Xanthippus' face was barely visible, Melaina saw clouds of concern gathered there. Leotychides ordered the standard bearer to signal the other ships ashore. The man came forward holding the flag upright, dipped right, then left, raised, lowered it, oriented the head one direction, then another. When the fleet had been so informed, Leotychides ordered his ship close to shore before the Persian palisade. A lead line sounded the depths to ensure they wouldn't run aground.

"Kallias!" he called. "You have the loudest voice onboard. Call to the Ionian Hellenes aligned with Persia to revolt when we attack. No Persian will understand you."

From shore, Melaina heard echoes of shouting workmen still hard at building the palisade, saw huge timbers dragged into place by oxen, and clouds of dust billowing skyward. Alongshore, the Persian infantry mustered in full battle gear.

Kallias stepped to the rail. Just as he looked ready to shout, Melaina said, "Give them a watchword, 'Hera'."

Kallias shouted across the water, "Men of Ionia! When going into battle, remember first your love of freedom, and next, a password for you to approach us, 'Hera,' whose beloved temple lays in ashes on Samos. Those in league with us will never regret it."

With that, they sailed east along the coast to where the rest of the fleet was offloading. Leotychides ordered the ship through the riptide, prow-first onto the sandy beach, and had the gangway lowered.

Kallias shouted to Leotychides. "That sanctuary," he said, pointing up the coastline. "The battle must be fought there."

Melaina exited with the men but stopped Keladeine at the boat's railing. "You're forbidden to come ashore," Melaina said.

"Leave me aboard? How ridiculous! With you suffering as you are," said Keladeine, "I'd be a comfort."

"Apollo has ordered you to Ephesus, not to be my handmaid. Stay here until it is safe."

Kallias had his own opinion. "That damn dog has come this far, he's going to fight for his food." He gave the order for Keladeine to offload with the rest. "Let's see if she can use that bow." He added, "And the Scythian. I hear the girlish bastards can fight in spite of their appearance."

But the Scythian wasn't all that agreeable. "I'll come with you if you show a little respect. I've found Hellenes less than accepting."

Kallias waved him off.

Melaina shook her head at Keladeine although she knew that

further argument was useless. "I see no reason to risk you. One of your mother's daughters has already given her life defending me."

The host set foot at a strip of beach lined with groves of dusky poplars and drooping willows. Fowl sprang up, a tumult of flapping wings over the meadows and marshes: geese, cranes, swans. To Melaina, it was as if all things fair had left Mykale, making way for the loathsome task before them. The air vibrated with armor's dull clank and came alive with the rush of warriors.

After the ships had been offloaded, but for the few oarsmen staying aboard, they pushed back from the beach and rode at anchor offshore. Each ship then let go a tethered iron mass off the bow and another at the stern to hold against broadsiding waves.

The divisions, commanded by Xanthippus and Kimon, then deployed on high ground, and as his troops did so, Xanthippus came to Melaina.

"My life is in danger from one our own," he said. "I fear Kimon will seize the opportunity to take it during battle."

Melaina had seen this feud simmer all the past year. Xanthippus was right. It should end now.

"Kallias!" she called. "Bring Kimon before me, if he will."

Kallias called Kimon from donning battle armour, and the three of them stood before her. She turned to Kallias. "These two are at speartips with each other, over the imprisonment and death of Kimon's father. Broker a peace that will see them through this battle without one of them seizing the chaos of battle to perform some deadly mischief on the other."

Kallias turned on both men. "I've seen this hatred simmer myself. Though both of you be generals, and me but a field commander, by all that's holy, if one of you dies, regardless the circumstance, I'll see that the other is charged with his murder." He grabbed both of them by the front of their armour. "Do you hear me? This is about saving Hellas, and not about person vendettas."

Kimon, large that he was, shoved Kallias back, looked at Melaina and then glanced away. "I admit that I have harbored hatred of Xanthippus over my father's fate. But never would I, nor will

I, strike at Xanthippus during battle. If there is a problem, I'm the one in danger of the coward's act."

Xanthippus wouldn't look at Kimon, or Kallias, but spoke to Melaina directly. "I'm not a man prone to violence, nor have I ever served more than divine Justice. I'll take Kimon at his word. Let this be the end of it."

All three of them dispersed to their commands without a further word. Melaina wondered at this man who'd married her, his fearless way with men more powerful than he. Proud she was to be Kallias' wife.

Kallias had but a regiment, and deployed it close by the sanctuary of Demeter. The soldiers stood in ranks at his right while sea waves raged to his left. Leotychides walked before them as commanding general. The troops complained of fighting on land. "Just when we get ourselves in the mood to fight at sea, you beach us on this desolate, beast-infested coast."

Melaina stood beside Keladeine watching a bewildered band of warriors. "They never thought they'd see battle when they came to Delos," Kallias said. "They're new recruits, a lurid rabble that enlisted at the last minute."

One with eyes the size of saucers said, "We're oarsmen, poor freemen come only to power the triremes."

"Surely you're not unlearned in evils?" Keladeine asked.

"I'll place them in the rear," said Leotychides, "to kill the wounded and despoil the dead."

Melaina shuddered, the horrors of war. She tried to walk away, but Xanthippus pulled her aside, again, his face molded to another great agony. "Back on Delos," he said, "you saw the future, all our fates. Will my men survive this land battle?"

"Not all can possibly escape such a bloodletting," she said. She walked from him again and stooped to lift an aged timber partially buried in sand.

But Xanthippus followed her, came closer. She realized his concern was personal. "I've a ten-year-old son," he said quietly. "When my wife Agarista was pregnant, she dreamed of being mounted by a lion. Within the week, she delivered. One day he'll be a great man if I can but live to raise him. He would be such a gift to Hellas. Would you speak to the Great Mother?"

Melaina looked in his eyes, saw fear lodged there and thought it was for his own hide, not that of his son. "Don't worry, Lord Xanthippus. Your son will have his father."

As he ambled off, she marveled at how easily she'd spoken this prophecy, her certainty he would live. Had she simply spoken out of frustration? She looked at the staff she'd retrieved from the sand. It was a crooked wand with a curved top and resembled a battle trumpet. It was an augur's staff. It looked familiar. Her heart leapt! Was this a miracle? Perhaps her grandfather, the Hierophant, wasn't dead after all. But just as she raised it clenched tight in her fist, she had another partial seizure as she'd had on Delos, and felt she'd taken hold of a lightning bolt. Saw the flash, felt the sizzle.

She saw an apparition, a hallucination of phantoms and wraiths. She couldn't speak but heard Keladeine shout and felt Kallias shake her. Quickly as it came, it left, but her eyes glazed over and her tongue felt thick. Her legs almost gave way. The generals gathered about her and the warriors pulled close, battle gear squeaking and rattling. Melaina tried to make sense of her vision. Her own words seemed to come from outside herself.

"I've witnessed…I've witnessed the battle on the mainland," she said, "just seen the Hellenes rout the Persian forces at Plataea. Mardonius…he's dead. A Hellene now rides his white stallion."

A great commotion arose among the troops, but some doubted she spoke the truth. They milled about voicing contrary words. "What's this?" asked Leotychides. "How can she know events on the other side of the Aegean?"

"It's the sacred sickness," said Kallias. "She's had a vision."

Xanthippus' worried eyes cleared. "We've taken back Attica!" he shouted.

A great bellow came from the troops. So eager were they for encouragement that disbelief was not possible. Fact it seemed, the words sweet as dinner-table dainties.

Melaina shouted into the crowd. "It seemed as though I saw through my own mother's eyes as she stood firm before the temple of Demeter in Plataea. They've overcome the enemy and now hold siege to Thebes."

Still Leotychides wanted more. "Give another word to help us with this prophecy, Lady Melaina, any further assurance to lighten our hearts."

As Melaina's mind cleared, she felt a flash of rage. Keladeine tried to restrain her, but Melaina broke free. "How many times do I have to tell you antelope hearts not to worry? Aaugggg...!" she shouted, then tried to control her anger, knowing it was a remnant of the seizure. She ordered Deiphonus, who stood nearby, to sacrifice a goat while she thought of a way to add to the omens. She turned back to Leotychides.

Keladeine warned her, "Take care, Melaina. Watch your words, lower your voice."

"I'm all right," she said. "I have control of my temper now." She turned to the generals. "This staff I just found here on the beach belongs to my grandfather, Hierophant of the Mysteries," she said. "The aged timber has been passed down from Eumolpus himself, the first to be initiated into Demeter's Mysteries. Ever since, initiates have taken turns holding it when observing the epiphany. Many times I've held it in my own hand. Only my grandfather could have left it here. The staff would not have left his hand but for a reason: Zeus willed it. Even now, Persians must hold him hostage in the palisade. It was left here as a sign."

A man came running from the forest toward them shouting, "Hera! Hera! Hera!" Leotychides ordered the man apprehended and brought before him. He was an Ionian escapee. After the Ionian caught his breath, he gushed news about the enemy forces. "Persian leaders place no confidence in the Ionians," he said. "They've confiscated all our arms. At their first opportunity, all Ionians will change sides. The generals are desperate to inspire courage in their soldiers. They say that Xerxes is coming with a mighty army of reinforcements. A great lie! Xerxes languishes in disgrace at Sardis. Their one hope is in numbers. Ever the generals scan your ranks to calculate their advantage."

Meanwhile, Deiphonus had completed his sacrifice. He shouted that Zeus had sent favorable omens. At this, Leotychides called a quick conference and proposed they further tempt the Persians by causing their own Hellene forces to seem smaller. After several moments of heated arguing, Leotychides decided to split the forces. He and his Spartans would proceed up a torrent into the thickly wooded hills to attack the Persian flank.

Xanthippus was beside himself. "Leotychides decides to beach the ships and attack the palisade, and now escapes to the safety of cover while we're left in the open to suffer Persian arrows and lances."

But the decision held, and as the Spartans disappeared up the ravine, Xanthippus climbed a sand hill and spoke to the warriors while standing on grass tufts.

"Don battle armor!" he shouted. "We fight for all the Hellene islands and for Ionia. The young priestess, Kynegeiros' daughter, has dashed all our doubts. Zeus himself stands beside us; fierce Athena urges us on."

Melaina raised her fist in the air and shouted, "Avenge my father, Lord Kynegeiros!"

Kallias then led Melaina and Keladeine, the Scythian trailing behind, from the beach to the small sacred village at the edge of the forest and to the temple of Demeter. The men stayed outside, and the women entered. Inside, Melaina and Keladeine found it vacated except for the occupation of a great stench. Melaina spotted what she thought was a wooden statue sitting on a throne, then realized that it was an old woman. The white-haired crone rose to greet them, a lifeless dream bowed over her walking stick. She crept forward on bony feet, fingering the wall as she went, her weak limbs trembling. Her voice was the creak of a rusty hinge, husky breath of death. "Long I've waited for the coming of the Maid. If you truly be she, I'll end this grievous old age, having spoken unbelieved prophecies for ten centuries. Now the god can unloose my spirit."

"What is that smell," asked Keladeine holding her nose.

"Is the priestess of the temple here?" asked Melaina, checking her own breath.

"Listen!" said the crone. "All able bodies have fled inland to escape my ill-smelling and noisome affliction. Ever I reek and rave. My life is my wound. I utter prophecies like matter from an oozing sore. Long I've been at this temple seeking Kore's mercy." The crone's eyes were like wells of deep memory.

"Who are you?" asked Melaina.

"Many the names I've had. At Thebes, I was first called Manto by my blind father. As Daphni, I delivered Delphi's oracular responses. As an unnamed poet, I invented Homer's best verses, and as Sibylla they still scroll my prophecies."

Melaina had no time to listen further. She spoke to Keladeine. "She can't possibly be Teiresias' daughter. She'd be eight hundred years old." She turned to Kallias. "I'll be safe here. Ensure Xanthippus realizes that the battle must be fought nearby. Don't let him siege the palisade, but urge him to await the Persian attack."

The old woman's scratchy voice questioned her. "You be truly the Maid, my cure? If so, you're as the rust from the sword that heals its own wounds."

Melaina and Keladeine were not listening to the old woman, but instead stepped outside to watch as the phalanx formed down the beach from the temple. Kallias mustered his regiment alongside the others. The old lady's coarse voice in the background kept up a steady stream, but Melaina ignored it. The late-summer sun cast long shadows as the hoplites rigged themselves in body armor: bronze helmets, bell corselets, greaves.

Kallias complained as he dressed, "Breastplates are always a bad fit and never distribute weight over the collarbone." He shuffled shields until, finally, he found one suitable for his arm length. "Many the time I've had a shield fly off." He searched through a pile of weapons for an iron thrusting spear, hefted one for weight and balance, and stuck a smaller blade into his belt. "When will they ever provide protection for the throat and groin?"

Melaina heard other warriors' worried grumbling of not having enough armor to go around. The men fought over breastplates and shields. Seemed no one possessed a complete panoply. One would have a new corselet but a primitive helmet, another no greaves. Even when all the hoplites were dressed for battle, no mustering order came, and the men were greatly displeased as they basked under the Aegean sun. "We'll suffocate!" they shouted, writhing inside their ventless armor.

Keladeine's Scythian took no armor. To Melaina, he looked something of a eunuch and seemed sluggish but stout, fat and hairless, with a sunburned complexion. He used bronze-tipped arrows, wore gold headgear, gold belt and girdle. Attached to his quiver, he wore three light-colored leathers, each with a large patch of hair.

Melaina had to know about the hides. "What are those?"

"Enemy skins," he said. Melaina was sorry she'd asked, but couldn't resist yet another question. "To what use?"

"Handkerchiefs."

She wondered if bring the Scythian had been all that necessary. His black dog looked fearsome enough, but Melaina didn't like him any more than she did his master.

The Scythian saw her looking at his dog. "My canine is famous as a hunter and distinguished for keen scent. No wild goat, fawn, or hare can escape him."

But Melaina thought the dog looked untrustworthy. It wouldn't meet her eye. "This dog is impure," she said.

Finally, Xanthippus raised the criers, and the call to battle went out. Auletes shrieked. She heard the whetstones screech as they grated against iron in the last-moment sharpening of swords. Men came crowding, and easily as herdsmen divide sheep mingled in pasture, so the officers formed combat companies. They advanced alongshore, making lines of hoplites ten deep, shields locked, long spears thrust forward. Then came the light-armed peltasts, javelin men, and stone throwers. Last came the defilers of the dead.

Melaina walked down from the temple and stood before Kimon's men. He was a great presence in armor, shield rattling against his spear tip. "At last! We get to bleed these Persian dogs," he shouted. "Think not of your own safety, men, but of the limbs you will sever from these pus buckets who burned your homes."

Xanthippus stood before all squadrons and shouted, "Steady your hearts! Remember, Mykale is ours! You're to but deal the death blow demanded by the gods." The general then approached Melaina and asked her to join him in reviewing the troops.

"But I don't know how. The warriors will never stand for it."

"Oh! You have no idea the violence a woman can stir in the hearts of men." He added, "Athena reviewed the soldiers with Agamemnon before Troy. Follow along with me."

"But she's a goddess," Melaina protested, following behind.

Oak-waisted and deep-chested as an ox, Xanthippus passed before his army, great strides bearing him along, and golden-haired, blue-eyed Melaina, heavy with child, kept pace, bearing the staff of the Hierophant. Immortal and august she seemed, golden tassels lofting in air. Down ranks that dazzling woman marched, stirring to the attack, and in each man she saw the heart grow stronger at her passing, war itself become fairer than return, lovelier than sailing home.

A shout rang out, and all turned toward the Palisade. Drawn up outside the timbered walls stood the Persian squadrons, flanked by officers, with the clamorous lines screaming slaughter, raging shoulder to shoulder. They wore little armor: leather corselets with bronze platelets, cloth head-coverings for sun protection, skin trousers and wicker shields.

The battle for Ionia was about to begin.

CHAPTER 15: THE BATTLE OF MYKALE

Xanthippus and Kallias stood surveying the enemy host before them. "Leotychides was right," said Xanthippus. "These Persians disdain us and emerge from their stronghold thinking of us as easy pickings. By Zeus, I hope they're wrong!"

As the opposing armies advanced, silence fell.

Quite without warning, another army appeared from the right. The Greeks, realizing it wasn't the Spartans' sneak attack, thought perhaps Xerxes' forces had arrived from Sardis. The Greeks fell into disarray, some shouting, "To the ships!" others, "Hold your lines!"

Both sides halted.

The Greeks then realized these were the rebelling, liberty-infected Ionians, who then fell in behind the defilers of the dead, since they were short on weapons. Xanthippus re-assumed his position leading the phalanx, and Melaina strode back to the temple. Another shout went up, a great eagerness for battle apparent as the Persians bore down screaming. A dense dust cloud rose, and the ground rumbled and groaned. A hail of arrows descended first, sharp points pelting shields like a mighty hailstorm. Voices carrying the paean broke out.

The phalanx charged, fifes splitting the air, front crashing against front, shield clanging against shield. Bucklers ground together, a toiling clamor. It was as if Terror, Rout, and Hate, Ares insatiable sisters-in-arms, walked the earth sowing ferocity, redoubling groans and cries of agony. Dust clouds soared heavenward. Throngs of Persians and Greeks lay strewn beside each other, and the earth streamed with mighty crimson torrents.

Keladeine and the Scythian stood their ground, protecting Melaina before the temple: Keladeine as tall as an Amazon, beautiful as queen Penthesilea who'd also roamed these shores and, as told of old, was killed in battle by Achilles. As the Persians grew ever closer, Keladeine and the Scythian stepped forward and turned loose the dogs. Lykos was a rage of howls and growls, ripping the face from one warrior, disemboweling another. Warriors fled before him without bothering to hurl a spear. The black Scythian canine worked along side Lycos, the two ferocious as lions.

Kallias' company was particularly hard put to it, shoved back against the very doorstep of Demeter's sanctuary. Kallias himself was disarmed, his shield shattered. He snatched a glittering buckler from a dead man and clashed amidst the assembled host, dealing death and courting it, all the time shouting, "Smite! Slay Persia's sons!" A thunder of war cries rang, roared. Men dropped, battered amid murderous streams of gore. Kimon gripped a fearful mace, swung it around like a sickle, lopping necks and heads, helmets clanging.

So the battle raged before Melaina, great numbers falling in both armies, neither winning an advantage, when, with a great crash, enemy forces closest the temple broke through Kallias' regiment, threatening the sanctuary. Melaina faltered, cold fear flooding through her, dissolving all her courage. She stood her ground although she knew not how, as before the gate, a Persian warrior stepped to the front, standing head and shoulders above the rest. He was the ugliest man she had ever seen.

"Tigranes!" she heard a Greek scream. As the shout went up, all Greeks before the great warrior gave way, no one willing to engage him.

"Melaina!" she heard Keladeine call, "back into the temple! Save yourself!"

Tigranes issued a great laugh and leapt into the fray where Keladeine and the Scythian loosed their arrows. He let the darting shafts thump on his shield, then scattered the Greek warriors.

Melaina lost sight of Keladeine as the lot of them were consumed in a flood of Persians. She herself started to run into the fray but remembered the child inside her, then again heard Tigranes shout nearby.

"Women! The Hellenes have brought their women to fight their battles. Hellene men are little more than children."

No sooner had Tigranes spoken the insult than Kallias accosted him, relying on the very skill he'd demonstrated in winning the Olympic pankratium.

"No! Kallias. No!" shouted Melaina. Surely he was no match for this giant.

But Kallias baffled the rush of his foe, noting the play of sword to judge strength and weakness, and exchanged brutal blow for brutal blow. As shipwrights smite timbers, thuds resounding, so helmets crashed, teeth clattered. Kallias and Tigranes stood apart, labored and gasped, then rushed together as bulls furious over a grazing heifer. Melaina watched the two battle and judged it not awkward but ordered, fierce Ares' blameless dance. But Tigranes quickly overcame Kallias, felled him with a stunning blow, then stood over him to wield death.

Melaina stopped herself from rushing to her dear Kallias. She had a better thought. "Here! Here!" she shouted. "Death beckons. Hear me!"

Tigranes, startled at hearing a woman's voice amid the battle cries, stepped over his fallen pray in favor of the sweet morsel before him. Tall and threatening this dark lord stood, a great shadow of despair falling over Melaina, his sword raised in eagerness.

Melaina stood her ground though by pale dread possessed. She'd have fled except for a curious thought: this man had killed her father at Marathon. A false wizardry worked her mind surely, but one she would not dismiss. A vision flashed of the severed limb, and she remembered Orestes wrath in avenging his own father's murder. Her heart flamed. Woman of Eleusis, courageous Kynegeiros' daughter, though swelled with child, she'd not cower before the might of Persia. Golden locks lofting about her shoulders, chiton wafting, she raised her grandfather's staff to ward off the blow and slumped to one knee to steady herself.

A cry of utter hatred split the air, a shriek of murder and madness, as down came Tigranes' grim blade. Her staff rang as if made of some sacred metal, notched but held even as her arms gave way. The sharp bronze ripped her garment, split her shoulder flesh and toppled her backwards into the dirt.

The fell lord bellowed, believing his blow had been fatal, hideous laugh ringing. But Melaina rose from her own wreckage, blood-stained, wounded, she stood again. The great shoulders gathered a second time to send her to the world of shades as she faced her enemy, on both feet this time, even more determined, and directed her own blow with the staff, a quick crack between dark eyes.

She knew not whether the snap was the staff's stiff wood finally giving way or if it was a skull splitting, but the man's eyes crossed, he stumbled, then toppled from his feet. As his dark shape crumbled to the earth, Melaina saw Keladeine looming over the fallen warrior and realized that she'd crushed the cranium from behind as had Melaina from the front. But Keladeine was swept up in the flow of battle, and the two were again separated.

Kallias then rose to his feet, blinking and bewildered. He looked around realizing that the two women had done his work for him. But he immediately responded to a call for help from Kimon.

Melaina swiftly stepped forward, grief over Keladeine's uncertain fate racking her insides, and seized the Persian sword. Anger over her father's severed limb grew inside, and she hewed the dark head of Tigranes from its shoulders. She lifted the heavy container-of-wits by the hair, shoved it down on the Hierophant's staff, and then resumed her position at the gate of Demeter's temple. She stood tall, blond hair shimmering, staff in one hand, sword in the other, blood trailing from shoulder to glowing skirt hem. Brains bled down the Hierophant's ancient scepter, a deadly admonition to all Persia. No one would pass Demeter's gate.

Leotychides' Spartans finally emerged from the forest and came screaming into battle. All Greeks found their courage as the flower of Persia broke for the palisade in terror. The troops of Leotychides and Xanthippus converged and pursued the barbarians into the moat surrounding the rampart, so close on Persian heels as to enter with them, leaving no chance for the barbarians to swing closed the gate and throw home the locking bolts. A great river of Greeks flooded over and through.

Since the battle no longer raged before her, Melaina searched for Keladeine among the nearby bodies to no avail. She reentered the temple. The old woman's voice had fallen silent. Melaina found her collapsed in a corner, just a heap of dust and bones, suffering an arrow through the chest although no blood flowed. Melaina thought the crone dead, but heard a faint squeak, mouse words.

"Burn not my body," she said. "Apollo's swift arrow has loosed me from interminable life and this oracular madness. Let me lie shamefully unburied. My black blood will seep through the earth and feed the green grass for herds of grazing beasts. It will infiltrate livers to foster prophets' foresight. Birds rending my flesh in ribbons shall gorge and prophesy mankind's woes." Her dull eyes raked across Melaina. "Daughter of Darkness, come for me at last." Then life left her, not as warmth ebbing, but as a cold puff of dust.

Melaina scooped the thin frame into her arms. It hardly felt the weight of a child, as she carried the body behind the temple and into the nearby woods. She heard wolves howling, yet laid it on the ground among the leaves of myrtle trees and hurried back to the temple.

She dismantled the head of Tigranes from her grandfather's staff, reuniting it with its shoulders. Anguish wrung her heart as she discarded the sword. She followed after the storm of murder, stepped through the carnage. The groans of the wounded matched her own throbbing shoulder, and she wished for the comfort of Kallias' arms. But she realized the truth about him.

Ever more was her grief. Melaina worried the spindle of shame over what she had done: helped Kallias and Keladeine kill a man, shouldered the wicked task of defiling the body. She heard the cries of the dying, the maimed, and remembered Sophocles' lament. He'd said it was because he'd slaughtered on the isle of Psyttaleia during the battle of Salamis. "Yea, I now know your burden," she said.

Searching for Keladeine, she followed after the warriors into the trench and up the other side through the stockade wall made of stones and tree trunks and crowned with spikes. Melaina stood inside peering down upon a city of beached ships, a great mustering of wood fishes: beaked bows with wide painted eyes gasping for breath, masts like gigantic fins, slack sails flapping, useless oars laying in sand.

As Zeus' great eagle had accosted Prometheus, so the Greeks swooped down upon the Persians, air ringing with screams as the warriors fed on gore. Melaina clutched tight Palaemon's golden broach. The stockade enclosed a thousand shapes of death. Greeks ever delivered to the helpless wounds, gashes, lacerations. Tears wet Melaina's cheeks as she thought what a dreary lot had seized her. "I've led them all to this," she said aloud. "Daughter of Darkness indeed, I've become the dreaded Daughter of Death." Melaina felt as though on this journey that started at Eleusis, she'd been on one long descent into the Underworld and had finally become dread Persephone herself, Mistress of the Dead.

Off in a corner of the palisade, the surviving Persians had locked themselves away in the only building, planning to await Xerxes' glorious entry. Xanthippus, however, set his own mind to fire. As a beekeeper smokes a droning swarm from its hive, so Xanthippus set fire to the timbers. The Persians remained steadfast until fear of becoming roast meat caused them to erupt from their prison. They scattered among the ships, this way and that, emitting wails and shrieks as they realized all was lost. Xerxes was not coming.

Word circulated that two Persian divisions, those under the

fleet commanders, had escaped into the deep forest. Greek warriors gave chase, but as dusk drew on, pursuit over the hills and gullies slackened. The warriors returned after hearing a lion roar and sighting a bear. Leotychides called off the hunt.

Melaina walked about in a daze, then ran onto the Scythian. Hope at last! "Keladeine," she shouted, "where is Keladeine?"

The Scythian said they'd been separated during the fighting, that he knew nothing of her fate. Melaina watched him hold a dying Persian's head in his lap and thought it touching, until the Scythian quickly slit around the neck, waited until the man bled to death, then slit around the ears. He skillfully slipped the skin and hair off the skull. She remembered his handkerchiefs.

Melaina was a blinking owl in failing light, wreck and disaster all around. She remembered her grandfather and knew he must still be alive. She turned bodies, questioned Ionians concerning an old sacred official of the Mysteries, a Hierophant.

She found Lykos whining over the body of the Scythian's black dog, who'd been hacked to pieces. Lykos took up with Melaina, walking at her side, as she sunk into deeper depression over Keladeine's fate.

Then Melaina saw a familiar face: a tall, broad-shouldered man, gentlemanly, yet grave. He was administering to the injured and dying. Alongside him, a young woman dressed wounds. They were the physician, Podaleirius, and Hygieiadora, his assistant, who'd examined Melaina at Eleusis. He'd taken possession of a portion of cleared ground. Also his serpent-entwined staff stood nearby staked into the soft sand. Hygieiadora recognized Melaina, nodding to her as she closed a patient's arm wound.

"Have you seen my grandfather," Melaina asked, "the Hierophant?"

The physician said, "Your grandfather was just here but is gone now."

Hygieiadora finished with the man and fell to cleaning and dressing Melaina's shoulder wound, applying a healing salve and wrapped her shoulder in fine white linen. She said, "Your grandfather was taken prisoner at Eleusis and kept alive although he was thoroughly disagreeable to his captors. Just moments ago, he was taken by force from the palisade when the two fleet commanders escaped."

Melaina talked to those who now returned from chasing the escaping Persians into the forest, but they knew nothing of the Hierophant. She realized that her grandfather's freedom would have to be won another day. "He's beyond liberation," she said, resignation filling her. "So be it." She took a deep breath. "Zeus has need of him in Persia."

Melaina watched as the Greek fleet beached at the palisade, and a great joy seizing her as she recognized Keladeine standing beachside. The young priestess of Artemis screamed when she saw Lykos, and ran to the canine, ignoring Melaina as though she weren't even there. Keladeine warbled over the animal until Melaina wondered if her friend cared about her at all. She shouted to Keladeine, but a great weariness had overtaken her. She sat on a stone beside the physician and Hygieiadora. "I've been very wretched," said Melaina, "not knowing if I'd see you alive again, Keladeine."

"So was I over you," Keladeine said. "And now I find you injured, blood drenched. You should have stayed in the temple as I told you."

Hygieiadora turned her attention to Melaina's pregnancy. "You've taken great risk with the child," she said. "From the seventh month forward, you should have given up violent movements and concentrated on perfecting the embryo. By breaking the chorion and losing the birthing fluids, you've ensured a dry delivery and endangered yourself and the fetus. Besides, of what use is a woman in battle?"

Melaina heard a scream from behind, then heard her name called. She turned to see a tall girl standing beside a sour-faced woman. Stately Anaktoria it was, Melaina's girlfriend from Eleusis, and her mother. Though captured, they'd both survived, along with a small group of women from all over Attica. They stood amongst the carnage, blinking and confused at having been liberated.

As the women raved at each others' remarkable survival, the warriors removed Persian treasure from the beached ships: golden bowls, goblets, silks, jewels, money chests. On the beach, they set up a great pile of common-stock plunder. From the dead they stripped anklets, chains and gold-hilt scimitars, embroidered apparel. All this fell activity shrouded by encroaching darkness. Warriors heaped the dead upon the beached ships, and Leotychides set afire the palisade. Melaina recognized the sharp aroma of Syrian cedar. The conflagration played along the wooden wall, blaze upon blaze leapt, flashing into the heavens. A great lion roared, silencing all but the raging funeral pyre. Warriors, oarsmen, and the two priestesses remained on the beach feasting throughout the night and tending hurts of the wounded. All the while, Deiphonus sacrificed to the immortals.

When the sun rose over dewy hills, waking roosters and shepherds, the fleet loaded the spoils onboard, loosed hawsers, and set sail back to Samos.

CHAPTER 16: A FINAL WORD TO THE GENERALS

Melaina couldn't stop the flurry of activity surrounding her. She'd already given voice to pains that had begun before leaving Mykale, so the women of Samos would allow her no peace. Chera swept her up at the first mention of discomfort, took her to the birthing chamber beside the temple, and sent for the midwife. Now women surrounded her, those from all over Samos as well as the few Athenian women saved from the Persians.

Melaina knew the child wasn't coming, yet the chamber reeked of pennyroyal, apples, and quinces to bring her back to her senses should the pain overcome her. Nearby, a fire-driven cauldron belched steam. Stacked about were wool cloths, linens, pillows, sea sponges, bandages for swaddling the newborn. The interrogating midwife was forever anointing her own hands with warm olive oil and probed Melaina's privates while frowning at the undilated uterus.

Melaina kept Anaktoria close, holding her hand and hugging her, unable to get enough of this human treasure retrieved from the Persians. Anaktoria cried frequently, lapsed into silent dejection and wouldn't talk. Her mother mourned the death of her child of less than a year while in enemy hands. Melaina worried about her grandfather. She'd sent Keladeine to snoop on the generals who'd been in council since their return to Samos. She'd heard Leotychides had already declared Ionia indefensible against Xerxes in the long term.

Melaina felt uncomfortable on Samos and desperately needed her mother. This troublesome pregnancy now caused her to feel as if she were again a child. She had faced the might of Persia, but cowered before birthing pains.

Keladeine returned, saying that the Spartans were dead set on relocating all Ionia to Attica, which greatly offended Ionians and Athenians alike. Melaina realized her labor was not progressing, so she sent for Kallias. The women scurried out except for Anaktoria, whom Melaina wouldn't let leave. Melaina stood to greet her husband, knees shaking.

"I must speak to the generals," she said, "a last word, Lord Kallias, to fulfill my commitments to the fleet and the gods. I realize the trouble I cause, but I must return to Eleusis. My mother should know that her father lives, and these other women from Attica should return to their families. A single boat, please."

Kallias said nothing but assisted her to the generals' council. It was a much smaller affair than those of the past: Leotychides and Xanthippus, the generals of Corinth, Sikyon, and Troezen, plus the three Samians who'd been at Delos. A handful set hard to the task of determining the future of Ionia. Kimon stood in a corner with Keladeine alongside.

They all fell silent and rose as she entered.

"I realize that for me to voice an opinion concerning the future of Ionia is against custom, but both Athena and Artemis, daughters of Olympian Zeus, came to me, concerned over your wavering. It would be a grievous insult not to tell you their will. This is what they've ordained. If you should give up Ionia and relocate its citizens, realize you forfeit Rhodes, Athena's birthplace; Ephesus, Artemis' greatest temple; and Samos, Hera's birthplace. Also, Manto, Teiresias' daughter, at the direction of Delphi, founded Colophon. The rocky island of Chios was home to Homer, favorite of the Muses. Several centuries ago, Immortal Zeus command all these places settled." Melaina stared at Leotychides until he dropped his eyes. "To even discuss abandoning them to Persia is blasphemy."

Her audience sat silent in the aftermath of her history lesson. Melaina felt tired and disillusioned, believing her words meant nothing to them. They'll find the path to greatest conflict and follow it, she thought. She turned to Kallias. "Please, I must go home."

Kallias said a few words supporting Melaina's position, then took his leave. "I'm escorting the women and injured back to the mainland," he said.

Melaina and Kallias left the council amid the rumbling of voices and sharp shouts from Xanthippus directed at Leotychides. "You'll turn all Olympus against Hellas with your isolationist attitude," he said.

At midnight, Kallias, Melaina and the other women boarded The Tragodia. Melaina balked when she saw the name, a tight grip of fear seizing her, but she gave herself and her child up to fate and stepped aboard. The physician and Hygieiadora accompanied them. Kimon also boarded and sought out Keladeine. The ship's lanterns created an eerie mix of shadow and golden light as Melaina said goodbye to Deiphonus, who stood on the dock looking up at her at the ship's rail, his face aglow with success.

"From now on, you can divine without worry. You have a reputation."

"Still, I could be found out."

Melaina smiled, thinking that this man's self-image was irreparable. "You're not a fraud. Study the craft, kind Deiphonus, and remember that each seer's art is unique."

"All my life I've wanted to be a diviner."

"Ancient Teiresias didn't think it a boon, and considered anyone who foretold the future a fool disdained by those who seek him. Even Agamemnon hated Kalchas for his divining."

"Everyone seems to appreciate your gift."

Kallias gave the order to disembark, and Melaina turned to her husband. "First travel along the coast of Asia to Ephesus, Lord Kallias. Apollo has ordered Keladeine there, and we can but deliver her."

Kallias spoke not a word of protest but motioned the helmsman north instead of west, the breeze billowing the white-linen sails. The oarsmen let the sleek pine rest in the tholepins, and the wind did the work for them.

Melaina looked at Keladeine, who was talking to Kimon. He was subdued, his voice reduced to gentle tones. He'd assumed a noble bearing, a tender look. Could it be that love inspired him? Melaina thought he was well worth the gaze of those initiated into Aphrodite's mysteries.

Not far up the coast, the trireme entered a quiet bay, light from the oil lamps of Ephesus aglow in the distance. Soon the ship entered the slip before a brilliantly lit temple, the most beautiful Melaina had ever seen, and so large that it dwarfed the Telesterion at Eleusis.

"You'll be in good hands," she told Keladeine. "I've simply been an instrument to get you here. What a magnificent temple! You'll have a life filled with purpose."

"I'll always feel empty without you beside me."

"Artemis will fill the void," Melaina said. "Mortals can't imagine the miracles worked by the divine."

"Come with me! Artemis could use you more than me."

"Insatiable necessity compels me forward, however bitter it is to leave you." Melaina then bent to pat the wolf. "Care well for your mistress, Lykos. She is truly one of the world's marvels."

Keladeine had a final word. "The great trireme will bear you home, lady, to the ashen ruins of Eleusis. Follow the ever-circling stars, and perhaps someday the gods' decrees will blow you my way again."

At the last moment, Kimon also stepped off, walking behind Keladeine and Lykos, Aphrodite in firm control of his heart and ever tempting the young priestess.

The warship finally set sail, following the stars' path west. Melaina and the rest of the women spent the remaining darkness below deck slumbering. With the sun, Melaina could no longer stay below. She left Anaktoria and went topside to care for the wounded. The slack sail billowed as though she'd brought along a bag of winds. One badly wounded warrior she held in her lap and eased him into his death. All day and night, the fresh wind bore the ship on, sleek trireme slicing silent through purple water.

CHAPTER 17: THE NEWBORN

Back in the ruins of Eleusis and within the Gates of Hades, Myrrhine relit the family hearth fire and set up residence. Palaemon tried convincing her to take a chamber in his home, but Myrrhine refused, preferring the Dark Lord's sacred grotto, where she sat awaiting her daughter's return from the far side of the Aegean.

Two days earlier, she'd watched the Greek forces rout the Persians at Plataea. She'd tended the injured, then returned to Eleusis with Aeschylus and Sophocles. The ruins of the Telesterion had become a great center for war casualties. Families and friends from both Attica and the Peloponnese congregated at Eleusis' crossroads to eye those returning from the north, question them about a husband, a son, a neighbor. By the wagonload came the injured and dying to be sheltered and nursed among the ruins. Gone was the glory of victory, left, only the unmerciful mutilations, the naked ghastliness of death.

When Myrrhine first returned from Plataea, she'd found Kallias' mother waiting for her. Hipparete had come to salvage what she could of Kallias' home in Eleusis. She told Myrrhine that Melaina and Kallias had gone with the fleet to Delos. With the annihilation of the Persian army at Plataea, Myrrhine hadn't been worried that Delos might be attacked, and knew Melaina would be safe to return a few days later. But Myrrhine couldn't understand why Kallias had taken Melaina with him to Delos at all. Hipparete, after much coercing, admitted that Melaina had had a vision, a prophecy of an Aegean battle.

"I know the truth then," said Myrrhine. "My daughter has had another seizure." Lady Hipparete nodded. She held Myrrhine's hands as they both cried. Myrrhine realized that her daughter's epilepsy hadn't been cured at Epidaurus after all.

At night, Myrrhine had been sheltering in the ashes under the overhang of the ancient grotto, and during the day, she stayed atop the hill overlooking the bay. Always she awaited the return of the warships.

While ascending the hill this day, she heard horse hooves along the road from Athens, then shouting in the ruins of the Telesterion. Young Sophocles, she thought, and called to him. He walked up as she started down to meet him.

Sophocles looked tired and worn, his tunic grimy. His eyes had lost their sparkle. Myrrhine realized that he didn't bring good news, and fear gripped the pit of her stomach.

"She's okay," Sophocles said, "but Melaina will not return soon. She's gone with the fleet to liberate Ionia."

"No! Sophocles, not to Asia!"

"Several days ago. This morning a ship returned from Delos with the news. A priest of Apollo mentioned her."

Although she questioned him unrelentingly, he knew little beyond those few words. Those who'd returned had given no reason for Melaina having followed the fleet. Sophocles had no word of Melaina's condition. Finally, he did remember that the priest had also mentioned that Melaina met another girl at Delos, a friend and a priestess of Artemis. She'd left with Melaina for Asia. A girl from the Isthmus.

Myrrhine thought a moment. "Keladeine," she said. "Melaina met her after the battle of Salamis. At least she'll not be among all those warriors without female companionship."

Two days later, Myrrhine sat on the Mirthless Rock before the entrance to the Gates of Hades, where divine Demeter had also sat awaiting the return of Kore. Myrrhine heard singing at the entrance to the sacred quarter and watched as choruses danced around the Kallichoron Well. These celebratory sounds mingled with the wails and moans of the injured still camped there. Myrrhine realized that this was the day of the Mysteries ceremony, and that people had come even though initiation was no longer possible.

Myrrhine climbed the hill's stone steps and stood at Melaina's favorite spot above the bay searching for ships that might signify Melaina's homecoming. The morning chill was deeper than usual. All day, Myrrhine remained on the hilltop, and as afternoon dragged, she noticed people streaming in from Athens along the Sacred Way. She thought she recognized the Iakchos song. The ruins of the Telesterion filled with people, both able-bodied and injured along with the dying and the dead.

Just before sundown, Myrrhine saw three sleek triremes slicing through the bay toward Eleusis. When they drew closer she could no longer contain herself and ran downhill, through the gate, and out onto the dock. Wind gusts created choppy waves as thunder rumbled in the distance. Others came running to join her at dockside.

Myrrhine stood at the gangway of the first ship but could see neither Melaina nor Kallias. The men who caught the hawsers and tied them over the landing lugs shouted back and forth at the men onboard. A great roar went up, so she could no longer hear.

"What's happened?" she asked a man struggling with the huge papyrus rope.

"Leotychides defeated the Persians at Mykale!" he shouted, but singing drowned the rest of his words. Another man spoke, "These ships bring the wounded and some of the dead." She saw the walking-injured struggle to the gangway. The bow officer was the first to step down.

"Have you seen a girl, a priestess from Eleusis," Myrrhine shouted to him over the din.

"Kallias' mistress? No one will ever forget her," he shouted back.

"She's dead then?"

"Next ship." He pointed at a trireme docking further down.

It was a featureless ghostlike ship in the gloom of twilight. As its gangway lowered, she saw Kallias carrying a bundle in his arms and rushed to him.

"Oh Zeus! How to interpret this? Is it a body?" she wondered aloud. "Kallias carrying a lump of humanity, bloodied, bandaged. Oh, if only I could see the face in this failing light. Is she Melaina? No! But who else could it be? Yes, it's my dearest Melaina, poor child. Am I dreaming?"

Kallias said something to the girl in his arms.

"Melaina!"

Lady Hipparete appeared from behind Myrrhine. She screamed, "Kallias, my son, you're alive! Ah, the worry is over!"

A flash of lightening lit the dock and another rumble rocked them. Myrrhine recognized the physician followed by more women from Eleusis, then Anaktoria and her mother, Myrrhine's own cousin. "Oh! Great Zeus in heaven," she said, "have they all returned alive?"

Melaina's face filled with pain. "Oh, mother! Your voice is the dearest music!" Tears came. "The wound is but a superficial nothing. I've been in labor off and on two days since the ship past Delos. I can't stand much more."

Myrrhine felt delirious upon hearing her daughter's sweet words, even if pain-filled. What exquisite complaint, she thought, running alongside Kallias as he carried Melaina through the stone gate, up the hill, and down the other side to the sacred quarter. Myrrhine took her daughter's hand, released it, took it again.

Myrrhine halted the small group and spoke quickly to Anaktoria's mother, hugged her and sent her and Anaktoria to find their burned-out homes. Then she turned back to her own daughter. "Through here," she said, directing Kallias to an opening in the hillside. "How could you do it? Lead her into such great danger."

"Me?" Kallias scoffed. "She dragged the entire fleet to Asia."

"You let them hurt her." She recognized one of her slaves hanging back and called him forward. "Off to Salamis with you," she said. "Bring Kleito. It's your life if she doesn't get here in time."

Kallias defended himself. "Zeus knows, it was not her life in danger. I'd not myself live today but for her."

Darkness came swiftly. They stepped out of the short tunnel and into the open space before Hades' cave, seemingly emerging from the Underworld itself. Lightning flashed, thunder crashed, announcing their arrival to those camped in the courtyard. A cry of wonder rose up from the field of wounded and dying who now spread before them as a gigantic plain of misery.

Aeschylus it was who came among them carrying a torch, grumpy Philokleia at his side, Palaemon limping behind. Aeschylus said, "The daemons Might and Force have announced your arrival to this primordial landscape. Bleak as Scythia this grotto seems among the ruins. I see you bring the injured daughter of my own brother. Is her life in danger?"

"Only from the child wishing to be delivered," said Myrrhine.

As Kallias placed Melaina upon a pallet within the grotto, Aeschylus questioned him. "How goes the defense of the Aegean?"

"Won!" said Kallias. "Ionia has been liberated along with the islands. What news of Plataea? Your presence here is surprising."

"We routed Mardonius four days ago. Pausanias lays siege to Thebes as we speak."

"Victory four days gone? Can it be, truly? Under that same day's sun we destroyed Xerxes' forces at Mykale and burned his fleet of ships."

"That very morning?"

"Afternoon and evening."

"We'd finished business and prepared a meal before you started."

"Ah, so it's true. Melaina had a vision. The troops believed her, took great heart in it. But the generals deemed it impossible that she'd know."

"Out with you, Kallias," said Lady Hipparete. "All you men, find another shelter from the storm." She shooed with her hands. "Women bring the newborn into the world. Off!"

"The staff!" said Melaina "Before you go, Lord Kallias. The

Hierophant's staff."

"The women have laid it on the ground beside you."

Myrrhine wondered at her daughter's words. How could the Hierophant's staff have fallen into her hands? "It burned with the Telesterion," she told Melaina.

"Not so, mother. I found it on Mykale's desolate shore. Grandfather is alive!"

"Mercy of the gods, what news! You saw him?"

"No. Although Anaktoria and her mother did. The physician also."

"Such relief! Where is he? Was he not aboard the trireme?"

"Our worries for him are not over. Persia still holds him captive."

"I'll worry him later. It's enough to know he's alive. But why did you make such a journey across the Aegean?"

"Please let me pass over that, not bring all the dangers to life again in the telling." She grabbed her abdomen, "Oh! It comes on again."

"The siege of birth pains?"

"Yes! This cursed plague. It burns me!"

"I'll get warm fomentations to ease the pain. Light a fire, Hipparete. Set a cauldron to boil."

Great thunderheads formed above, as night grew deadly dark inside the cave. Bitter wind swirled about them, kicking up ashes among the towering ruins. Yet nothing could dampen Myrrhine's spirits. Her mind whirred. *Melaina returned safe, my father back from the dead, the Persians routed both on land and sea, Ionia liberated. Is it possible to retrieve so much happiness in all these ashes?*

The slave reappeared with Kleito, little Euripides at her side. "Found her at the dock," said the slave, "her mind already bent on serving you."

"Oh Kleito! Good news comes so quickly, I can hardly catch my breath. Lady Hipparete is here to help, but has no herbs for birthing afflictions."

"Lost during the evacuation," confirmed Hipparete.

"I never travel light. Always have remedies at the ready." Kleito hefted a leather satchel. "These all be herbs for delivering as well as healing. Who'll do the midwifery?" Kleito looked ethereal, dressed in a silvery robe, golden belt around her waist, her face veiled. Myrrhine thought her friend resembled a sorceress. Kleito pulled the veil forward over her brow.

Myrrhine waited before answering, knowing she'd have to admit her barrenness. "I will. My womb is empty even at this early age. Artemis wishes it so. She gave me one child to gain experience. You and Hipparete can assist."

"Hurry, Kleito!" cried Melaina. "The fiend attacks again. Oh agony!"

"Steady," said Myrrhine, then turned to Kleito. "Give her something for pain and check her shoulder. She's been injured. Heat the olive oil, Hipparete, while I soothe her with warm hands. Soak some rags."

"Her shoulder is fine. Some professional has already treated her," said Kleito.

Agido rushed into the grotto, screamed, and fell upon Melaina.

"What a joy to see you, little friend," Melaina said, "but the pain! Mother, help!"

Myrrhine kept an eye on Kleito as she retrieved a small pouch from the satchel. "What's that?" Myrrhine asked. "Tell the heritage of each medicine before administering."

"Don't trust me after the hellebore?"

"I asked you here, didn't I?"

"Dittany, peculiar to Crete." She spread flakes over the surface of a cup of steaming cauldron water. "Relieves pain during difficult labor, and resembles pennyroyal in looks and taste. Goats go crazy over it, graze it to nothing. It's scarce. If you prefer I not…."

Myrrhine hesitated. "Smells of lemon."

Melaina said, "Yes! Kleito, yes! Give it to me." She held Agido's hand so tightly that it looked as though blood might drip from the fingertips.

Kleito faltered, as if she'd withhold the medication, given the questioning. Melaina grabbed the cup from her.

"The epilepsy," said Myrrhine to her daughter, "are you in danger of a seizure?"

Melaina sipped. "No, Mother. No symptoms."

Still Myrrhine worried. "Kleito, do you have anything to forestall seizures?"

Kleito said nothing but dipped another cup of hot water from the cauldron, sprinkled a bit of dried leaf upon its simmering surface.

"Mmmm," said Melaina putting aside one steaming cup for the other. "Thyme."

"From the slopes of Hymettos not far from our home in Phlya. It's usually given to revive from a seizure."

"If I could rest, a little sleep. I'm so tired."

As the women chattered, the blazing fire cast dark shadows onto the grotto walls, shapes shifting about like Underworld creatures. The chorus, who'd been dancing around the Kallichoron Well, came to the sacred grotto in a long train, followed by a chorus of warriors who had finally made it back from the battle at Plataea. With them, came the children of the silver mines at Laurium, the worms so dear to Melaina. The children scampered, sang, and scurried about the temple ruins like crazed Korybantes. The chorus formed about the birthing scene, drowning Melaina's cries with wild shouts and the lusty beating of swords against battle shields.

Through all the din, Myrrhine went about her business laying hot cloths across Melaina's swollen abdomen, then inserted her finger into Melaina's privates.

Melaina jumped, trembled. "Where are you touching me? You'll kill me! It leaps again! The evil pain rouses up!"

Myrrhine shook her head. "You've already lost your water. Why didn't you tell me?"

"It happened at Delos," Melaina confessed, "ten days ago."

"A dry birth? No wonder the problems. Your isthmus is still closed after two days labor." She filled a goat's bladder with olive oil, shoved the small end inside her daughter and squirted till it ran out.

Again Myrrhine inserted her finger, lubricated the orifice, and pulled slightly to dilate it.

Melaina groaned. "Get your hand out!"

"It's open barely enough to admit two fingers, but getting larger. Feel it?"

"Yes! It has hold of me!" said Melaina raising from bed. "The burning flames again! What have you done?"

Myrrhine ignored her daughter's agony to observe Kleito retrieving a terracotta jar of gray balls from her satchel. "This good charm is cyclamen," Kleito said. "It produces rapid delivery. I harvest the root, burn it, and steep the ashes in wine to form balls." She looked at Myrrhine directly, her eyes cold, hard.

"What else is it good for?" asked Myrrhine.

"Pessary."

"It prevents conception? Okay, that makes sense. Give it."

Melaina said, "Ah! No need. It's gone now. Just please be quiet. Don't wake the slumbering malady."

"The pain will grow," said Myrrhine.

"Chew," Kleito said, giving Melaina one of the balls. After Melaina had chomped, Kleito gave her a small cup of wine. "Sip."

"Oh, Kleito! It leaps up again. So soon, the evil pain blazes forth."

Myrrhine stooped again to check the dilation. "Time for the midwife's stool. Oops! We have none. It burned in the fire!"

"Kleito," said Hipparete, "you're robust. We'll use your lap."

"Euripides," Kleito said to her son, "stand back against the stone wall, out of the way. You touch that fire, I'll have you by the ear." Then quickly she loosened her golden belt, stepped out of her silvery robe. She slipped on an apron, gathering it midway to her thighs, then sat upon the slaughter stone. Myrrhine helped her groaning daughter onto Kleito's thighs, placed her daughter's thighs outside Kleito's. "Melaina is so light in the hips," said Kleito, "no wonder she's having trouble."

Myrrhine sat before Melaina, anointed her left hand with olive oil and turned to Hipparete. "Has this oil been used for cooking?"

"No," said Hipparete, "it came from underground storage and hasn't been touched by the kitchen."

Another quick check revealed that Melaina was now dilating rapidly.

"Eyie!" screamed Melaina. "The vile pain has me in its clutches. Pray for me, Mother. Call forth Eileithyia."

"Can you hold her, Kleito?" asked Myrrhine.

"She's feather light but writhes like an eel."

Myrrhine wondered how she could have forgotten the birthing prayers. She rose to her feet, raised her palms to Heaven. "Venerable goddess of swift birth, Eileithyia, hear my prayer. No one sees bright day without your aid. Sweet sight are you to those in travail, laboring women. Years ago when I gave birth to Melaina, I called you. Then, you came and saved us both. Now again, I call you to us. Speed this delivery. Share Melaina's pain, freeing her from terrible distress, and I promise a great golden-threaded necklace in return. Come to Melaina's aid, rescue her child. It's your nature to be savior of all."

Myrrhine then prayed to Hera, that she not restrain Eileithyia, divine midwife, so Melaina would deliver quickly. She also prayed for Artemis to assist, for she had helped her own mother, Leto, during Apollo's birth.

Though the chorus ranted continuously, the heavens had remained quiet but now broke loose during the prayers. No lightning stuck the ground, but licking tongues of fire danced along the clouds. Thunder rumbled and echoed.

Myrrhine placed a blanket on the cold stone before Melaina and sat on it, looking up into her daughter's pallid eyes. "Expel the baby, dear. The pain is nothing to fear."

Melaina took a deep breath, strained till the blood veins

popped out on her forehead, then sent forth a scream.

"Keep the breath above, child. Groan, don't scream. Let the groan drive breath downward into your flanks. Let down her hair, Kleito, loosen her wraps."

Myrrhine again placed her left hand over her daughter's womb, inserted her oiled finger, and, with a circular movement, dilated the orifice. "Ah," she said. "The chorion has ruptured. Won't be long now. I feel baby hair!"

Though Melaina grunted and strained, strained and grunted, the baby wasn't coming. Myrrhine read exhaustion on her daughter's face. Her own mother had died giving birth. She couldn't bear thinking of Melaina suffering the same fate. She felt inside Melaina again. "The orifice is large enough, but the head is wrong. Maybe something beside it. Move her around, Kleito. Shift her."

"Perhaps she conceived a monster," said Philokleia, who'd kept silently back until the first hint of disaster. "That's known to cause difficult childbirth."

Myrrhine fixed her with a stern look. "We'll have none of that."

"Is something wrong with the baby, Mother?" asked Melaina.

"No, child. The baby is fine. It may be turned the wrong way."

Kleito put Melaina on the pallet, raised her feet, and shuffled her body about, then resumed her seat on the slaughter stone, Melaina astride her thighs.

"The orifice breathes also," Myrrhine said to her daughter. "First it opens, then contracts. Wait for my word to push…. Now!"

"Perhaps it's stillborn," said Philokleia. "That also causes trouble."

"Shut up!" said Kleito, with uncharacteristic venom. "Don't jinx the birth. Make yourself useful, Philokleia. Watch little Euripides so he doesn't toast his fingers in the fire."

Myrrhine ignored them. "Now, Melaina, push!" and a few seconds later, "Again! Deep breath, push it into the loins."

Agido wiped sweat from Melaina's brow.

Melaina sucked air, groaned, strained. She repeated again and again at Myrrhine's bidding. Just as Myrrhine thought that her daughter had passed into unconsciousness, given up, Melaina raised slightly, opened her eyes with new resolve.

"I'll not have my child stillborn," Melaina said, growling under her breath, hot anger flushing her face.

Myrrhine sensed Melaina put great pressure into her body, felt the child's head slip. "Yes!" she cried. "The baby comes! More, Melaina, more!"

Another loud groan.

"The head is through!" Myrrhine slipped her fingers around the child's chin, pulled the head forward. "Quickly now, before the orifice closes about the neck. Yes! The shoulders are free!" Slowly she pulled out the child, umbilical cord trailing. Myrrhine looked up into Melaina's astonished eyes.

"My baby! I have a child!" cried Melaina, then fell back into Kleito.

The chorus that had kept up a steady vocal stopped. The silence in the sacred grotto was broken only by the infant's squeaky wails.

"A girl!" cried Myrrhine. "A granddaughter!" She took the warm rags from Hipparete and rubbed them gently over the smooth skin, raked aside waxy goo and blood. The baby stopped wailing and opened its eyes, blinked, lips formed as if to speak. "The navel cord, Hipparete. No, a steel blade is of ill omen. Bring a sharp piece of glass. There, cut it four fingerbreadths." Myrrhine squeezed clotted blood from the remaining length of cord.

"She's mine, Mother," said Melaina. "I want her." But she grunted again, groaned. "Ohhh! How's this? The gripping comes again! Is there no end?"

"Something is wrong," said Hipparete. "The chorion is left behind, won't fall clear and makes trouble."

"Eyie!" screamed Melaina. "It's devouring me!"

Again the chorus' voices lofted, swords clanged against shields, thunderbolts crashed. A few drops of rain fell. Kleito felt Melaina's abdomen, then laughed. "She has another loaf in the oven. Hurry, Myrrhine! That it not fall on the ground."

Myrrhine handed the first baby off to Hipparete and again sat before her daughter. With her left hand, she felt inside the hot, bloody opening to her daughter's womb. "You're right, Kleito. A slick, bald head." She looked up into Melaina's agony-filled eyes, saw tears, felt a knot in her own throat. "One more time, dearest. Twins! No wonder they've come early and with double trouble. This one'll be easier."

"I haven't the strength. My whole body is ruined."

Myrrhine could see her daughter's exhaustion written across her drawn face. "A few deep breaths. You must start again. The baby calls." She watched as Melaina roused herself, groaned.

Surrounded by lightning, neither cowering nor afraid, the women trusted in Zeus as would innocent children, that he'd not strike them dead amidst his own mystery. Crash after crash struck the mountain, illuminating the grotto scene witnessed by the spellbound audience as the chorus continued its crescendo of voices, laced with the twang of a minstrel's lyre brought to song by the plectrum. The chorus mimicked dances of the immortals, cosmic dances, twirling to imitate the course of planets through the heavens.

The second child did come easier, Myrrhine pulling at the infant during dilation, giving way when the uterus drew together. Myrrhine, lit by strobed lightning flashes, handed the baby to Hipparete, then turned to work the chorion. She inserted her left hand into her daughter's uterus before it closed, grasped the embryonic pouch by its roots, gently moved it from side to side to ensure it was unfettered, and pulled. While Melaina strained, Myrrhine applied a light but steady pressure, careful not to capture the uterus. Finally, the quivering mass of purplish jelly, with nerves, veins, and blood-filled arteries, pulled free. She set it sizzling on the fire.

"What's the second, Lady Hipparete?" asked Melaina. "I'll die if you don't say."

"Bright-eyed boy! Bald as a gourd."

"Let me have them before swaddling."

"Not so fast," said Myrrhine. "We've the cleanup work left."

While Philokleia stood back out of the way, sulking that all had gone well, Hipparete and Kleito bathed Melaina first with cloths doused in hot cauldron water, followed by heated olive oil, washed her genitals and padded them to absorb the drainage. For the breasts, which had already begun to swell with warm milk, Kleito applied fomentations with sea sponges squeezed in a decoction of aromatic fenugreek.

Myrrhine cleaned each child, first beating fine powdery salt with honey, besprinkled it over the child, avoiding the eyes and mouth, washed it with a great quantity of warm water. This she repeated, besprinkling and washing, with even warmer water. Then she squeezed thick mucus from the nose, cleared the mouth and injected the eyes with olive oil. With her little finger, she dilated the anus. She bent the naval cord double, wrapped it with a lock of wool. So, the second child.

Melaina took a child in each arm and soothed the wails with patting, gentle coos, put them inside her own blanket. Two naked little bodies pressed against their mother's warm skin.

Myrrhine watched her daughter, proud, jealous waves sweeping her. "May I take one?"

"Mother! You've seen them more than me."

"They need swaddling."

Melaina, baby cradled at each breast, said, "The man at Epidaurus had it backwards. The gods give two blessings for a single trial."

Melaina finally gave up the little girl. Myrrhine gently laid her on a blanket in her own lap, gathered soft wool bandages threefingers width. She held the babe's left hand and felt its fingers grip her thumb, fell in love, so tiny. She kissed them. She wrapped the fingers, wound the palm, forearm, biceps. Wrapped the other arm. She wound a larger bandage around the tiny chest and bound the breast tight, the loins loose.

She looked away, then spoke again, but her voice cracked, felt a sob in her throat. "The little girl, all that hair. She's but a duplicate of you, Melaina."

Each leg she swaddled separate, so to the toe tips. Then she placed the arms tight against the sides, the feet ankle against ankle, and with a broad bandage wrapped the babe from chest to toes to prevent twisting and inordinate movement. About the head, she wrapped a soft clean cloth. Thus, she also wrapped the little boy, but loosened the chest bindings and tightened them about the loins. More seemly for a male.

She passed both babes off to Melaina.

The warriors and slave children of Laurium had vanished, leaving only the women's chorus's soft song and the quick floating rhythm of tender feet. It was a vision of the cosmos: the twin primal forces of music and twirling dance setting order amid chaos, the ethereal elements woven tight by gesture and movement as even the very planets coursed the heavens.

Agido beamed at the babies as if they were her own.

"May I give them a nipple?" Melaina asked. "Both are making smacking noises."

Melaina then took each nipple in turn, wet her babies' lips with them. They set to sucking. Melaina first winced with pain, then smiled as intense pleasure spread across her face.

While Melaina nursed them, Myrrhine set torches about, and Zeus continued his lightning and thunder. The babies trembled at each flash, frightening crash. Like flaming pillars, the bright bolts stood and vanished, yet lingered in the mind. The chorus parted to give the audience more than a glimpse. A deathly stillness fell.

A final lightning bolt struck the cave itself, setting afire the wobbly-hinged Gates of Hades. The crowd cringed back from the crash, women ran screaming as if having viewed light from the Elysian Fields. Great shouts of surprise and amazement erupted.

When the commotion subsided, and the fire on the wooden gates became but smoking embers, young Sophocles made a short appearance. He'd only just heard of their return from Asia and rushed to the ruins. He was surprised to see Melaina with two babies. He smiled to see such tiny humans, blushed before Melaina, then walked away.

Little Euripides finally came to see, touched his finger to a tiny nose, then took up residence beside Melaina, snuggled against her shoulder.

Melaina spoke to Hipparete. "Have you seen Kallias?" she asked.

"Gone to Athens," she said. "Melaina… He'll not have the children as his own."

"I know," she said. "I've watched him agonize over me and the pregnancy for several days. Finally he's decided."

Myrrhine saw a cloud descended over her daughter, but she breathed a sigh of relief. "This is all for the best," she said. "I don't believe either of them. Not Kallias, not Aeschylus. Your father would never have given a Eumolpid to one of the Kerykes and upset the balance of power in the Mysteries."

"But Kallias described Father's death scene to me. How the two of them were alone and Father close to death. Father gave me to him for my protection. So Kallias tells it."

"Aeschylus wasn't there?"

"No, according to Kallias."

What great liars, both of them, she thought. She'd not trouble her daughter further with this. Not only Kallias, but also Aeschylus would have some explaining to do. Myrrhine saw the blacksmith approaching.

Palaemon told her, "Bring mother and children to my home. This is no shelter for the newborn."

CHAPTER 18: Journey to the Elysian Fields

Myrrhine stood at the makeshift loom she'd pieced together, listening to the clang of the blacksmith's hammer and swoosh of bellows at the opposite end of the courtyard. Palaemon had been better than his word. He'd moved himself out and given Myrrhine, Melaina, and the babes the best chamber in his home, small though it was, having swept and scrubbed it during the night. He'd left the furnishings and found new bedding. Myrrhine realized that Akmon and Damnameneus had performed much of the work and reluctantly felt indebted. She hoped to get her own home rebuilt soon. The oath the generals took before the battle of Plataea, to not rebuild the burned sanctuary, still worried her.

Kleito spoke words of departure while giving Melaina a supply of kakhry, fruit of the herb libanotis. "It smells like frankincense but brings breast milk, should you be slow to lactate."

Melaina accepted the leather pouch, thanking Kleito for the remedies against birthing travails. "I'd still be in labor but for you."

Kleito left by carriage for her home at Phlya. "It's nearly burned to the ground and ravaged by Persians," she said. "But it's where I belong." She retrieved Euripides, who was pestering Agido by pulling at her braids, and set off.

Myrrhine put her mind to names for the babies. Two of them! Kynegeiros would be proud. A grandson! She tried not to think of Kallias trying to take control of the Mysteries by marrying Melaina. Aeschylus had remained nearby while the two family additions came into the world. Myrrhine thought of his alliance with Kallias and wondered if Aeschylus realized how close that scene had come to the epiphany of the Mysteries.

"Theonoë," said Melaina. She'd been up and around since

yesterday with Agido begging to help. Myrrhine had never seen such swift recovery. Melaina and Agido bathed the babies at the back of the chamber, then lay them down to sleep.

"What?" Myrrhine asked, fitting a scorched shuttle with soft thread.

"Theonoë. Fits her perfectly. Her little eyes project wisdom. She'll know the gods' designs, both what is and what will be."

"And the boy?"

"Zakorus, for Grandfather."

Agido giggled. "That's a big name for a small child."

"One day he'll be Hierophant."

Myrrhine wondered if her daughter was right. She'd not tell her of the generals' oath. Could Greece really exist without the Mysteries? The last two years, Eleusis had conducted no official ceremony. Yet, the Hierophant had held that initiation of the dead before the battle of Salamis. And the scene with Melaina giving birth two nights ago, lightning and thunder crashing around them, could be viewed as the epiphany with Zeus himself officiating.

"I knew Kallias would reject me when we returned," said Melaina. "You were right, Mother. Men have no stomach for aberrations in women. He'd support me as long as I served his needs, but won't tolerate me running his home."

"It's all of little consequence."

"Why so? Children need a father."

"If your grandfather returns, perhaps he can solve this problem. It will not be difficult to find a more suitable match for you, one who will love and foster the children."

"Agido," said Melaina, "find some lamp black and papyrus for me. Please?"

Myrrhine checked the weights at the ends of the warp, fingered the threads, slid the shuttle through. "More poetry?" she asked.

"Through all the years since Father's death at Marathon, I've longed for some word from him. Just any memory meant for me alone. I'll write a short scroll for each of these, my babies. I'll

not have them raised without a heartening word from me. Bad
enough they won't have a father. I love them so."

"They'll have years of memories of you."

"I need to tell you something, Mother. Seriously."

The gravity of Melaina's words alarmed Myrrhine. She turned
a weary eye toward her daughter.

"My seizures have become progressively worse. The one at
Kallias' home almost marked me permanently. When on Delos
and again on the beach at Mykale, I had partial seizures. I didn't
fall, but trembled and had visions."

"Surely this shows improvement. Definitely not cause for
concern. Perhaps they'll stop altogether."

"Oh Mother! How I love your eternal optimism! Ever you
see the bright side of a dark reality. I felt the closeness of death
following my last full seizure at Kallias' home. Since then, I've
noticed a gathering storm, some great anger approaching. The
partial seizures delayed it, but only while giving birth have I been
sure I'd not have an attack."

Melaina fell silent as Agido returned.

"The lamp black is of no great quality," Agido said. "The papyrus is from my father's private store." Her voiced cracked. "He'll
not need it in the Underworld. I couldn't find a stylus."

"I already have one," Melaina said. "You're a dear to give such
precious stores. Now you must leave me alone with my mother,
sweet Agido. We've something to discuss." When she protested,
Melaina said, "Shush, be brave little Agido. And always remember,
I've never loved any friend more than you."

When she was gone, Melaina added. "Kallias has my dowry."

"Oh dear Demeter! I knew it, though Kallias wouldn't admit
to it."

"Though he's rejected me, he still may try to keep it for himself. And I won't be here to see that Theonoë gets it."

"You can't be serious. You're recovering remarkably."

"Grave are the days coming! Worry the dowry, not for me, but
for little Theonoë. It's hers henceforth."

"Surely you're wrong. Perhaps you'll have another seizure but be fine afterward."

Melaina told her, "I never foresee a seizure's day or hour but can feel a disposition toward one. Plus," she said, her voice cracking, "I read it in the entrails of a sacrificial victim while on Delos."

Myrrhine felt as though her daughter had stabbed her with a kitchen knife. "Surely, you're wrong about this. Demeter wouldn't permit such a thing with the children meaning so much to the Mysteries."

Melaina didn't respond, but continued to write scrolls to the children, stopping now and then to nurse or change their soiled cloths. Melaina bathed and dressed herself becomingly, and afterward Myrrhine caught her talking to the babies as she took each in her arms, fondly kissed them. "Never shall I see you dance the Bear, Theonoë, or you, little Zakorus, lead the initiates to Eleusis. Farewell, my babes, little orphans. Live glad lives in the light."

Into evening, Myrrhine's vigil continued as she grew increasingly apprehensive of her daughter's state. Late that night, Melaina came to her, took her hands within her own, as she'd not done for so long. "Ensure they build a temple to Artemis here at Eleusis," Melaina said. "Artemis demands it." She fell quiet again. "I wanted so to remain virgin. And never wished to be married. I wanted only freedom, but once married, learned a sort of love for Kallias. Just as the gods wouldn't allow me to stay virgin, so they also took my marriage."

Myrrhine told her, "Freedom is an illusion here on earth, and is only real in the Afterlife. All we see and know is a but metaphor of the eternal."

"Such I've learned. Now I can imagine nothing greater than being mother to my babes. But Zeus will take them from me, too. It's as if first he makes me see what I've renounced, ensures I love it, then takes it from me as punishment."

Myrrhine saw a nervous twitch in her daughter's eye. A slight trembling in the limbs. "Are you certain you'll have another seizure?"

"More so than ever. Do not, Mother, I pray, store bitter sorrows, for you'll only become a bird of ill omen. Promise if I should die you'll summon cheerfulness and a peaceful spirit. Now tell me of the Underworld."

Realizing that her daughter might be right, Myrrhine bid Melaina sit. "Should it happen," she said but faltered, then gathered her courage. "Inside Hades, a spring flows on the right, and beside it grows a white cypress. Descending souls cool there, but you should pass on without drinking as the water contains forgetfulness. Further on, guardians will ask why you're wandering Hades. Tell them you are a daughter of both Earth and Uranus, desiccated with thirst, and wish cool water from the Lake of Recollection. Afterward, you'll come to a meadow, be stripped naked and judged wearing only life's deeds. Zeus appointed King Minos of Crete to hold court in this meadow, where the path branches to the Isle of the Blessed and Tartarus. Holding his golden sceptre, he scans your soul. Those who've suffered at the hands of the gods have been cured of evil deeds, and thus, go to Elysium. Those guilty of heinous crimes are past cure and sent to Tartarus. You needn't worry. You're headed for eternal oneness alongside the divine."

"How can you be sure?" said Melaina, grasping the golden broach of Arrogance. "I killed and beheaded a man in Asia."

"That was in war. Besides, you've abandoned bodily pleasures and devoted yourself to knowledge, afitted your soul with courage and selflessness. You're devoted to others and country. Look at all you've suffered for the sake of Hellas. I'd think your concern would be that you've lived so little, been cheated of a full life, not of where you're going."

"Oh, not so! Remember? Grandfather told me, I've been blessed with two fates. Kynthia at Brauron died that I might live a while longer. Before she stepped between the assassin and me, I saw my own death. Favored I've been, not cheated. Yet, it is with dire dread that I leave you, Mother. What happiness can I have even in the Elysian Fields without you?"

Myrrhine saw the muscles twitch in her daughter's cheeks. Melaina took a deep breath. Her hands trembled. "Oh Mother, I feel a tightness between the shoulders and hear ringing in my ears. Eyie! Sparks, fiery circles. Ah! They come!"

"Who, Melaina? What's happening?" Her daughter seemed to be looking through her to something beyond.

"First comes the dark lady, dread Persephone, though beautiful beyond words. Then comes dear Hermes, guide of souls, followed by Father, your husband. Aha! His hand has been restored. In the distance, I see Charon, death's ferryman, with his two-oared skiff lurking at the dock, his hand impatient upon the boatman's pole."

"Are you really leaving me?"

"Don't worry. Father will care for me. Though you live a long life, it will be as tomorrow you shall join us."

"Ah me! What'll I do without you?"

"One last thing. We owe a cock to Asklepios. Don't forget it." Melaina reached for the leather strap but couldn't grasp it, gave a strange cry. She fell backward as the bodyquake took hold, rent her legs stiff, and turned up the whites of her eyes.

Though she'd prepared herself, Myrrhine was shocked at the power, the ugliness of it. "Off!" she screamed, "the child is not yet yours." She searched the fold of Melaina's chiton and found the leather strap, forced it between her daughter's teeth although the struggle was fierce. Already, foam formed at the mouth's corners, and Melaina was slick with sweat. Her arms beat the ground as if they were drumsticks in the hands of some madman.

The shaking stopped, but Myrrhine knew it wasn't over. Melaina's eyes flitted back and forth, her limbs tensed. The seizure struck again. Melaina was beyond her help. Myrrhine turned her daughter loose and stepped back as the entire body was lifted from the ground, thrown about.

As quickly as it began, all was silent, still. Melaina was at rest, but breathless, lifeless. "Oh! Hermes, no!" Myrrhine screamed. "Don't take her. Mark her if you must. Cross an eye, wither a hand, but don't take Melaina from me."

Again the sickness seized Melaina's limp form, as if it were some god in the midst of a terrible rage. It shook her until Myrrhine thought the body would be dismembered.

"Leave her alone!" cried Myrrhine. "Can't you see she's dead?" Myrrhine wept, again took Melaina in her arms, her darling daughter, and prayed her not leave. "Already I yearn to stand in the light with you, but gone are all our times together."

Myrrhine fell on the neck of her dead daughter, wept her miserable heart out. "Would that on the day I heard of Kynegeiros' evil death, I'd straightway given up my own life and gone among the shades. Once I was admired among Eleusinian women. Now I'll pine away, ill-fated for love of you, my only child."

Then Myrrhine made a long, frantic appeal to Asklepios. "Divine healer! I know you possess blood from the Gorgon's right artery that heals the dead. Bring some swiftly for Melaina." Although she realized that Zeus had killed Asklepios because of such an act, still she argued her case. "Zeus is wrong to have allowed Melaina's death. Your healing act will be justified. Please! Asklepios, please!"

Myrrhine held tight to her daughter's limp frame, felt the warmth dissolve. She rose to her feet, stood over the body, and prayed long with one arm outstretched, palm upturned, the other fist clenched over her heart. She beseeched dear Hermes to be gentle with Melaina, to guide her swiftly to the Elysian Fields. She evoked Charon, Hades, told gracious Persephone how much Melaina loved her, begged her grace.

Just before dawn, one baby cried and woke the other. Myrrhine left her daughter covered with a blanket and went to care for the children but had nothing to quell hunger wails. She walked to the chicken coop. She witnessed the cocks' first crowing and carried home a warm-feathered rooster. At the slaughter stone before the sacred grotto, she lopped the head with an ax and let the rooster's black blood flow as its flapping wings created great gusts of dust in the temple. She stood with arms outstretched to the god but could find no words to propitiate him.

She returned.

Myrrhine checked Melaina again. Yes, she was dead. Reluctantly, ever so tenderly, Myrrhine closed her daughter's eyes, released her soul.

CHAPTER 19: THE FUNERAL

A gido couldn't stop screaming. Her face swelled to bursting, veins dilated and blue against her forehead, cheeks flushed crimson. Still her screams echoed along Eleusis' streets, unconsoled even by Anaktoria.

Morning came without a breath of air, and the sunlight filtered through a dull haze. Myrrhine's cheeks were wet and her heart in agony when she sent runners to Athens for Aeschylus and Kallias, to Kolonus for Sophocles, and Phlya for Kleito. She walked the length of the courtyard to the smithy, where the crippled blacksmith sat in silence as if awaiting his own death sentence, bellows not breathing, fires but dying embers. She heard the far-off thud of axes as woodcutters felled giant timbers to warm the hearths of Eleusis.

"Come witness," she said, "the corpse of she who was not merely loved, but the loveliest of the beloved."

He hobbled after Myrrhine to the chamber where the body lay. He fell before it pouring torrents of tears, his words now marked by the Ionian dialect. Around the lifeless form, he pranced on dwarfed legs like some dumb beast. Grief expended, he spoke with uncharacteristic pessimism. "The gods never take villainy but by chance, the noble always."

"Melaina never felt that way."

"Her generous nature wouldn't allow as much," he said, "but I've seen the wicked given excellent care, Hades never calling rogues and knaves but gleeful in stalking the valorous and just. The gods want the most precious with them."

"Be grateful they allowed her with us as long as they did."

"A grievous task we have to live a bleak existence without the one who makes it bearable. Never has the world seen the like of this one."

While awaiting the arrival of family and friends, Myrrhine rummaged her small store of clothing, holding out sable-hued grieving rags. She had nothing suitable in which to dress the corpse and began to worry about it. Before the gates of Palaemon's home, she placed a bowl of lustral spring water and sheared a lock of Melaina's blond hair for the threshold. Palaemon set giant Akmon and Damnameneus to scavenging wood for the funeral pyre and digging the grave. Melaina would lie beside her father at the family cemetery close by.

Helios had already reached the zenith and begun his descent when Hipparete arrived, followed shortly by melancholic Philokleia, Aeschylus' wife, fully within her element and weaving her web of woe. "Punishment for the way you raised her," Philokleia said.

Myrrhine was staggered by the cutting remark but remained silent. Neither Aeschylus nor Kallias were among the mourners. Myrrhine thought it strange, but knew that sending the dead to their final destination was women's work. Hipparete brought a glorious white, ankle-length himation for the deceased, so that was one worry Myrrhine could set aside. No word of Kleito. Perhaps Mnesarchides wouldn't allow her to come.

"Thank goodness you're here, Hipparete," Myrrhine said. "You can help keep my emotions within bounds."

Myrrhine sought restraint in grieving. Law prohibited loud wailing or other unseemly excesses. She didn't know how she could possibly watch the body burn. Just then, all Melaina's best traits came to full bloom. How gentle she was with children, her willingness to give, her devotion to country. There'd be no more illuminating questions, no prophecies. The wonder had gone from Myrrhine's life.

Myrrhine would allow no one but herself to handle the body and trusted others only to retrieve fresh sea water, the origin of all life, and dowse the sponge. But Myrrhine took the sponge herself and tenderly, gently caressed her daughter's body with it, as might a lover, using soothing strokes. She washed the breasts, dabbed dried milk from the nipples, rubbed them with perfumed olive oil as if for a wedding. She washed with particular care the navel where Melaina had been connected to her own body fifteen years before, the tortured privates where Melaina had given birth, smoothed away blood crusts. The limbs were most sorrowful, rigid already with death's creeping stiffness.

The face she washed last, most painful, and allowed herself a single mournful wail. "I hoped you'd nurse me in my dotage, deck my corpse with loving hands." Delicately she washed away caked foam from the lips, affectionately scrubbed the nose, eyelids, fondled the ears. She fixed the golden silk hair, soft, manageable. How many times she'd brushed and braided it, felt its rich curls between her fingers. Lastly, she cut two locks and rolled one within each of the scrolls that Melaina had written for the babes.

The women moved the body to the death couch, Hipparete and Philokleia helping slip on the himation, prop the head with a pillow. Myrrhine added her daughter's favorite earrings and necklace just before Palaemon returned with a gold lip-band to hold Melaina's mouth closed and a gold strophion to grace her head, add queenly presence.

Myrrhine was content with a single bronze obol slipped between the lips, but Palaemon wouldn't have it and substituted two gold-foil coins he'd made himself, Charon's pieces. Myrrhine put a honey cake in Melaina's hand to distract Kerberos when she arrived at the Gates of Hades, and remembering the eagle broach, pinned it between the breasts.

"Yes," said the smith, "she wore it well."

The dark, smelly forms of Akmon and Damnameneus moved the couch upon the high-standing bier and set it in the center of the chamber, feet facing toward the door. Myrrhine draped it with a white cloth and spread myrtle branches over the feet. She swept the chamber and the floor of the smithy, saving the sweepings in a leather pouch.

Death's garniture was complete.

As darkness descended on the ruins of Eleusis, strangers journeying by sea and land gathered before the blacksmith's home. Unaccountably, they'd heard of the death. Observing great composure and quiet, they entered, said prayers bierside, then lingered in the courtyard. Many brought sacrificial animals, slaughtered them, and held their own funerary banquet.

From among them emerged Pindar, the famous bard Myrrhine had seen at the Isthmus. "I'm on my way to witness the siege of Thebes, my home, see it burned or saved. Never would I have thought that the little priestess I saw dance at Poseidon's temple could be dead.

Myrrhine asked if he'd sing before continuing on his way. "Rather than a dirge to incite an unseemly tempest of grief, let it be inspirational. Melaina would have wanted it so."

Pindar accompanied himself on the lyre and sang standing before the crowd in the courtyard, his voice lofting a forlorn refrain.

> The death yoke comes hard for all us left behind
> but even Kronos, father of all,
> can undo none of the Fates' determined endings
> whether in right or wrong. The good soul,
> pure from all dishonorable deeds, passes
> where ocean-breezes blow round the Isle of the Blest
> and flowers of gold blaze from radiant trees.
> For them, Helios shines in meadows red with roses,
> shaded by the incense tree laden with golden fruit.
> So shall it be for the deceased here.
> Pure was her heart, loyalty to Hellas ever her cause.

Afterward, a chorus of maidens clapped their youthful palms and danced around the bier. Myrrhine let it go awhile, enjoying the sweet voices that reminded her so much of Melaina's. Finally, she stepped forward. "Hold the hymn, stay the dancers!" she called. "Enough! Time for bed. Fatigue is the enemy of us all. Let the mourning continue at the procession early tomorrow."

She thanked Pindar and sent him on his way.

Myrrhine hadn't slept in two days and went to bed hoping for at least a little rest. They'd all be up long before first light. By law, the burial had to be complete by sunrise. She hugged the crying babies to her, each frail squeak reminding her of their need for nourishment. She'd tried goat's milk without success. Little Theonoë spit up, and Zakorus got mad about it, clenching his little fists and wrinkling his brow. She'd find a wet nurse in the morning after the funeral. Before bed, she ingested the rest of the herb Kleito had given Melaina, the kakhry, to produce milk. An overdose taken all at once, it was worth a try. She dozed thinking that she had become her own daughter. Both babes were so precious.

Myrrhine woke several times, reasoning that Melaina's death had been a dream, and finally felt it so strongly that she rose and walked into the death chamber, only to find Melaina still on the bier, flesh cold and firm, tight within the grasp of death's stiffness. She stood over the body expecting Melaina to awake, sit up. She remembered that Death and Sleep are twin brothers who dwell in the country of dreams. She kissed Melaina's face, couldn't quit kissing it, the cold lifeless flesh sweet nectar to her lips. She returned to bed.

A ruckus in the house, followed by the babies' wails, woke her. She started at a chill across her bosom, then realized that her bedding was soaked. Tightness in her breasts caused her to pull open her nightgown. Milk flowed copiously. The kakhry had worked. She put a child to each breast, as had Melaina, an elbow cradling each. She felt that sensual, sexual heat creeping into her bosom that she'd not known since breast-feeding Melaina. How she'd missed that feeling. And how different were the two babes. Little Theonoë quietly sucking, placid, pensive, gentle at the nipple, sighed. Shiny-headed Zakorus' greediness already showed, sweat puddles under his eyes as he worked hard at the warm breast, butted when flow slowed like a kid at the nanny's udder, squealed. Guilt swept over Myrrhine, enjoying Melaina's children so.

Myrrhine arrived late at the procession, the bier already upon a funeral wagon. Ghost-like shapes wailed about it. Why the hearse? she wondered. The walk to the family cist tomb is but a short one. Pallbearers would be more appropriate. Dogs stretched awake, yawned. Birds rustled at their roost. Bright stars broke the black overhead. Arkturus, the star that ushered in the harvest of grapes and pears, hung well above the horizon. Oh, how Melaina had loved sweet pears! Kallias' four high-spirited black horses, barely visible in the darkness, stood impatiently before the train. All was ready, waiting. But the procession faced the wrong direction, west not east.

Aeschylus stood before the horses ready to give the command forward.

Just then, Kleito arrived by carriage. Waterfalls of apologies poured forth from her along with tears upon seeing Melaina's corpse atop the bier. Myrrhine hugged her, passed a babe to her, the other to Hipparete. Myrrhine turned back to question Aeschylus.

"She'll not be buried in the family cist," he said.

Fear seized Myrrhine. Aeschylus seemed no longer her late husband's brother, but some evil spirit hovering about the death train. "But Kynegeiros' daughter demands burial alongside her father."

"Not so," he said.

"But the pyre and grave have been made ready beside him."

"I ordered them changed last night, timbers moved, trench filled."

Myrrhine saw Agido and Anaktoria nearby and did not want them to witness her hostility, then thought it better that they learn early men's unjust nature. Rage flamed in Myrrhine's heart, a great hurt fueling it.

"What idiocy! Have you gone mad?" She turned to Kallias. "Why shield yourself behind Aeschylus, Kallias? Is this your doing? You want your wife buried with your family?"

Kallias shuffled his feet. "She'll not be interred there either. Our marriage was never consummated."

Myrrhine, standing close to Kallias, felt a sudden hatred for him, had to check her fists. She had never hit a man. "Melaina warned me of your fickle heart. She saved your life in Asia. Think about what you're doing." She turned back to Aeschylus. "Still, the procession points in the wrong direction. Burial along the Sacred Way is to the east."

"The Sacred Way has nothing for this corpse."

"Cowards! Why didn't you reveal this maliciousness last night? I'm a woman, not one to reverse men's dictates."

"We'd not trouble you unnecessarily," said Aeschylus. "It's the epilepsy. I'll not have the frenzy pollute those already laid to rest."

"Many the hero who died with the falling sickness, yet was given a glorious burial."

"None's death was caused by it."

"Where's the burial to be then? Some dark world corner to hide this shame that is my lovely daughter?"

"West of the city."

"Hence the hearse instead of pallbearers. But all that lies out there is the burial site of those disgraced centuries ago by the futile siege of Thebes, the leaders of Argos' armies who died in the struggle between Oedipus' sons. That is a burial site for commoners, slaves, and those humiliated by defeat."

"The same."

"Melaina during life was infinitely kind. Even as a child, she'd invite my breast to other infants, serve them at her own bountiful table. Remember her prayer before the battle of Salamis? Her call to you to find your own courage? Surely you'd not reward such kindness, such honor, with ostracism."

Aeschylus stood silent.

"Enemy within my own family! I should have known your mischief wouldn't end with marrying off my daughter without me. But this cunning deception strikes at the heart of divine justice. Many an evil will this act spawn."

Myrrhine shrieked, then left the lot of them and returned inside the house. She took up a dull blade, chopped at her hair, scraping at it angrily until it was cut close about her face. She noticed broad streaks of gray that had come upon her overnight. Then she turned her nails upon her cheeks and unleashed sharp pain that lured ever deeper. Runnels of bright blood merged with her tears' stinging torrents. She cherished the sharp pain, delighted as her nails stripped skin from her own flesh. She rubbed filth into her grieving cloths, ripped them, covered herself in hearth ashes.

She returned, unleashing her fury anew on Aeschylus. "In this bosom festers wrath and hate immeasurable."

Aeschylus shook his head. "Don't surrender to unwarranted grief and rage. The law requires natural sadness and goodwill instead of wild, frenzied mourning."

"You forget," she said, "when Zeus apportioned honors, Grief asked and Zeus granted a share."

"Yes, but only a share."

The procession moved slowly through the dark city gate. Kleito held a babe in one arm and helped Myrrhine walk with the other. They left cobblestone for the dirt road west toward Megara, past the earth-scarred quarry to a stone enclosure at the edge of town where the ancient Argive warriors lay buried. Beside the enclosure, Myrrhine saw a tower of timber and a hill of dirt beside an open grave.

Myrrhine turned on Aeschylus again. "Do not do this evil thing," she said. "Lead us back beside her father's grave."

Aeschylus remained silent.

Myrrhine clenched her teeth, so her words hissed through them. "The procrastination of the divine in punishing the wicked is infamous. But never you mind the slow grinding. The mill of the gods ever turns. Soft though she treads, divine Justice in her own season seizes them unawares, deals the fatal blow." Then she put him out of her mind and turned back to her daughter.

Myrrhine fell to her knees on the soft, fresh earth. Here she'd have the last glimpse of her daughter in this life. She climbed upon the bier, took Melaina's stiff hand in hers. "Ah me! What mournful dirge shall I sing to you? O Melaina, how can I now go through life? Hear me, sweet daughter. Never did I realize how much I loved you. My life is gone, my heart in ruins. Hear me, daughter. It is I who call! Ruined me, printing a kiss on your dead lips." With great spasms of sobs she fell upon her daughter, embraced her, cuddled her face.

Finally, she stepped down, and Aeschylus and Kallias hoisted Melaina upon the funeral pyre. Myrrhine saw Palaemon, his twisted shape never looking so burdened by deformity, hovering about, stepping forward as if to help, then stepping back shaking his head.

Myrrhine took a torch from Aeschylus and stepped up to the felled timbers. "O Melaina! Forgive me, dearest! Had I Orpheus' tuneful voice to charm Demeter's daughter, I'd descend into the Underworld and return you to life. Not even Kerberos, Hades fell hound, could hold me from restoring you." A great pain seized Myrrhine's chest as she touched flame to tinder. She circled the pyre, spreading fire along its flanks.

The greedy blaze leaped along the timbers, wetting each limb with cleansing flame, licked her daughter's garments until they also burned. "O divine Demeter, I release my daughter to the fire to make her immortal. Receive her into your care. If it weren't for these two babes, my limbs would be stretched beside hers on these same flames."

Myrrhine saw the dark shapes of Akmon and Damnameneus hovering just outside the firelight and thought of a use for them. "The grave pit must be larger, deeper," she said. That set them grumbling about the first pit they'd covered in, but still their huge shapes again bent hard over their shovels. Myrrhine's mind was a whir of odious thoughts.

She cast her eyes over the desolate landscape, then looked out over the bay. These were the deep black bogs where frogs croaked, dread children of lake and land who live in both worlds representing both the living and dead, speaking their, "ko-ax, ko-ax," from the depths of marsh rushes. Myrrhine made up her mind to work something dirty to repay Aeschylus for burying her daughter in this forlorn moorland.

As the flames rose skyward, loosing their roar of sorrow, Myrrhine stepped back from the heat, then stepped forward again, relishing the pain it caused her lacerated cheeks. Her daughter was on her own, lost from view by the conflagration. Loud cracks scattered coals, and sparks soared skyward, trails of brilliance dancing into the heavens. Ever higher, upward it burned, the purifying flame soaring amid the stars, all accompanied by Myrrhine's wails of woe as her daughter winged her way to Elysium.

As the fire died, glowing skeletons of coals ribbed the pyre. The iridescent timbers gave way and crashed to the ground. Myrrhine stood within the ashes, searching for her daughter's remains. As the glow faded, she decided against letting anyone help bury Melaina's bones. Fetching the babes from Hipparete and Kleito, Myrrhine passed them off to Palaemon despite their whimpers of protest, then turned on Aeschylus.

"Off with you, scoundrel!" she shouted. "I'll not have you at the burial."

Aeschylus stood his ground. "I fear you devise some cureless ill against us all. Say you'll quench your thirst for this sea of misery."

"I do only what benefits my daughter. Should I catch you here when I sacrifice, I'll slit your throat and throw your blood-drained body into the pit along with her urn of ashes." She picked up and threw a clod from the burial mound, hit him in the chest.

Aeschylus was visibly shaken, and Philokleia stopped her ranting. Both slinked grudgingly off into the darkness.

Myrrhine hugged Agido and Anaktoria, bid them leave with their parents, then told Kleito to wait at the grotto. "No need for you to be part of what I am about to do," she said. Kallias and Hipparete had already left aboard the carriage.

With them gone, Myrrhine realized that Sophocles had not attended the funeral. No matter. She quickly turned to the smith. "I'll need Akmon and Damnameneus to do something dirty." She then faced the two dark shapes, feeling camaraderie, fidelity, great comfort in their presence. "If you're not up to it, say so. I'll not hold it against you. My anger rages out of control."

Myrrhine knew the two tended to be short on words, and now only heard a grunt from each, something low, harsh, favorable.

"I want the four black stallions. Can you get them?"

"Kallias will not part with them willingly," said Palaemon.

"He need not know. Follow him, quickly! Steal the horses!" An inspiration seized her. "Also, bring a single thin sheet of lead, enough for a curse tablet, and a nail. Bring Kallias' chariot. Steal everything breakable, pots, jars, from wherever. And most of all, a sharp blade of the finest bronze, a hammer, and an apple."

Akmon and Damnameneus didn't wait for Palaemon's okay. They disappeared, hungry to execute a fell deed.

Myrrhine did not douse the coals with wine, nor did she loiter as the embers cooled. She collected the ashes, skull, rib bones, knuckles, ankles, charred vertebrae while relishing the sting of the hot coals as they singed her daughter's cinders into her own hands. She scooped the melted metal, puddles of gold left by the eagle-broach, headband and strophion, then draped herself in Melaina's hot ashes that they might burn her daughter's essence into her.

All this she placed alongside the delicate bones within the funeral urn: blackened joints first, next the fine fingers and toes as were left, gold puddles, all capped by the skull. The ordering she changed several times, unable to get it right. Only the smith's troubled countenance hovering over her put a stop to it. She looked up into his face, set aglow by the coals of the burned out pyre, heard the children wailing in his arms.

"Forgive me," he said, "for what I'm about to ask, but I've seen you harden yourself to this task such as I'd never believed possible." He stopped talking and stood blinking in the dark.

"Though I've the words, I lack the courage to speak."

"Don't tremble so, Palaemon. I know nothing but good could cause your questioning."

"It's thoughts of Medea troubling me."

Myrrhine wondered what on earth could be the connection with the Kolchian sorceress of ancient days. Then, she realized. Medea had killed her own children. "Brave Palaemon, I read your heart, and I'm sorry for causing such concern. Never could I steel myself to slay the children. Rest assured, I've not calculated such a murderous deed."

Myrrhine climbed down into the grave pit, dark scar in Mother Earth, and brought Melaina's metal urn with her. Her sandals bogged in the moist earth, and she noticed the musty, earthy odor of the Underworld.

"Dear daughter," she said aloud, "I'll leave here for now what remains of your earthly form. But never think I'll rest until you're laid alongside your father."

Myrrhine climbed to the surface amid the rhythmic clap of horses' hooves. Kallias' carriage careened into sight, the black steeds greedy at the run, puffing steam, the chariot stacked with clanking vessels of every shape, size, and material. Akmon worked hard at the reins, bringing all to a halt, while Damnameneus labored to keep the clanging jars from cracking.

Myrrhine asked for the nail and lead sheet first, and as would a schoolchild writing upon a tablet, she scratched harsh, querulous words into the soft surface.

May Aeschylus, the tragic poet, go to Tartarus,
and likewise Kallias, the richest man in Athens.
I bind Kallias before Hermes the Restrainer and Persephone,
the tongue of Kallias, the hands of Kallias, the soul of Kallias
the feet of Kallias, the body of Kallias, the head of Kallias
because he deserted his wife, my daughter.
I bind Aeschylus before Hermes the Restrainer,
the hands, the feet, the tongue, the body of Aeschylus,

the will of Aeschylus for improper burial of Melaina.

Myrrhine labored over each word, ensuring the letters were of uneven size and written in different directions, upside down. Greater the disorder, the more powerful the curse. She folded the tablet and, taking the bronze nail into her hand, grew large and menacing, the likeness of some awful goddess of inevitability, she seemed, divine Fate herself. Through cold lifeless lead, she hammered home the nail as if marking the close of an age, then tossed the curse tablet into the grave alongside the urn.

Akmon and Damnameneus unharnessed the carriage beside the grave and took the horses behind the ancient gravesite wall. Myrrhine asked for the sword and saw that they'd thieved the glorious blade that Aeschylus had captured from a Persian at the battle of Salamis. "You've exceeded all my hopes," she said.

She asked that they bring forward the first horse.

The black stallion trembled in her presence, nervous ripples cascading along its obsidian flanks. She spoke sweet warbled words into its ear, reached for the flowing mien, then slit its throat in one swift stroke. The horse didn't bolt, just stood dumbfounded while its gaping wound waterfalled blood into the grave. Slowly its legs gave way before collapsing in a heap in the grave.

Myrrhine wiped the blade on her gown, asked for the apple and the second horse. "Blindfold it," she said, knowing it'd bolt at the sight of its felled companion. She split the apple and rubbed it on the horse's nostrils, let its molars crunch the pulp, so it'd not smell the fresh blood. Each of the remaining three she sacrificed in this way, said a prayer over the stack of fresh bodies, and finally, threw Aeschylus' sword in on top.

"Throw the jars from the carriage here on the ground," she said, "and give me the hammer." Then she loosed her rage.

They carefully set the first pot at the side of the grave, and she smashed it with the hammer, shoved the pieces in on top of the horses. Bewildered, the two gently set the next jar on the ground before her, and she smashed it as well. Akmon and Damnameneus finally caught the mood and began throwing jars to the ground, crashing them into the grave pit. They'd brought more than pots and serving dishes, having stripped Kallias' stable of all his saddles, bridles and blankets.

The medal urns Myrrhine smashed with the hammer, clanging like a dull bell ringing over the plain and out into the swampy bay, sending word to all the Underworld that a beloved was coming amongst them. The grave brimmed, and they heaped dirt upon it, packing the mound tight as the bright morning sun broke the eastern horizon. Myrrhine deposited the house sweepings she'd brought with her, then scattered brilliant flowers over the mound.

Myrrhine hurled herself to the ground and hammered the earth with her fists as if pounding the gates of the Underworld. Long she beat the nourishing earth, bent forward on her knees, wailing to Hades and cold Persephone, tear-soaking her lap. She finished with a call to Melaina. "Daughter of Kynegeiros, have a happy life in Hades. Pass swiftly through the golden gates of Elysium. No year-long mourning will I keep, but all my life."

CHAPTER 20: THE COST OF SALVATION

A s dawn stretched its rosy fingertips over Eleusis' ruins, a monstrous screech arose. Kallias had discovered his horses missing. The entire city fell into an uproar, everyone missing something. Myrrhine's heartache was replaced by a consuming loneliness of the soul, an exile of the spirit that left her feeling so frail she felt she could be whisked away by a puff of wind. This was the first day she'd spend with her daughter gone from the world.

And what a glorious morning! The sun had never been so bright, birds never sung so sweet, children's voices never echoed with so much laughter. Soft breezes buffeted about, lofting limbs of trees laden with fall's first fruits. It was an inheritance, a great gift given to the world by some unknown god or blushing goddess of pure heart and gentle spirit. Myrrhine nursed the babies who basked in this afterglow and was nourished herself by the innocent faces pressed against her flesh.

Later, Myrrhine busied herself preparing for the Amphidromia, the ceremony where she'd officially name the children and accept them into the family. The babes would be five days old tomorrow.

By afternoon, the slaves completed rebuilding the roof over one of the chambers in her burned-out home, so she moved there from the smith's quarters, glad to be back in the arms of Eumolpid soil, although it reeked of smoke. She relit the hearth fire in the center of the courtyard, obtaining a new flame from that brought from Delphi, and sacrificed while praying to Hestia, divine mistress of eternal fire. Myrrhine prayed that Hestia restore the family of the Hierophant, "though the father of this flame is imprisoned far across the Aegean." She stood the Hierophant's staff against the fireplace as a symbol of his presence.

Ordinarily, the rest of the family would have been invited to the Amphidromia, but she'd alienated Aeschylus and Hipparete and felt relieved to have the children to herself. That evening, she stacked enough wood on the fire to create a sizeable blaze and sacrificed a swine before the hearth, calling first on Kynegeiros, then divine Demeter and Kore to renew their presence in the home and see to the welfare of the children. She burned, then ground an anklebone from the swine together with a snail. She then unwrapped the swaddling cloths of each child and pulled off the withered umbilical cords, revealing the pink, blood-speckled navels. She molded the thick mixture into two spinning whorls and pressed one into each umbilicus cavity.

She stripped herself and the babes naked and lofted each over her head while running round the fire singing aloud the child's name. Then she held each over the flame as closely as was safe, though they screamed and squalled at the heat, to burn away the pollution of birth.

As she finished rewrapping the swaddling bandages, smelling the fragrant fumes of roast pork on the kitchen fire where she prepared her own feast, she felt a presence behind her. She turned and jumped at Aeschylus' dark form lurking in the shadows.

She stepped between him and the children as he advanced, his dark figure laced with firelight.

"You've performed the Amphidromia without a man officiating?" he asked.

"In the name of the Hierophant."

"He's dead. You and your offspring belong to me."

"He lives. He was taken by the Persians to Sardis. Melaina said as much, even returned with his staff she found on Mykale's far shore. Anaktoria and her mother confirm this."

"A fanciful tale. I saw him die. You found his charred bones here in the Telesterion and buried them yourself."

Myrrhine knew arguing this was futile. "Still, the Amphidromia is finished. I'm Melaina's mother, her children are more mine than yours."

"No true mother exists. Women but incubate men's live seed. Men are the only true begetters, the progenitors of life. Kynegeiros was her only sire."

"A lie! You don't even believe that yourself. This is but Cyclops vision, one-eyed wisdom."

"Melaina was my ward. I'll determine her offspring's fate."

"If you take the children for fathering, I realize that I can't stop you."

"They're not to be raised. Both are polluted. They are but lifeless phantoms and not worth carrying around the hearth."

"You can't believe that. Melaina's epilepsy wasn't something she could pass to them. Why are you doing this? What are you not saying?"

"You'll expose them on Kithaeron's slopes."

"They're healthy. It would be murder." She walked to them, loosened their swaddling clothes. "See for yourself. When I put them upon the earth, they cry with reasonable vigor, not weakly as they would with an unfavorable condition. They're perfect in all members and senses, orifices free from obstruction. Every function is natural, neither sluggish nor weak. The joints bend and stretch, have no undue size or shape. Come here, Lord Aeschylus," she begged, "press a finger against the surface of the body or prick it. See that they suffer pain. These are the ways the ancients taught to determine an infant's worthiness."

"True, but you give only half a method. The ancients also taught that the mother should spend her pregnancy in good health, for sickness also harms the fetus and enfeebles the foundations of life. Melaina suffered a killing epilepsy. Second, they should be born in due time, best at nine months. These two came at eight. An obvious show of weakness. Further, the mother should not overly exert herself. Melaina was beaten and jostled about during the crucial late months. Kallias tells that she wielded the blow that saved his life at Mykale. She witnessed the horrors of the battle's aftermath. No telling the insanity that could produce in the unborn."

"That they survived at all and remain healthy shows their strength, not weakness. Some believe they're divine. The priest of Asklepios at Epidaurus was certain of it. To expose a divine child, two of them, would provoke the wrath of Zeus himself."

"You think this is easy for me.? These are my brother's grandchildren; the male child, his heir. I've affection for them you can't guess. My grief is tenfold yours. I'll hear no more. Expose them."

"But dear Aeschylus, I see now your crossways attitude toward the children is because of my ill manners during Melaina's funeral. Please forgive me. Don't inflict punishment rightfully mine upon the newborn."

"I've spoken. Do my bidding. I rule here."

"Please, hear just this final word. The Mysteries must be reinstated. These children are the only direct descendants of Eumolpus. The male is the only legitimate heir to be Hierophant, the daughter the only one to replace me as priestess of Demeter. All Hellas hangs in the balance. See the wrong of exposing them, Lord Aeschylus. This decision cannot stand. Rule by choosing to be overruled."

"This is but idle chatter. The Mysteries haven't been held for two years, and during this time, we've repulsed the world's mightiest army."

"Dear brother of my beloved Kynegeiros, don't throw away your own sibling's grandchildren. Look!" Myrrhine threw back her wrap to expose her breasts. "The goddess gave me milk. See! My breasts swell with nourishment for the babes. Never did I even think it possible except for a goddess. Hera's milk returned to feed the infant Herakles."

Aeschylus didn't look at her breasts, but turned his back and walked off. "You'll have until tomorrow evening. Give them to a slave to expose on Kithaeron. I warn you. If you try to escape, I'll have all three of you put to the sword."

That night Myrrhine went to bed but couldn't sleep, her grip on the babies so tight that she worried she'd crush them. Many were the names of ancient heroes who'd survived being exposed on Kithaeron's shady slopes. Oedipus had survived to unwittingly kill his father and marry his mother. And Herakles, Greece's greatest hero. Paris, who kidnapped Helen and caused the Trojan War, had been exposed on Mt. Ida.

She cried through the night, getting no sleep, but by morning had a plan. She'd give the children to Kallias. As Dadouchos, he'd understand. She hated to see them become Kerykes, but if it would save their lives, she'd do it. One day they'd be the Hierophant and Priestess of Demeter. Having the sacred officials within the Kerykes had been his one desire. Would he know about the horses? Oh how she wished she'd not been so venomous over Melaina's burial.

★

Kallias was defensive at first. His guilt over not allowing Melaina to be buried within his family plot showed. His shoulders sagged, and he had no spring to his gait. Still, Myrrhine couldn't help but wonder if part of it was caused by sadness over the death of Melaina. He spoke to Myrrhine while shouting to his slaves where to look for his horses.

Myrrhine spoke words of sympathy over their disappearance.

"Ah! We'll find them," he said. "I've a list of those who most coveted them for the Olympic games. They'll not be gone long."

Then Myrrhine approached him about the children. "Please, Lord Kallias," she said. "It would be a crime against the Mysteries, Demeter herself, to allow the children to be exposed."

"The loss will be unfelt," he said, a great arrogance seeming to come upon him. "The two sacred offices can be filled from within my family, the Kerykes."

"You can't be serious. The Hierophant and priestess of Demeter have come from the Eumolpids since Demeter herself initiated the Mysteries."

"That's of little concern. I can't take the children. I'm to be married."

The Cost of Salvation 207

"Again? So soon after Melaina's death? It would be unseemly."

"My marriage to Melaina was never consummated because she was pregnant. The marriage was never official."

"Kallias, you're my last hope. Aeschylus orders that they be exposed."

"Elpinice would never agree. We'll have our own children."

"Elpinice? Kimon's sister? Surely this can't be! Elpinice has been cohabiting with her brother in a shameful union. Every woman in Hellas has words of their filth on her tongue. She's even been over-intimate with Polygnotus, the painter. This will cast a shadow on the Mysteries. After all, you are the Dadouchos."

Kallias backed up and motioned Myrrhine away with a sweep of his hand. "She's been living with her brother due to poverty. She has no dowry. Until now, that has excluded her from a suitable match. I'm also to pay her father's fine, which cost him his life. He died recently in debtor's prison."

"But Kallias, have pity! Save these innocent lives."

"I'll hear no more. You've become abusive of late. Out with you!" He turned his back to her.

"I know you have Melaina's dowry. I'll expect it back."

Kallias didn't respond.

Myrrhine turned on him, her voice reeking vengeance. "I've always thought stories of you getting your wealth by theft and murder at Marathon were lies, but be they true or false, Kallias, you touch so much as one obol of Melaina's dowry, I'll slip you hemlock."

Myrrhine then walked to the toppled icons of Demeter and Kore outside the ashes of the Telesterion. "Dear goddesses, soften someone's heart toward the babes. Deliver them from cruel death on Kithaeron."

She carried them about Eleusis' ruins, searching for she knew not what. She spotted a horse coming along the Sacred Way, a lone rider slumped over its mane. It was young Sophocles riding a pony. As he came near, she realized that he didn't recognize her. With her long chiton, Myrrhine felt as though she didn't walk but glided upon the earth, as would a wraith soon meant for the Undergloom. Her hair, which she'd chopped short before the funeral, had turned solid silver in the last five days. She'd lost so much weight that her cheekbones pushed beneath the skin. Her face was skeletal and scabbed from the clotted mourning lacerations.

"Young Sophocles," she said, "please recognize me. I'm Melaina's mother although I've changed so in but these few days. All the desperate forces of the universe have sent you to me."

Sophocles dismounted and stood beside the pony, reins in his hand. Myrrhine knew he too had been grieving. "You're right, I didn't recognize you," he said. "But I've also been decimated by Melaina's death. How little compassion the gods have for such suffering. Her demise is shameful for them and pitiful for us."

"Oh noble Sophocles, how welcome are your words for Melaina. I'd thought the whole world abandoned her memory."

"No more honorable one has ever been than she. But please, I'm anxious to continue my journey. Make your plea, and if it's within my power, I'll grant it."

"Aeschylus speaks death for the children."

"How could anyone choose that, unless fiends had made his mind witless? Did he give a reason?"

"Pollution from epilepsy. But some other devious calculation lies behind it, I'm sure. Just realize, he means the death of them."

"I know you speak the truth because I've wondered myself why, when they were hardly out of the womb, Aeschylus unleashed a campaign against them. He prevented me from attending Melaina's funeral. I can't imagine what has hardened him so."

"Dear Sophocles, Melaina held you in highest esteem. Would you take them, save them from an evil fate?"

"I'm on my way to Delphi on an urgent mission for my father, but I believe these children are destined to fulfill a design of the gods. They may not be divine as some think, but I'll do what I can. Even so, I can only find a safe place for the male child. You'll have to find another for the female."

Myrrhine felt doomed. She'd not thought of splitting them up. Surely they should be raised together. "Alright," she said, feeling as if the words came from another's mouth. "Take little Zakorus. I'll find another savior for Theonoë."

"I'll do one further thing to keep Aeschylus off their trail. When I return I'll tell him you gave both to me and that I exposed them. The lie will ease his mind and set his conscience to worry. But you must get the little girl out of Eleusis. If he hears of her again, surely it'll mean her death."

"Oh gallant Sophocles, ever I'll be indebted. May the gods watch over you always."

"I greatly esteemed your daughter. Sweetest maiden I've known in my short life. Even in legends such valor was only found in Antigone, daughter of Oedipus. I'm off now, but beware! Aeschylus lurks about. I saw him talking to Kallias."

Sophocles mounted his pony, and Myrrhine handed up the male child with the papyrus Melaina had written for him safely tucked within his wrappings. Overwhelming grief stopped her. She pulled back little Zakorus. He'd voiced a sweet noise, and the stark reality of his impending departure overcame her. She summoned more courage than she thought possible, realizing that the child's life depended on her giving him up.

Myrrhine took a deep breath and passed the child up to Sophocles, again. The pony, with Sophocles astride him and the babe cradled in his arms, disappeared into the failing light, leaving Myrrhine with the emptiness of the child's absence. She hugged little Theonoë. "Girls are worth so little in this world," she said. "Who can I find willing to give you love and shelter?"

Myrrhine walked to the blacksmith's shop as if blown by some holy wind. There, she stood amid hammers clanging hot metal, smelled the sweet easy sweat of men at heavy work. Akmon and Damnameneus seemed golden spirits of providence since they'd become her partners in crime. Finally, Palaemon noticed her.

"I've come for another miracle," she said. "I need you to save Melaina's daughter."

The smith looked older than his years, his deformity over-powering. "Oh, priestess, surely another's help would be more suitable. What's an old cripple to offer a child?"

Myrrhine knelt before him, tears streaming her scab-scarred cheeks. "I come to you as a suppliant. Never have I been more desperate. O dear Palaemon! I found a savior for the boy, but you are the little girl's last hope. She's been ordered abandoned to Kithaeron's cold slopes on penalty of both our deaths. Take her and flee, to what destination I know not, nor care. Just fly far from Eleusis so that her enemies never cast eyes on her sweet face."

The smith took her by the shoulders and raised her to her feet. "What can I possibly offer that another, any other, can't duplicate manyfold?"

"Life itself. For only in your arms will she find safety. I've tried all others and feel ashamed for not coming to you first."

"What a terrible fate then is hers. Of course I'll do it, since you know it's no mistake to put the child in my care."

"Will it be such a burden to help the little one?"

"You've given me a joy such as I've never dreamed. My life has always been lacking. Not only will I do it for sake of moral virtue but also from deep sympathy for this child. Already, I love her more than life itself. I've been thinking of returning to Ionia since the Persians have been driven out. Eleusis is in such a desolate state. I hear they'll not rebuild the Telesterion. Never fear, I'll care for the infant as if she were my own."

Myrrhine looked straight at him, squeezed his callused hands in hers. "No! Not 'as if.' She must never be brought back here. She's yours! Henceforth, you are her father." She sat the bundle in his arms and fled, fled from her own weakness, knowing one look at the little girl or one small sound from her could overcome her resolve.

On her way home, Myrrhine saw in the street a girl who reminded her of Melaina. She chased but lost sight of her, then broke into tears, ran again, only to collide with Aeschylus. His large form, reeking of body odor, took hold of her, shook her.

He shouted at her, "Kallias tells me you tried to convince him to take the children. You went against my word as soon as my back was turned."

Myrrhine felt her body quake, shiver with cold. "Kallias had to be told of the twins' fate. When he married Melaina, he said he'd be their father. I could have died at his hand if I'd exposed them without telling him. But he rejected them also, so I've done as both you bid. Young Sophocles is on his way to Delphi by way of Kithaeron and has agreed to expose them. Ask upon his return, if you don't believe me."

He gave her a stern look and still held her by the shoulders, as if he'd like to shake her brains out. "Exposing them will end Kallias' claim to them and put your precious Mysteries back in the hands of Eumolpids. Eleusis will keep its power structure, and all I've done will be erased. Let this be the end of it. The stain of epilepsy will also die with them."

"In doing so, you'll slay me too. Go ahead, kill me if that's your desire," she said. "You've already murdered my soul."

When he was gone, Myrrhine sensed still more strongly her daughter's presence. Finally, she spoke aloud, "Ah me, what can I do bereft of thee?" and returned home.

★

The next day, Myrrhine visited her daughter's grave, then again on the ninth and thirteenth days to pour a libation and say a prayer. Thereafter, she returned each month until the Genesia year was up. She had developed a wicked insomnia and took to walking at night, a homeless, dislodged spirit seen hovering along the roadways and footpaths of Eleusis.

Then one day, Myrrhine said goodbye, calling upon the hills, meadows and sea beating in the bay where her daughter had so often walked. "Farewell, land of Eleusis," she said. "Waft upon me a peaceful silence that my own will dissolve and I submit to this grim fate the gods have dealt me."

She doused the family hearth fire.

Some said the priestess of Demeter entered the sacred grotto and descended to Hades. Others believed they saw her return each year on the anniversary of Melaina's death to carry a pale torch about the gravesite. Many who passed it late at night heard crying and great lament but saw no one. Mention of Melaina's exploits was forbidden since it was unseemly to speak of women in public, but she lived in people's hearts and private whispers. Many believed that the mother and daughter had been Demeter and Persephone returned to Earth to save Greece. They had spent what time it took and departed.

CHAPTER 21: XERXES' BRIDGE CABLES

Following the victory at Mykale, and after Melaina and Kallias had departed, the Greek fleet sailed north along the coast of Asia, past Ephesus to the Hellespont where Xerxes had crossed over into Europe a year and a half before. Hard-set they were upon destroying the bridges Xerxes had built of biremes, triremes, papyrus and flax cables. When they arrived, they found that the strong-hearted brothers Boreas and Zephyrus had already demolished the bridges. The rest of the Greek fleet, including the Spartans, returned home, but the Athenians under Xanthippus made port on the Chersonese, where they laid siege to Sestos, the most heavily fortified town in the district. Refugees had fled there and taken the bridge cables with them. The town was still under the command of Xerxes' governor, Artayctes.

When the siege dragged on into the bad-weather months, the occupants of Sestos resorted to boiling their leather bed straps for nourishment. Finally, Artayctes and the rest of the Persians, who'd held the district under their yoke, fled, and the Greek residents opened the gates. Artayctes and his son were captured and brought back to Sestos, where Artayctes offered to pay two hundred talents for his life. But Xanthippus and the locals were in no mood for reconciliation. They dragged him to the spit where Xerxes had winched the bridges.

That cold day in the fall of the year, clever, corrupt Artayctes begged not for his own life as they nailed him to a plank and lofted him high into the air, but for that of his son whom they also brought forward. Not content with the crucified man's physical suffering, they stoned his son before his eyes.

The Athenians then sailed home with the bridge cables Xerxes had used to span the Hellespont. The Persian invasion was over. Xanthippus had indeed survived to raise his son, as Melaina had promised. The child's name was Perikles.

★

After his retreat from Greece following the battle of Salamis, Xerxes had spent the past year at Sardis, where he fell in love with his brother's wife. Xerxes' own wife had the woman's tongue torn out, her breasts, nose, ears, and lips cut off and fed to the dogs. Xerxes' brother then tried to stir up a revolt against Xerxes but was caught and executed. A general decadence fell over his empire, and Xerxes himself eventually succumbed to an assassin.

Here ends Volume Two, *The Mysteries: The Dadouchos*. Volume Three is titled *The Twice Born*, which tells the story of the two outcast children who lead the struggle to reinstitute the Mysteries of Eleusis. That volume is in process and will be available at a later date. For updates, please check www.themysteriesofeleusis.com.

THE END

SOURCES

Sources

Cover Illustration

The cover for *The Dadouchos*, as was the cover for *Daughter of Darkness*, is the product of close collaboration between the author and illustrator. I conceptualized the cover illustration. Richard Sheppard created the cover layout, design and illustration. I provided source material for the cover illustration and Richard painted a watercolor that he overlaid with text. My source material was as follows: The man on the cover represents Kallias, the Dadouchos (Torchbearer) of the Mysteries, as best we could imagine him. His overall appearance came from a famous vase painting of a Dadouchos that may actually be a drawing of Kallias himself. It was painted around the time of Kallias' death and was found in a grave at Eleusis. His long hair and short beard were taken from several statues of ancient Greeks. His facial expression was taken from a statue of Hermes, Kallias' divine ancestor, from a picture I took of an ancient Greek statue in the National Archaeological Museum when I was in Athens in October 2009. The image of Melaina defending herself from a Persian warrior (Tigranes) in the near background was sketched from a staged scene in my own home. Marilyn Mueller, my editor, was the model for Melaina, and I was the model for Tigranes. It represents a scene from the Battle of Mykale. Mylaina's attire was taken from *Costumes of the Greeks and Romans* by Thomas Hope. The depiction of the battle between the Persians and Greeks and the palisade came from a combination of online images and ancient Greek vase drawings.

Primary Sources

See *The Mysteries.*, Volume One: *Daughter of Darkness*.

Genesis of The Mysteries

See *The Mysteries*, Volume One: *Daughter of Darkness*.

Sources for Chapter 1

1. State of the troops and the location of the Persians at this particular time is well documented by Herodotus, *The Histories*, IX, 13-15, as well as the fact that after starting to withdraw from Attica they turned about and ravaged the countryside all the way to Megara, by necessity passing through Eleusis to get there. Although Herodotus doesn't state it explicitly, Mardonius also burned Eleusis, as verified by archaeological evidence.

2. The burning of Eleusis is addressed at length by George E. Mylonas, in *Eleusis and the Eleusinian Mysteries*, pages 88-91. Although the city may have been burned earlier, my supposition follows that of Mylonas that it was burned just before the Persians pulled back out of Attica and positioned themselves south of Thebes for the final land battle.

3. What happened to the sacred objects at Eleusis is solely a matter of conjecture. Mylonas, although he presents (pages 84 and 90) his speculation as fact, says "It can be considered as certain that the Hiera of the Goddess were transported from Eleusis to a safer place when the Persian menace was drawing near." I've taken a different approach. I've assumed that the Persians turned about and flew into Eleusis so rapidly that advanced word of their coming never arrived. That Eleusis would not have been completely evacuated earlier is also conjecture on my part, but is possible since Delphi was never evacuated. The fate of the Hiera as presented in *The Mysteries* is not known for sure. Volume 3 provides a fully fictional account of their fate.

(As an aside, I would wonder what happened to the Hiera in the 5th century AD when the Mysteries were abandoned. The priests and priestess had to decide what to do with them. Did Christians destroy them? My guess is that they probably did. But we have no definitive answer. Do they still exist? That is a really interesting question.)

4. The actual spot where the Persians broke through the wall is shown in Mylonas, Figure 28. Kimon's administration repaired this breach sometime during the years to come. The spot where the Hierophant was believed to have stood his ground in the novel is shown in Figure 4, H10, although this figure has several configurations superimposed for the archaeological site and is difficult to follow without intense study of text and figure. The date when the Telesterion was rebuilt is also a matter of speculation, and, although Mylonas says it must have been rebuilt immediately, I don't believe it was because of the oath not to rebuild any of the temples burned by the Persians, which was taken by the generals only a few days later.

5. The presence of Sophocles and Aeschylus here while the Persians burned Eleusis is fictional. All I can say is that they had to be somewhere, and I've used their presence to suit the purposes of my storyline.

6. The blacksmith's use of turkey wood, which "springs about and emits sparks" (but was used by blacksmiths) to create a little fireworks, comes from Theophrastus, *Inquiry into Plants*, Volume I, pages 209-11.

Sources for Chapter 2

1. Mardonius' retreat after burning Eleusis and Megara to just south of Thebes is documented by Herodotus, IX, 15.

2. For the fort at Eleutherai at one time being on the boarder between Boeotia and Attica but hatred of Thebes driving them to align themselves with Athens, see Pausanias, *Guide to Greece*, I, 38[8]. Also, N. G. L. Hammond, *The History of Greece to 322 BC*, pages 191/2, which also contains a list of references on the subject.

3. The scene from the pass: "To the north they overlooked the deme of Boeotia that had gone over to the Persians, including Thebes and Orchomenus between which the Kopaic Basin, with its eel-infested swamplands, glinted in sunlight," comes from Pau-

sanias, IX, 24[1] and partly from Katie Demakopoulou and Dora Konsola, *Archaeological Museum of Thebes*, pages 11/12. The swamp was drained sometime in antiquity, as it has been more recently, and is now farmland. See also Hammond, page 12, and Sarantis Symeonoglou, *The Topography of Thebes*, page 5.

4. The location of Demeter's temple is found in Pausanias, IX, 4[2,3]. The description of the "old temple of Eleusinian Demeter standing amongst a grove of trees: pine, mighty elms, pears, apples. Though it was late summer, water gushed in a stream coming from the slopes of Kithaeron," comes, at least in part, from Plutarch, *Lives*, "Aristides" page 444 (The Modern Library).

5. Myrrhine refusing to drink or freshen herself follows the lead of Demeter in *The Homeric Hymn to Demeter*, Lines 49/50.

6. The description of Demeter's icon has been taken from Lewis Richard Farnell, *The Cults of the Greek States*, Volume III, pages 268/9.

7. For the location of Moria Bridge, see Peter Green, *The Greco-Persian Wars*, pages 235 and 242.

8. The description of the Persians ("fish-scale mail," etc) comes from Herodotus, VII, 61.

9. For the blacksmith's comments concerning the inferiority of Persian armor, see Snodgrass, *Arms & Armor of the Greeks*, page 75 and all of Chapter IV, and Herodotus, IX, 60-86.

10. For the extravagant tree cutting of Mardonius, see Herodotus, IX, 15. The descriptive words ("men-giants," etc.) come from Callimachus, *Hymn VI, To Demeter*, Lines 33-9.

11. The description of the slaughtering area ("camels, horses, oxen, asses, deer, and smaller animals, ostriches, geese and cocks") comes from Athenaeus, *Deipnosophistae*, IV, 145e.

12. For Mardonius' solid-brass manger, see Herodotus IX, 70.

13. For the layout of Mardonius' camp ("Some dined out of doors in full sight, others inside. When she reached the tent entrance, she saw that even those inside didn't eat in the presence of Mardonius for he had two separate rooms. His advisors ate in one, and he in another with a chorus of his concubines playing the

lyre and singing...”), see Athenaeus, *Diepnosophistae*, IV, 145a-d. All this and the following description assume Mardonius is living like a Persian king, which is reasonable since he covets the position.

14. The description of Mardonius’ accommodations (“The tent floor was covered with beautifully-designed carpets containing miniature figures of Persian heroes. Tables were furnished with cups and mixing bowls of silver and gold. Upon the fire burned the spine and gallbladder of an animal.”) comes from Athenaeus, *Diepnosophistae*, IV, 146b and e.

15. Mardonius’ banquet is described in Athenaeus, *Diepnosophistae*, IV, 147

16. Myrrhine’s comment to Mardonius that “flatterers, worms that bore into a man of simple character,” comes from Athenaeus, VI, 254d.

17. The disposition of Mardionius’ table leftovers is described in Athenaeus, VI, 145f.

Sources for Chapter 3

1. Mylaina being “kidnapped” and married off by order of her father is in keeping with the story of Persephone. See Helene P. Foley, *The Homeric Hymn to Demeter*.

2. Myrrhine’s objection (“How could this be? Only I can marry her off. Who raised the bridal torch?”) and the words of Aeschylus have been patterned after that of Klytemnestra in Euripides’ *Iphigeneia at Aulis*, Lines 992/3 and those following.

3. For Pausanias’ youthfulness, see Green, *The Greco-Persian Wars*, page 232 and Note 11.

4. For Tisamenus, his background and his reputation as a seer, see Herodotus, IX,33-5.

5. The famous “Oath of Plataea” was probably given at Eleusis, but no one knows for sure. See Bradford, *Thermopylae*, page 226, and Green, *The Greco-Persian Wars*, page 239/40. As for the actual oath, see Green, page 240, and Diodorus Siculus, XI, 29, 3-4.

6. For the nature of oaths, them being “surrounded by Furies,”

etc., see Burkert, *Greek Religion*, pages 250-54. The "preamble" to the oath comes from Homer, *The Iliad*, Book III, Lines 300f.

7. An oracle did come from Delphi saying that the Greeks must fight before a temple of Eleusinian Demeter. See Plutarch, *Lives*, Vol. I, "Aristides," page 443/4. The Greeks' difficulty locating the temple was as dramatized in the novel.

8. Myrrhine's fasting, refusing wine, and accepting the drink, kykeon, and even Myrrhine's words come from the *Hymn to Demeter*.

9. Myrrhine arguing with Kallias and Aeschylus follows that of Demeter in the *Hymn to Demeter*.

Sources for Chapter 4

1. The scene at the pass where they view all Boeotia spread out before them comes from Green, *The Greco-Persian Wars*, page 241.

2. The loss of a wagon train of 500 is told by Herodotus, IX, 39.

3. For the confrontation between Aristides, general of the Athenians, and Arimnestus, general of the Plataeans, where the Plataeans give up their land to Athens, see Plutarch, Lives Vol. I, "Aristides," page 444. Myrrhine's reasoning, that it is necessary to gain the aid of Athena, although not a part of the argument provided by Plutarch, is sound. For the fight between Ares and Athena in which she wounds Ares, see Homer, *The Iliad*, Lines 470-80.

4. Liver reading. For Tisamenus, I've adopted the liver reading method of the ancient Etruscans. The position of the Etruscan seer when reading a sacrifice was always the same, left foot on a rock, the liver in the left hand, the lungs on a table. A good example of this is Figure 8 of Otto Willhelm von Vacano's *The Etruscans in the Ancient World*. The figure comes from the backside of an Etruscan Mirror. Also see the Frontispiece.

5. Tisamenus' "uniform" is indeed that of the Etruscan harus-

pex, but I must admit that we have no evidence Tisamenus himself was educated in his art by the Etruscans. The Etruscans were known as the most religious people in the world and were quite skilled in liver reading. The story of Tages is from von Vacano and can be found in many ancient sources, but the primary one is Cicero, *De Divinatione*, XIII.

6. The "uniform" of the Etruscan haruspex is shown on page 254 of *Etruscan Life and Afterlife* edited by Larissa Bonfante.

7. My source for the group of people Tisamenus has with him is a famous scene on the backside of an Etruscan hand mirror. The blond woman with the four horses represents the Goddess of the Dawn. The scene is only made complete by Myrrhine filling in for the woman just to the haruspex's (in this case Tisamenus') right. This is a ritual scene, and all the figures can be identified except for the woman Myrrhine replaces. See *The Etruscans in the Ancient World* by Otto-Wilhelm von Vacano, pages 44-8.

8. Tisamenus' comment that he is haruspex, not a fulguriator has been taken from Bonfante, page 265. A fulguriator read divine will from the sky by use of thunder and lightning.

9. The description of the two groups arguing, finally the generals rising to their feet with a roar, no decision and wanting it both ways, comes from Homer, *The Odyssey*, Book III, Lines 157-9. The argument actually occurred. I have only used Homer to describe it.

10. The visit of King Alexander of Macedonia to the camp under cover of darkness is documented in Pausanias, *Lives*, Vol. I, "Aristides," page 446, and in Herodotus, IX, 44/5.

11. All the sacrificing with negative results, the shortage of sacred sacrificial victims, and the Persians coming upon them, actually happened, along with the prayer to Hera by Pausanias. See Herodotus, IX, 61. For suffering a shortage of sacrificial victims and using a bullock yoked to a wagon instead, see Xenophon, *Anabasis*, VI, IV, 20-7.

12. The horsemen entering the sacrifice area and being beaten back with staves and whips is according to Plutarch, *Lives*, "Aris-

tides," page 448/9, as is another version of Pausanias' prayer to Hera. For the marriage of Zeus and Hera on Kithaeron, see Kerenyi, *Zeus and Hera*, pages 142-7. The finding of a sacred swine is my invention.

13. The entire scene with Sophocles, Myrrhine, and Auroriana climbing the temple wall to look out over the battlefield has been taken from Euripides' *The Phoenician Maidens*, Lines 88-201. The scene in that tragedy has Antigone and her aged attendant overlooking the battlefield of Seven Against Thebes.

14. As for Pausanias' speech to the troops, I've taken much of it from Xenophon in a similar situation. See Xenophon, *Anabasis*, VI,V 17 and 24.

15. For the description of the battle, see Xenophon, *Anabasis*, VI,V, 27/8.

Sources for Chapter 5

1. The ferryman here is patterned after Charon, the grumpy ferryman of Hades, who ferried souls of the dead across the river Styx. He charged one obal. The description comes from Euripides' *Alcestis*, Lines 252-9, and Aristophanes' *Frogs*, Lines 138-40 and 180-269. I've even used the words for shoving off and slowing as they come into dock. His question, "Who's for Kerberia or Lethe's plain?" also comes from *Frogs*.

2. For the relighting of the hearth fires, mentioned both at the beginning and the end of this chapter, see Pausanias, *Lives*, "Aristides," page 451.

3. Kleito's methods for examining Melaina are in accordance with Owsei Temkin's translation of *Soranus' Gynecology*, page 44, (which comes directly from Hippocrates), and page 57.

4. The daughter belonging to the uncle at her father's death is as described in *Birth, Death and Motherhood* by Nancy Demand, page 3.

Sources for Chapter 6

1. For the family gods, see *The Ancient City* by Fustel de Coulanges, pages 21-5 and 34-9, and for the ceremony before the hearth fire, pages 25-33.

2. Melaina's statement, "Let me take heart with my misfortune as might a philosopher," comes from Plutarch, *On Exile*, found in *Moralia*, Volume VII, LCL 405. The ideas she expresses in this paragraph can be found on pages 521-29.

3. The Temple of Artemis Brauronia on the Akropolis is documented in *Death and the Maiden, Girls' Initiation Rites in Greek Mythology* by Ken Dowden, pages 26-8.

4. For Kallias' family, the Kerykes, see *Sacred Officials of the Eleusinian Mysteries* by Kevin Clinton, pages 47-68. Kallias himself was an actual person and famous throughout Greece, not only in sacred circles but also in politics. The story of Laertes not being Odysseus' biological father is told by Hyginus, *Fabulae* 201. The naming of Odysseus by his grandfather, Autolycus, comes from Homer, *The Odyssey*, Book 19, Lines 392-466. The descent of the Kerykes from Hermes is signified by the name (herald in the ancient Greek is κερυξ, as used by Xenophon, *Hellenica* II, IV, 20). Also see Kerenyi, *Eleusis*, page 23. Hermes was Zeus' divine herald.

5. Melaina's vow comes from Xenophon, *Oeconomicus*, VII, 8.

6. Mention of the Lessor Mysteries at the temple on the banks of the Ilissos is from Kerenyi, *Eleusis*, pages 48-52.

7. The nuptial bath and wedding ceremony comes from *Pandora*, Ellen Reader editor, pages 3-73 and 126-8. Also see pages 161-174.

8. The description of Kallias' wedding attire comes from a red-figure stamnos or amphora (jar or vase) in the museum at Eleusis. The words are patterned after those on page 48 of Kevin Clinton's, *The Sacred Officials of the Eleusinian Mysteries*. It is entirely possible that Kallias himself was used as the model for this painting. So what we may have here is a 2400 year old painting of Melaina's husband as he was dressed the night of the wedding,

although in the painting Kallias is leading a procession of initiates in the Mysteries ceremony.

9. As for Kallias having a eunuch for a doorman, see Plato, *Protagoras* 314c-e. (Pages 313-4.)

10. The relationship between Melaina and her mother-in-law is as described in *Birth, Death, and Motherhood* by Nancy Demand, page 15.

11. "Argos" was the name of Odysseus' dog, see Homer, *The Odyssey*, Book XVII, Lines 290-328. I've used it here for Kallias' dog. But the description of Argos comes from Ceberus, the watchdog of Hades, as depicted in *Gods & Heroes of the Greeks, The Library of Apollodorus* tr. and Intro. by Michael Simpson, 2.5.12, and Hesiod, *Theogony*, 310-12, 769-74.

12. The scene of Melaina's unveiling comes from *Pandora*, Ellen Reader editor, 123-6.

13. For Sophocles not being an aristocrat, and "doesn't know how to throw his cloak over his shoulder from left to right," see Athenaeus I, 21c.

14. Kallias' "teachings" to Melaina come from Xenophon, *Oeconomicus*, VII.

15. Kallias' statement, "To bed with us then. I'll strip off and work the land," comes from Aristophanes, *Lysistrata*, Line 1173.

16. Kallias' statement that he wished "to weave our souls beneath this tapestry," comes from *The Craft of Zeus* by John Scheid and Jesper Svenbro, Chapter 4.

17. Hipparete's concern over her position within her son's family now that he was married was a real one during this time period. See Nancy Demand, *Birth, Death, and Motherhood in Classical Greece*, pages 5, 15-17.

Sources for Chapter 7

1. For the effect of epilepsy on the eyes, see Temken, *The Falling Sickness*, page 376. For other physical effects of the seizure, see Figure 6, page 358.

2. As for Herakles having epilepsy, see Aristotle, *Problems*, Book XXX, Lines 10-18.

3. For trouble with the equipment and crew on a ship, see *Financing the Athenian Fleet, Public Taxation and Social Relations* by Vincent Gabrielsen, pages 105-25 and 146-9.

4. For the Pythia at Delphi on Apollo's tripod speaking with the voice of Apollo, see Fontenrose, *The Delphic Oracle*, Chapter VII, "The Manic Session."

5. The Greeks' actions during the winter are described by Herodotus, VIII, 133 and evaluated in *Athens and Samos, Lesbos and Chios 478 - 404 BC*, by T. J. Quinn, pages 3-6 and *The Greco-Persian Wars* by Peter Green, pages 227/8 and 277.

6. The tone of Melaina's discussion here, "I see our fate clearly now and know what must be done," has been patterned after Iphigeneia's speech, Lines 1845/6 in Euripides' *Iphigeneia at Aulis*.

7. Melaina's statement that "in ancient times all prophets were women," comes from Pausanias X, 5.4. "... the greatest and most universal glory belongs to Phemonoe: that she was the god's first prophetess and the first to sing the hexameter." (Olen was a possible exception to this.) But "No record goes back to any other man, only to prophetic women."

8. Melaina and Kallias leaving for the docks has been patterned after a similar situation in *Argonautica* by Apollonius Rhodius, Book I, 268-70 (LCL).

9. The scene at the early morning docks comes from *A Day in Old Athens* by William Stearns Davis, page 120.

10. Kallias' prayer to Hermes has been inspired by that of Jason to Apollo in Apollonius Rhodius, *Argonautica*, Book I, Lines 410-24.

11. The last words of this chapter were taken in part from *Argonautica* by Apollonius Rhodius, Book I, 530-6.

Sources for Chapter 8

1. Cape Zoster (Girdle) and Leto's own trip down the coast

of Attica (the Apollo Coast as it's now called) is given in Pausanias I, 31.1. The description of the narrow strip of land is given in Scully, *The Earth, The Temple and the Gods, Greek Sacred Architecture*, page 117.

For a map of Delos and the nearest islands, see, *Delos, Monuments and Museum* by Photini Zaphiropoulou page 7. Mykonos is off to the east.

2. For a good look at Cape Sounion, see the chapter by that title in my travelogue, *Oedipus on a Pale Horse.*

3. The forming of the Greek islands by Poseidon is given in Callimachus' poem "To Delos," Lines 30-40.

4. Delos as a "wave-beaten haunt for gulls" comes from Callimachus' poem "To Delos," Lines 1-10.

5. For a description of the port at Delos, see Lionel Casson, *Ships and Seamanship*, page 362.

6. Many of the physical details of Delos I've taken from Scully, *The Earth, The Temple and the Gods, Greek Sacred Architecture*, pages 117-120: the harbor, the rush-grown marsh, Mt. Kynthos. For my own trip there, see my blog http://palehorseblog.com, October 16, 2009.

7. For Delos as the birth of Apollo and Artemis, see *The Homeric Hymn to Apollo.*

8. For the Cyclades as a dancing chorus around Delos, see Claude Calamae, *Choruses of Young Women in Ancient Greece*, page 36.

9. For a map and description of Delos as well as the archaeological ruins, see Dr. Fotini Zaphiropoulou, *Delos, Monuments and Museum.*

10. Just as at Epidaurus, Melaina learns that Delos also will not allow women to give birth on the island, but the priest states that they have no official ruling on the matter. Their concern at this time is my speculation. Actually the island was purified in 426/5 BC and births were no longer permitted. See Thucydides, *The Peloponnesian War*, Book III, 104.

11. The scene of Melaina appearing before the generals is set

within the Ecclesiasterion, (used for assemblies of the city council) which is Number 42 on the map in Zaphiropoulou's *Delos,
Monuments and Museum.*

12. The description and general layout of the interior of the
building also comes from Zaphiropoulou's *Delos*, but I have em-
bellished it with words from Homer, *The Odyssey*, Books IV, Lines
44-77 and VII, Lines 85-100.

13. The Greek seer, Deiphonus, was indeed a real person.
Herodotus tells us of him and his father in *The Histories*, IX, 92-
95. Deiphonus' credibility, however, was questioned, just as I've
presented here. Herodotus says, "One account ...declares that he
was not really the son of this man, but only took the name, and
then went about Greece and let out his services for hire." If so, he
was a fraud, as I've depicted him.

14. Kallias' quick list of those who had epilepsy is from Aristotle, *Problems*, XXX, 1.10-30. Aristotle adds Empedocles, Plato,
and Socrates, all of whom came later.

15. Xanthippus' words of praise for Melaina's speech have
been influenced greatly by those from the mouth of Menelaos in
Homer's *The Odyssey*, IV, 203-15 in praise of the young Telema-
chos, Odysseus' son.

Sources for Chapter 9

Relationship with the rest of the novel: The end of this chapter constitutes the three-quarter point in the novel (Volumes One
& Two). In terms of pages, it is within one page. In terms of plot,
it is the second plot point. At this time, Melaina has lost most of
her own self-centeredness and is primarily interested in the fate
of Greece and working the will of the gods, if she can. In a sense,
the gods have won her over. This is also the point where the
Greek fleet has little choice but to pursue the Persians. The deci-
sions the Greeks make in this chapter, and will make in the next,
will seal their fate.

1. The Deliades were an actual chorus of dancing girls alluded

to by Hesiod in the *Hymn to Apollon*, Lines 157-64:

> There is also a great wonder of everlasting renown,
> the Delian maidens [Δηλιαδες, Deliades],
> followers of the lord who shoots from afar.
> After they first praise Apollon with a hymn
> and now again Leto and arrow-pouring Artemis,
> they tell of men and women who lived long ago
> and sing a hymn, charming the races of men.
> The tongues of all men and their noisy chatter
> they know how to mimic; such is their skill
> in composing the song that each man might think
> he himself were speaking. (Athanassakis translation)

Sources for Chapter 10

Relationship with the rest of the novel: The end of this chapter depicts the key to a favorable resolution of the conflict between the Persians and the Greeks.

1. For the primordial (cosmic) nature of the dance, see Lillian B. Lawler, *The Dance in Ancient Greece*, page 12, and Lucian, Volume V (LCL), page 221. The other influence here is the Plato dialogue *Republic* X, 616/7. In combining the dance with this spiritual hallucination of Er during his "near-death" experience, I hope to closely represent the nature of the cosmos as perceived by the ancient Greeks and as experienced by Melaina.

2. The description of Melaina's incomplete or aborted seizure comes from Temkin's, *The Falling Sickness*, pages 319/22 and 391/2.

3. The description of the Skythian comes from Herodotus, I believe, but can no longer find the reference. The story of them eating the elderly is actually an accusation against the Massagetae, but the Skythian customs were frequently confused with theirs. It comes from Herodotus, I, 216. I've taken the name, "Coalaxais" from a Scythian king in Herodotus, IV, 7. For more on Scythians and the Scythian culture, see Herodotus, IV, 1-142.

4. The lake called the "Wheel" has now been drained to keep

down disease, but the row of lions standing guard is still there. See my pictures on my blog at www.palehorseblog.com. The actual lions have been removed and taken into the museum on Delos. Replicas now stand in their places.

5. The description of the top of Mt. Kynthos comes from Za-phiropoulou, *Delos*, page 44.

6. The scene back inside the council chambers comes from Herodotus, IX, 90-1.

7. Melaina's history lesson and her contention that, in the gods' view, Ionia was Athenian is firmly based on fact. Herodotus mentions Kodrus (IX, 97) and the founding of Miletus.

Sources for Chapter 11

1. The theory behind divining the will of the gods from reading the liver of sacrificial animals is discussed in detail by Plato in the *Timaeus*, 71-72b, from which I've taken Melaina's lesson to Deiphonus, which of course I've supposed she learned from Udaeüs at Epidaurus. The actual practice is discussed in detail in L. B. Van Der Meer's *The Bronze Liver of Piacenza*.

2. That the liver was viewed as a model of the heavens, see Der Meer's *The Bronze Liver of Piacenza*, page 3, plus the list of sources for dividing the heavens on pages 27-9. The relationship between the Etruscan gods and those Greek is discussed throughout that reference.

3. The incident involving the portent of the Samians' names is given in Herodotus, IX, 91, except that Kallias mistaking the identity of Hegesistratus is my invention.

4. Melaina's statement that "What holds democracy together is the oath," comes from Burkert, *Greek Religion*, page 250. This reference also contains a complete discussion of the oath's importance in ancient Greek society, pages 250-54.

5. The small islet west of Delos where Melaina and Kallias draw Styx water is mentioned by Kerenyi, *The Gods of the Greeks*, page 60. It was called Hekatesnesos, Hekate's Island, and Kerenyi

tells us it was also sacred to Iris, the Oathgiver. The following is the passage from Hesiod's *Theogony* describing where she gets the Styx water:

> Then Zeus sends Iris far away to fetch in a golden jar
> the legendary cold water by which the gods swear great oaths,
> water that tumbles down from a steep and soaring rock.
> This water flows through the black night
> from a sacred river, far below the earth of the wide paths.
> It is a branch of Ocean allotted one tenth of the water;
> the other nine parts wind round the earth and the broad-backed sea
> and, silver-swirled, cascade into the briny deep,
> but this one branch--this bane for the gods--runs off a cliff.
>   Hesiod, Theogony, lines 784-94

I've used these lines to set the scene where Melaina and Kallias get the water. The penalty for lying after taking the oath is from Lines 793–804.

6. Melaina's oathgiving that starts, "This water bears a curse...," comes from Hesiod's *Theogony*, Lines 785–805.

7. Slinging hot iron masses into the sea as a part of the oath was common practice. See Herodotus I, 165; Aristotle, *Constitution of Athens* 23; and Diodorus 9.10.3.

Sources for Chapter 12

1. The halkyon (we know him as the halcyon), kingfisher, as a mythical bird that nests at sea is documented in Apollonius Rhodius, *Argonautica*, Lines 1078-1102. Much of Melaina's musings here come from Apollonius, but even more comes from Euripides, *Iphigeneia Among the Tauri*, but the translation I've used is that of Edward P. Coleridge from *The Great Books* by Encyclopaedia Britannica, Inc. The translation of the Chorus (Lines 1089-1105) reads as follows:

> O bird by ocean's rocky reefs! thou halcyon, that singest thy hard fate
> in doleful song, whose note the well-trained ear can catch, and know

that thou art ever moaning for thy mate; with thee I match my tearful plaint, an unwinged songstress, longing for the gatherings of Hellas, for Artemis our help in childbirth, whose home is by the Kynthia hill with its luxuriant palm and sprouting bay and sacred shoots of olive pale, welcome Latona in her travail, beside the rounded eddying mere, where tuneful swans do service to the Muse.

2. Melaina's statement that Kallias should "Look at it through mine eyes, and see the right of it," etc., comes from words spoken by Iphigeneia in Euripides' *Iphigeneia at Aulis*, Lines 1848-46.

3. Melaina's statement for Kallias to "Put me where you will, in the bilge, on the prow, at the stern. Wherever I'm least likely to cause disruption," comes from Sophocles' *Philoctetes*, Lines 480-3.

4. As for the giant Orion walking on water, see Kerenyi, *The Gods of the Greeks*, page 203.

5. For Scythians blinding their slaves, see Herodotus IV, 2.

6. Aristagoras did stand lookout on the lead ship, see Herodotus, IX, 94.

7. The sentence, "Crews frapped their ships, undergirding hulls weakened during the battle of Salamis with papyrus cables to withstand the violent sea," was composed from words taken from *Ships and Seamanship in the Ancient World*, by Lionel Casson, page 91.

Sources for Chapter 13

1. The crew's paean is an edited version of Pindar, *Isthmian II*. Since Pindar was from this time period, use of his paean is about as authentic as it gets.

2. The line that they "...watched as gusts shook the shrouds, billowed the fine-linen sail, and oarsmen turned profitless oars aside ship like the wings of sea birds," comes from Ovid, *Metamorphoses*, XI 474-7 and *Greek Oared Ships 900-322 BC* by J. S. Morrison and R. T. Williams, page 310.

3. All sailing speeds of boats throughout *The Mysteries* have been carefully calculated using the techniques presented in *Greek*

Oared Ships 900-322 BC by J. S. Morrison and R. T. Williams, Chapter 12, "Handling" and also Chapter 12 of Lionel Casson's *Ships and Seamanship in the Ancient World*.

4. Melaina's prayer to Leukothea (Ino) has been inspired by "To Leukothea" from *The Orphic Hymns*, Number 74, page 97, translated by Apostolos N. Athanassakis.

5. Melaina's action, when she gives her veil to the helmsman, comes from Homer, *The Odyssey*, Lines 346f.

6. Much of the paragraph on the sailing of the ship comes from Apollonius Rhodius, *Argonautica*, Book I, Lines 1153-62, and 1358-62.

7. The scene when Melaina and Keladeine go below deck would be as shown in Figures 101 and 102, of Lionel Casson's *Ships and Seamanship in the Ancient World*.

8. The spray from oars containing little rainbows is from Aristotle, *Meteorology*, Book III, 374, 30. Aristotle, however, does not make the connection between the rainbow and Iris, messenger goddess. I've taken that from Greek Lyric I, *Sappho and Alcaeus*, page 369, and from Kerenyi, *Hermes, Guide of Souls*, page 15, and *The Gods of the Greeks*, page 60.

9. Melaina taking over for the aulete, "her aulos playing a stout measure for the long-stroking oars, now a swift stroke, now a pause for the blade of pine" comes from *Greek Oared Ships 900-322 BC* by J. S. Morrison and R. T. Williams, page 196, but actually has its origin in Euripides.

10. The words "treasured water tun" were compiled from Lionel Casson, *Ships and Seamanship in the Ancient World*, page 177 and note 49.

11. The creaky beam of old oak from Dodona at the prow of Kallias' ship comes from Apollonius Rhodius, *Argonautica*, Book IV, Lines 580-5.

12. Both the ships being lit at night using lanterns, so they could see each other, and the line "the bo'sun lit the ship's three bronze lanterns" comes from Lionel Casson, *Ships and Seamanship in the Ancient World*, pages 247–8, particularly Notes 91 and 92.

13. Melaina's and Keladeine's singing and the comments about Sirens comes from Apollonius Rhodius, *Argonautica*, Book IV, Lines 891-915.

14. The Persians leaving Samos and heading for the coast of Asia Minor is discussed by Herodotus, IX, 96-8.

15. In the burning of Hera's temple at Samos, I've followed the lead of Peter Green, *The Greco-Persian Wars*, page 278. I've tried to verify the burning of the temple, and all I've found to support it is a few words in Pausanias, VII, 5.2. Pausanias gives no date at which the Persians burned it, nor does documentation of the excavations make mention of it. See the article, "The Heraion at Samos," by Helmut Kyrieleis in *Greek Sanctuaries*.

16. For a description of the harbor at Samos, though it might actually be further north of the temple of Hera, see Herodotus, III, 60.

17. "Chera" (widow) is the name of a priestess of Hera, and it comes from Kerenyi, *Zeus and Hera, Archetypal Image of Father, Husband and Wife*, page 129-30. Hera herself was known as "Chera" after her falling out with Zeus.

18. The description of Chera comes from Athenaeus, *Deipnosophistae*, Paragraphs 525e-526a, from her bracelets, her flowing hair, and her robes.

19. The purification ceremony with the torch comes from Euripides, *Helen*, Lines 865-72.

20. The Greeks' uncertainty after learning that the Persians had given them the slip is discussed briefly by Herodotus, IX, 98.

21. Tigranes' good looks are attested to by Herodotus, IX, 96.

22. Divining by lightening is discussed by Cicero, *De Divinatione*, XVIII.

23. The theory behind an "offered" and a "requested" sign was taken from David Potter, *Prophets & Emperors*, page 153.

24. At the end of the chapter, Leotychides tells them to "Clear the decks of masts and sails. Bring up the boarding bridges." This comes from Lionel Casson, *Ships and Seamanship in the Ancient World*, pages 120/1 and 235/6,

Sources for Chapter 14

1. For shortages aboard ship, see Vincent Gabrielsen, *Financing the Athenian Fleet*, pages 146-9.

2. Melaina's question, "How is it men by the thousands give their lives for Greece, yet you bemoan a single woman..." follows the trend of thought again of Iphigeneia in Euripides' *Iphigeneia at Aulis*, Lines 1867-82.

3. The oarsmen putting up "side-screen leathers, shallow tents extending along both sides of the ship to protect themselves from the rain of Persian arrows" comes from *Ships and Seamanship in the Ancient World*, by Lionel Casson, page 249 and *Greek Oared Ships 900-322 BC* by J. S. Morrison and R. T. Williams, pages 119 and 302.

4. Herodotus says nothing about battleship formation, but the line-abreast and line-ahead formations mentioned here make strategic sense. See "Battle Tactics" in *Greek Oared Ships 900-322 BC* by J. S. Morrison and R. T. Williams, pages 313-20, but in particular 314.

5. The setting for Samos and Mykale both come from *The Earth, The Temple and The Gods*, page 49/50 and 52-4. I've also relied on Peter Green, *The Greco-Persians Wars*, pages 283 and 302, Note 27.

6. The sequence of events at Mykale comes from Herodotus, Paragraphs 99-108.

7. The standard bearer signaling another ship by waving a flag is described in *Ships and Seamanship in the Ancient World*, by Lionel Casson, page 246-8.

8. The founding of the temple of Demeter here is documented in Herodotus, IX, 97. The significance of this being a temple of Eleusinian Demeter is extremely important and is not mentioned by any of the scholars I've read. That the battle had to satisfy the oracle from Delphi is critical, and even though Herodotus doesn't mention it, it must have been on the minds of the generals when

they made the decision to fight on land.

9. The call from the ship for the Ionians to revolt is real (Herodotus IX, 98). I've used Kallias for the herald because he was a descendent of Hermes, the divine herald, and he would have had to have a good voice to be the Dadouchos of the Mysteries.

10. After the beaching of the troops, Herodotus (IX, 100) describes the finding of a staff, and, at the same time, word from some unknown source that the Greeks had defeated the Persians (Mardonius) at Plataea. I've seized the opportunity to connect this with Melaina's epilepsy. I place the clairvoyance squarely on her shoulders with the coming of another partial seizure. Peter Green in *The Greco-Persian Wars* has another theory (pages 281/2) of how the word of the Greek victory on the mainland was received at Mykale so quickly. I'll not go into it here, but I would like to say that as a practical matter, I thoroughly agree with him. That the staff belonged to the Hierophant, of course, is purely my invention.

11. The organization of the hoplites comes from Xenophon, *Hellenica*, II, IV, 12 and *Anabasis*, VI, V, 26-30.

12. Xanthippus' description of his wife Agarista's dream of being mounted by a lion just before giving birth to Perikles is true. See Plutarch, *Lives*, "Perikles," pages 203.

13. Just before the battle started, the Spartans did run off into the bushes. This part of the story is questionable but comes from Diodorus, Book XI, 36.

14. The stinking old woman comes from *Argonautica*, Book II, Lines 178-231, where I've taken the attributes of an old man for my old woman. The description of her death by Apollo's arrow and leaving her body unburied comes from *Prophets & Emperors* by David Potter, page 71. As for the old woman's three names (Manto, Daphne, and Sybil), Teiresias' daughter was known by all three, (Diodorus, IV, 66.5-6), and the old woman in Potter's book, a Sybil, claimed to be one thousand years old. Potter even mentions a connection to Demeter and Persephone, so that Melaina

finding the old woman here in Demeter's temple wouldn't be extraordinary. Furthermore, Manto came to Kolophon (just north of Mykale) to found a colony at the order of Delphian Apollo (Pausanias, VII, 3[1]) and would have died there in Ionia.

15. Kallias' comment, "When will they ever provide protection for the throat and groin?" comes from an actual complaint documented by A. M. Snodgrass, *Arms & Armor of the Greeks*, page 56. Kallias' other complaints are documented in Victor Davis Hanson, *The Other Greeks*, page 245.

16. Melaina reviewing the troops with Xanthippus comes from Homer, *The Iliad*, Book II, Lines 515-31.

Sources for Chapter 15

Relationship with the rest of the novel: The end of this chapter resolves the central conflict between the Greeks and the Persians.

1. The lines, "Terror, Rout and Hate, Ares insatiable sisters-in-arms, walked the earth sowing ferocity, redoubling groans and cries of agony. Dust clouds soared heavenward," comes from Homer, *The Iliad*, Book IV, Lines 532-38.

2. The words that describe Kallias fighting, "He snatched a glittering buckler from a dead man, clashed midst the assembled host dealing death and courting it, all the time shouting, "Smite! Slay Persia's sons! A thunder of war cries rang, roared," was inspired by Euripides, *Suppliants*, Lines 696-72, both the Way and Coleridge translations.

3. The details of the fight between Kallias and Tigranes (which of course is totally fictional) come from Apollonius Rhodius, *Argonautica* Book II, Lines 75-97. However, Tigranes did die in the battle. Kallias would have been a good opponent for him since he won the pankratium at the Olympics.

4. Melaina's words while grieving over killing Tigranes and not having Kallias to comfort her comes from the lament of Medea in Apollonius Rhodius, *Argonautica*, Book IV, Lines 1062-7.

5. The Greeks swooping down upon the Persians like Zeus' great eagle accosting Prometheus comes from Apollonius Rhodius, *Argonautica* Book II, Lines 1247-59.

6. Xanthippus setting fire to the timbers, to rout the Persians, "as a beekeeper smokes a droning swarm pent up in a hive," comes from Apollonius Rhodius, *Argonautica* Book II, Lines 130-6.

7. Melaina smells Syrian cedar, the wood out of which the Persians actually built their ships. See Theophrastus, *Enquiry into Plants*, V.VII "Of the Woods Used in Shipbuilding." This reference contains a good discussion on the use of woods in shipbuilding, obviously.

8. For the Scythian skinning his victim's head see Herodotus IV, 64.

9. Hygieiadora's admonition for Melaina not guarding her pregnancy comes from *Soranus' Gynecology*, pages 45 and 55.

10. The spoils described here are taken from Herodotus IX, 106 and also 80.

Sources for Chapter 16

1. In the second paragraph, the preparations for childbirth are taken from *Soranus' Gynecology*, page 70.

2. The argument over relocating the Ionians is from Herodotus IX, 106.

3. Melaina's words and their origins are as follows: "Rhodes, Athena's birthplace [Pindar, "Olympian Ode VII," Lines 30-40]; Ephesus, Artemis' greatest temple [Pausanias IV, 318]; and Samos, Hera's birthplace [Pausanias VII, 4.4]. Also, Colophon was founded by Manto [Pausanias, IX, 33.1], Teiresias' daughter, at the direction of Delphi. As for Chios being the home of Homer, this comes from the *Homeric Hymn To Apollon*. In the 5th century BC, it was believe that Homer had written the *Homeric Hymns*. Few scholars now believe that to be true. These are the lines to which Melaina refers:

> I ask you to call me to mind
> in time to come whenever some man on this earth,
> a stranger whose suffering never ends, comes here and asks:
> "Maidens, which of the singers, a man wont to come here,
> is to you the sweetest, and in whom do you most delight?"
> Do tell him in unison that I am he,
> a blind man, dwelling on the rocky island of Chios,
> whose songs shall all be the best in time to come.

This also led to the belief that Homer was blind.

4. They leave aboard a ship named *The Tragodia*. All the names of ships in *The Mysteries* have been taken from actual ones documented in Lionel Casson, *Ships and Seamanship in the Ancient World*, pages 348-54.

5. Kimon's bearing here, "subdued, his voice reduced to gentle tones," is from Xenophon, *Symposium* (Banquet) I, 10.

Sources for Chapter 17

1. Initiates danced around the Kallichoron Well (Well of Beautiful Dances) during the initiation ceremony for the Mysteries. In the following chapter, I've used the structure of the Mysteries throughout and patterned events after some in the ceremony. See Kevin Clinton, *Myth and Cult, The Iconography of the Eleusinian Mysteries*, pages 27/8. The initiates danced in the courtyard by the Well for the return of Demeter's kidnapped daughter, Kore (Persephone). For the full sequence of events during the initiation, see Kevin Clinton's article, *The Sanctuary of Demeter and Kore at Eleusis*, in *Greek Sanctuaries, New Approaches*, pages 110-124, edited by Nanno Marinatos and Robin Hägg. A better understanding of the entire sequence of events would come from a careful reading of the *Homeric Hymn to Demeter*, edited by Helene P. Foley. Foley's book contains an excellent new translation as well as the ancient text. For more on the archaeological site and the Mysteries' connection with the ancient Greek religion, see the chapter in my travelogue, *Oedipus on a Pale Horse*, "Eleusis." For a picture of the

Mirthless Rock see Figure 1 of Kevin Clinton's *Myth and Cult, The Iconography of the Eleusinian Mysteries*, page 24. The discussion of the Mirthless Rock is on pages 14-27. Many pictures of all this are on my blog at www.palehorseblog.com.

3. The opening in the hillside that leads to the Gates of Hades is identified by Clinton, pages 87-9.

4. Aeschylus' statement that Might and Force have announced their arrival is from the opening to his play *Prometheus Bound*.

5. The discussion here between Aeschylus and Kallias concerning the two battles, that at Plataea and Mykale, occurring on the same day is from Herodotus, IX, 101.

6. Melaina's refusal to retell the events of the past few days comes from Ismene in response to a similar request in Sophocles' play, *Oedipus at Colonus*, Lines 361-5.

7. Melaina's expression of pain during childbirth (in several places) I've taken, believe it or not, from those expressed by Herakles in Sophocles' *The Women of Trachis*, Lines 1004-10, 1023-43 and 1046-57. To check the appropriateness of this, I've had two women, who between them have given birth seven times, read it (one of them a published novelist herself) and both agreed with the depiction.

8. The language throughout this entire birthing scene ("warm fomentations," etc.) comes from *Soranus' Gynecology*, pages 70-6.

9. Under normal conditions a birthing stool would be used (as shown in Fig. 13-14 of Elaine Fantham's *Women in the Classical World*, page 38), but a birthing stool is not available here, so Kleito provides the support of the chair as dictated by common practice. See *Soranus' Gynecology*, pages 73/4, as follows:

> There should be three woman helpers, capable of gently allaying the anxiety of the gravida [pregnant woman] even if they do not happen to have had experience with birth. Two of them should be at the sides and one behind holding the parturient woman so that she may not sway with <the> pains. But if the midwife's stool is not at hand, the same arrangement can also be made if she sits on a woman's lap. However, the woman must be robust, that she may bear the weight of

the woman sitting upon her and be able to hold her firmly during the pangs of labor. Moreover the midwife, after having covered herself properly with an apron above and below, should sit down opposite and below the laboring woman; for the extraction of the fetus must take place from a high towards a lower plane.

10. The herb dittany, peculiar to Krete, and its benefits for women in childbirth, comes from Theophrastus, *Inquiry into Plants*, IX, XVI, 1.

11. Kleito's description of thyme and where it grows comes from *Ancient Herbs* by Jeanne D'Andrea, pages 84-6. Also see Theophrastus, *Enquiry into Plants*, VI, VII, 1-3.

12. The children from the silver mines at Laurium, the "worms," singing and scampering about the temple ruins like crazed Korybantes comes from Kerenyi, *The Gods of the Greeks*, pages 82-5. I've appropriated the "Worms" for the task. When Rhea gave birth to Zeus on Mt. Ida, as told on Crete, the Kory-bantes were in attendance to the goddess and "made a din with their iron weapons, to drown the wailing of the child so that Kronos might not hear it." These creatures lived underground and were sometimes known as Daktyloi. They "were servants and instruments of the Great Mother, obstetricians, smiths and magi-cians, who may also be described, by reason of their seemingly small stature, as craftsmen–dwarfs."

13. For a difficult delivery, see *Soranus' Gynecology*, pages 184-9. Specifically for the case when the woman's water has already broken, see *Soranus' Gynecology*, page186: "If, however, the fluid has already drained forth, one should instill some greasy fluid into the vagina by means of a small syringe." Thus Myrrhine's goat bladder. Soranus mentions olive oil for situations like this on page 185.

14. Myrrhine lubricating and dilating the orifice is from *Sora-nus' Gynecology*, page 75.

15. Kleito's cyclamen, the "good charm" for producing rapid delivery, as well as the harvesting technique, "burn it, steep the ashes in wine to form balls," comes from Theophrastus, *Enquiry*

into Plants, IX.IX.3.

16. Eileithyia was the goddess of fast birth and was called throughout antiquity to assist in delivery. See the Homeric Hymn "To Apollo," Lines 97-117. The prayer here has been influenced by the hymn "To Prothyraia (Eileithyia)" in *Orpheus, The Orphic Hymns*, page 7 (Hymn 2).

17. Myrrhine's admonition for Melaina to expel the child, that the pain is nothing to fear, and to groan not scream while driving the breathing down into the flanks, all comes from *Soranus' Gynecology*, page 74.

18. Pilokleia's statement, "Perhaps she conceived a monster, ... That's known to cause difficult childbirth," comes from *Soranus' Gynecology*, page 180.

19. Women "not very heavy below the hips have difficult labor," comes from *Soranus' Gynecology*, page 176.

20. Difficult labor because of twins comes from *Soranus' Gynecology*, page 179.

21. The opening and closing of the uterus orifice comes from *Soranus' Gynecology*, pages 75/6.

22. The cutting of the naval cord with a piece of glass as opposed to a steel blade is from *Soranus' Gynecology*, pages 80/1.

23. The cosmic quality of the chorus' dancing and singing is from *Lucian*, Volume V, LCL, pages 221 and 223.

24. For Myrrhine's method of removing the chorion, see *Soranus' Gynecology*, page 76, Note 20, and pages 198/9.

25. Myrrhine cleaning the child is in accordance with the explicit instructions in *Soranus' Gynecology*, pages 82-4.

26. Melaina's gentle cooing sounds, etc, are as directed in *Soranus' Gynecology*, pages 113.

27. Swaddling of both a girl and a boy child is in accordance with the instructions in *Soranus' Gynecology*, pages 84-7.

28. The argument over letting Melaina nurse the babes immediately is from *Soranus' Gynecology*, page 89.

29. Testing the breast milk comes from *Soranus' Gynecology*, pages 94-7.

30. The action of wetting the baby's lips is from *Birth, Death, and Motherhood in Classical Greece* by Nancy Demand, page 126.

Sources for Chapter 18

1. Kakhry as the fruit of the herb libanotis, smelling like frankincense, but bringing breast milk if lactation is slow, is documented in Theophrastus, *Enquiry into Plants*, IX.XI.10.

2. The childs' name, Theonoë (the purpose of god), comes from Euripides' *Helen*, Lines 13/4. Theonoë is a priestess who "knew Heaven's will for things that are and things to be."

3. Epileptics frequently know when an attack is going to occur, although they may not know how far away in time. See Oswei Temken, *The Falling Sickness*, page 39.

4. Myrrhine's discussion of the nature of the Underworld comes from Plato, *Phaedo*, 114e.

5. Melaina's farewell to her, "little orphans. Live glad lives in the light," comes from Euripides, *Alcestis*, Lines 270-3.

6. Melaina's words to her mother, "Do not, I pray Mother, store bitter sorrows, for you won't save me but become a bird of ill omen. Promise if I should die you'll summon cheerfulness and a peaceful spirit," comes in part from Plutarch, *Moralia*, Vol. VII, "Consolation to His Wife," Page 573.

7. Melaina being "blessed with two fates" comes from *The Greek Way of Death* by Robert Garland, pages 100/1.

8. Melaina seeing "sparks, fiery circles" at the start of her seizure comes from Timken, *The Falling Sickness*, page 38.

9. Melaina's vision of the "dark lady, dread Persephone" along with the rest of her entourage comes (except for the appearance of Melaina's father) from Sophocles, *Oedipus at Colonus*, Lines 1545-50, where he describes the death of Oedipus.

10. Melaina's vision of "Charon, death's ferryman, with his two-oared skiff lurking at the dock, his hand impatient upon the boatman's pole," comes from Euripides, *Alcestis*, Lines 252-7.

11. Melaina's last words, "We owe a cock to Asklepios. Don't

forget it," come from Plato *Phaedo* 118a. These are the last words of Socrates, and have been the cause of much wonder as to what they mean. Of course, anyone with even a superficial knowledge of Asklepios knows that he is the god of resurrection and that the dead meet him on the way to their resurrection in the Elysian Fields. Small wonder that a dying person would request a sacrifice to the god of resurrection.

12. Myrrhine's words, "Would that on that day when, I heard of Kynegeiros' evil death, I had straightway given up my own life and gone among the shades. Once I was admired among Eleusinian women, but now pine away, ill-fated for love of you, my only child," have come from a reference that I can no longer locate.

13. The story behind Myrrhine's appeal to Asklepios for "blood from the Gorgon's right artery" to bring Melaina back from the Underworld, comes from *The Library of Apollodorus* 3.10.3.

14. Closing the eyes to release the soul of the dead is discussed in *The Greek Way of Death* by Robert Garland, page 23.

Sources for Chapter 19

1. Myrrhine's statement to the blacksmith to "Come witness... the corpse of she who was not merely loved, but loveliest of the beloved," comes from Euripides, *Alcestis*, Lines 230-3.

The procedures of Melaina's funeral are from *The Greek Way of Death* by Robert Garland, page 27.

2. The blacksmith's statement that "The gods never take villainy but by chance, the noble always." and "I've seen wicked given excellent care, Hades never calling rogues and knaves but gleeful in stalking the valorous and just. The gods want the most precious with them," comes from Sophocles, *Philoctetes*, Lines 434/4 and 446-52.

3. In dressing the corpse, the line "a glorious white, ankle-length himation for the deceased" comes from *The Greek Way of Death* by Robert Garland, page 24.

4. The laws on mourning are expressed beautifully in several

places in Plutarch, *Moralia*, Vol. VII, "Consolation to His Wife."

5. Preparation of the body for burial is in accordance with *The Greek Way of Death* by Robert Garland, pages 23/6.

6. Pindar's poem has been edited from his "Olympian Ode II," Lines 15-20, 68-74.

7. Myrrhine's changed approach to grieving, chopping short her hair, turning her fingernails upon her cheeks, and rubbing filth into her grieving cloths, ripping them, covering herself in hearth ashes, is in keeping of everything that had been outlawed. Again see Plutarch, *Moralia*, Vol. VII, "Consolation to His Wife."

8. Aeschylus' statement, "Don't surrender to unwarranted grief and rage. The law requires natural sadness and goodwill instead of wild, frenzied mourning." Followed by Myrrhine's, "You forget," she said, "when Zeus apportioned honors, Grief asked and Zeus granted a share," come from Plutarch, *Moralia*, Volume VII, "Consolation to His Wife," Paragraph 609F.

9. Myrrhine's statement "The procrastination of the divine in punishing the wicked is infamous. But never you mind the slow grinding. The mill of the gods ever turns," comes from Plutarch, *Moralia*, Volume VII, "Delays in Divine Vengeance," 549D-E.

10. Myrrhine's statement, "Soft though she treads, divine Justice in her own season seizes them unawares, deals the fatal blow," comes from an Euripides fragment quoted in Plutarch, *Moralia*, "Delays in Divine Vengeance," 549A.

The location at Eleusis of the ancient graveyard of the humiliated generals of Argos is shown in the upper right of Figure 32 in Mylonas, *Eleusis and the Eleusinian Mysteries*.

11. Melaina's burial place was indeed believed to be the graveyard of the Argive dead killed during the futile siege of Thebes. See Euripides *The Suppliants*, Lines 1210-12, Pausanias I, 39, 2 (page 109) and Plutarch, *Lives*, "Theseus" 29 (page 19).

12. The sacrifice of horses, even four of them, is not without precedence in ancient myth or archaeology. Achilles sacrificed four on Petroklus' grave, and skeletons of at least three were found in a 10th century grave. See *The Greek Way of Death* by Robert

Garland, page 35.

13. For destructive sacrifice at the gravesite see *Greek Religion* by Walter Burkert, tr. by John Raffan, pages 192/3.

14. For frogs representing both the living and the dead, see *Dance and Ritual Play in Greek Religion* by Steven H. Lonsdale, page 128.

15. The phrase, "her daughter winged her way to Elysium" comes from Euripides *The Suppliants*, Lines 1141/2.

16. Curse tablets, the physical composition and writing, are documented in *Curse Tablets and Binding Spells from the Ancient World* by John G. Gager. Much of the language of Myrrhine's curse comes from this reference, pages 175 and 162/3, as well as the fact that chaotic writing strengthened the curse.

17. Myrrhine driving home the bronze nail through the lead curse tablet comes from a practice of the Etruscans, and the portrayal of her here as Atropos, one of the three fates (the one who cut the length of the Thread of Life), comes from *The Etruscans in the Ancient World* by Otto-Wilhelm Von Vacano, page 12. Atropos driving home the nail of destiny to end the year and eventually to end the Etruscan civilization comes from *The Etruscans in the Ancient World* by Otto-Wilhelm Von Vacano, page 10.

18. The last paragraph of this chapter is fashioned from Homer, *The Iliad*, Book 9, Lines 565-80.

19. The last sentence of this chapter comes from Euripides, *Alcestis*, Lines 336/7.

Sources for Chapter 20

1. The Amphidromia is documented in *Studies in the Use of Fire in Ancient Greek Religion* by William D. Furley, pages 65-70.

2. The directions on how to handle removal of the umbilical cord is from *Soranus' Gynecology*, page 114.

3. Aeschylus' statement that "No true mother exists. Women but incubate men's live seed. Men are the only true begetters, the progenitors of life," is from his *Euminides* where he expressed the

opinion through the words of Apollo, Lines 656-66.

4. Exposing unwanted children on Kithaeron's slopes was common practice. Baby Oedipus was exposed there (Sophocles, *Oedipus Tyrannus*, Lines 1086-1185).

5. Myrrhine's methods of determining a healthy child is from *Soranus' Gynecology*, page 80, but Aeschylus' reasoning against the children is just as valid and also from *Soranus*, page 80.

6. Aeschylus' reasons for not keeping the kids are also justifiable by ancient reasoning. See *Soranus' Gynecology*, page 48.

7. Myrrhine's statement, "Rule by choosing to be overruled," is from Sophocles, *Ajax*, Line 1353, spoken by Odysseus, tr. by E. F. Watling (not very literal but useful here), *Electra and Other Plays*.

8. Myrrhine's words that the goddess Hera's milk returned to feed Heracles are my speculation.

9. Kallias' horses were highly coveted. He won the horse race at Olympic games but was second in the four-horse chariot race. See Herodotus VI, 122.

10. Kallias did marry Elpinice, Kimon's sister, even though gossip told of Kimon cohabiting with her. The explanation Kallias gives here is the one told by Kimon. She'd even been accused of being over-intimate with Polygnotus, the painter. Other tales of her and Perikles came later. See Athenaeus, *Deipnosophistae*, XIII, 589e-f. Also Plutarch, *Lives*, Vol. 1, "Pericles," page 209 and 225; and "Kimon," page 644/5 and 654.

11. Myrrhine's statement, "Ah me, what can I do bereft of thee?" comes from Euripides, *Alcestis*, Line 380.

12. The last few paragraphs concerning Myrrhine's visitations to Melaina's tomb come from *The Greek Way of Death* by Robert Garland, pages 104/5 and Herodotus IV, 26.

Sources for Chapter 21

This short chapter is a dramatization of events described by Herodotus in *The Histories*, Book IX, Paragraphs 107-122.